A Town Called Potato

Galactic Detective Agency
Book 1

Gary Blaine Randolph

ISBN: 978-1-7347741-2-2 (paperback)
ISBN: 978-1-7347741-3-9 (ebook)

For Gabe …
The first person to call me Daideo and the first to imagine a town called Potato.

Contents

Chapter 1

My Used-to-Be Life

A blue light pierced the darkness, a *whomp* slicing through air, fabric, and wood to cut a fiery fist-sized hole through the armchair right beside me. Resisting the urge to duck and cover, I bolted after my assailant down the line of chairs, the line made all the longer because the chairs were huge — each one as tall as my garage back home and as wide as a couch. Darting under a giant end table, I peered through the gloom, searching for signs of movement. A shadow passed in front of an enormous ottoman. I raised my blaster and took a shot. It missed wide to the left, causing the fine red upholstery to burst into flames as the shadowy figure darted under a giant couch.

They hadn't hired me to burn down the place. I ran to the ottoman and patted out the embers, wishing I had spent more time in blaster practice. It had seemed so easy in the daylight … with targets that didn't shoot back.

A rustle sounded from the direction of the couch, and I hit the deck in time to see another blaster shot whiz past where my head had just been, blowing a wooden table into kindling. I rolled under the ottoman, regretting several of my recent life choices. I mean, last week nobody was shooting at me. Last week I didn't even know that blasters and planets with giant aliens and any of this existed.

I muttered, "How did I ever get myself into this?"

I can tell you how I got myself into this.

It started the day that guy out in Plainfield called me. Seriously, that's the name of the town — Plainfield. I was in my home office, working on my computer and writing software for clients when the phone rang. I stared at it for a moment since my preference is to be texted or emailed. The number wasn't anybody in my contacts list. Probably a telemarketer, I thought. But when you're in business for yourself, you take just about every call. You never know. I tapped the pickup button.

"Gabriel Lake here."

"Yeah. Hi," the voice drawled. "I have a trucking company out here in Plainfield. Your website says you do phone apps. Is that right?"

"Just like the website says," I replied.

"Okay. See we have to do these load tickets with fuel and mileage and stuff. Government regulations. I'm having a hard time getting my drivers to complete them, and I thought an app might help."

"It might."

"How much would something like that cost?"

It's never a great sign when the first question from a potential client is about cost.

"It depends on how complicated it all is," I said. "Tell you what. I can do an analysis, no charge. Can you email me the information on what you need? I'll check it out."

He paused for a beat or two. "Could you maybe come see me?"

I hated going out on appointments, but I said, "Probably. You said you're in Plainfield?"

"Yup."

"Okay. Sure. I can run out. You can show me the form and explain what goes into completing it. Then I can give you an estimate."

"I have some time this afternoon."

"Sounds good. How about four o'clock?" I thought that way I could get some stuff done first and then end the day with the meeting.

He gave me his address, and we hung up. Turning back to the laptop, I noticed by the clock in the corner of the screen that it was time for lunch. I rolled my desk chair back and padded from my home office into the kitchen. Scrounging through the fridge failed to locate any lunch meat, so I pulled out my phone and added cold cuts to the growing grocery list. I fixed myself a peanut butter and banana slice sandwich and sat down at the dinette table.

Reaching for the Raymond Chandler detective novel that was face down on the table, I opened it at the scrap of paper I was using for a bookmark. I chomped down the peanut butter while following Philip Marlowe through the dark and seedy streets of mid-twentieth-century Los Angeles. Marlowe was digging up clues, and they all pointed in one direction. But maybe they were red herrings. Perhaps the real culprit was someone no one suspected. It might even be the gal Marlowe was starting to fall for.

I finished the chapter and the sandwich, then grabbed a couple of cookies from the package on my way back to my home office (a.k.a. the second bedroom in the little bungalow). My afternoon job was to get a data import running for a different client. I finished it by three o'clock, giving me plenty of time to change from jeans into khakis and check out a few funny videos on the Internet before leaving for my meeting with the trucking guy.

I grabbed a jacket as I left the house. Early March can be chilly in Indianapolis, and on this day the sky was gray. From my bungalow in the Fountain Square district, it was only about a thirty-minute drive to Plainfield across, as Philip Marlowe might say, the mean streets of Indy. Except Indy streets aren't really that mean. They can be rough, though. Especially during pothole season, which lasts about six months from mid-winter to whenever the city's new budget kicks in.

I pulled into the gravel parking lot at 3:55 and walked up the concrete steps to a mobile trailer with a sign on it that said: *Office*. A bull of a man with a square jaw and thinning hair sat behind a metal desk covered with folders and papers. Metal filing cabinets stood behind him, also strewn with papers. A table nearby held a dirty coffee maker and yet another mound of papers.

"Are you Lake?" he asked without standing. I nodded, and he waved me toward a chair. It too had a folder on it, which I perched precariously on top of one of the piles on the desk before taking a seat.

The meeting turned out to be less than productive, though it certainly lasted long enough. In addition to information about the proposed app, he had to include a rant against government regulations in general and a few of his drivers in particular. The app turned out to have more complexity to it than I had first anticipated. So when I shot him a ballpark price, his eyes widened in surprise.

"Son, I ain't planning on taking you on as a dependent. What are you driving out there, a Cadillac?"

"Apps are complicated," I said with a shrug. I knew I could suggest some things to trim the cost. But with his long-windedness, I wasn't that enthusiastic about having him as a client. I could see every meeting and every phone call turning into a marathon session. I let him turn me down, and I left the trailer and got back into my car. For the record, it's a ten-year-old Honda.

As I started the engine, my phone buzzed. I tapped it to life and saw a text from my friend Adam.

Coffee 9AM Buzz House. B there?

I tapped the suggested answer for *Yes* and started the car.

As I rolled across the lot, the phone buzzed again. I wasn't on the street yet and nothing was around me, so I tapped the screen. Sarah had received Adam's text, too, and had replied with a thumbs-up emoji. Good. It was going to be the whole gang.

On the way home I had to stop to fill up the tank, and right beside the filling station was a very tempting Steak 'n Shake. I succumbed to the temptation. So by the time I got back to Fountain Square, stuffed with a steak burger, thin fries, and a chocolate shake, the early March twilight was coming on.

As I got out of my car, I noticed someone standing on my porch, draped in shadows. The figure wore a dark robe. It was long like a duster coat you might see in Westerns but with a hood covering the head.

I stepped around the car and mounted the sidewalk. The figure stepped off the porch and moved toward me. In the fading light, the face was hidden inside the hood. What little of the cheek and chin I could make out seemed to have an olive cast. Not what people call olive-colored skin, which is just a term for someone with a Mediterranean complexion. No, this skin appeared to be literally the color of a green olive. I assumed it was some weird trick of the light.

"Can I help you?" I asked.

The robed figure opened its mouth, and a series of hissing sounds emanated from it. The form took another step toward me, giving me a better view. The hooded robe was made of soft leather, opened down the middle and cinched at the waist by a belt and ornate buckle. Heavy leather boots extended below the robe's hem. The figure hissed some more and took yet another step.

I began backing away. What in the world was this thing? "Look I think you have the wrong address. I didn't order anything. I'm already registered to vote. I don't need gutter guards."

More hissing sounds. I was ready to turn and make a dash for my car when the figure raised an arm and pointed something at me. It was shaped vaguely like a gun.

Whomp!

A sharp pain shot through my leg. I glanced down and saw a hypodermic needle sticking out of my thigh.

Chapter 2

A Shot in the Dark

I stared down at the dart sticking from my leg. Who was this creature? Why did it shoot me? How does something like that even happen to a guy who's just minding his own business? My head started swimming, and I dropped to my knees. I knew I couldn't stay where I was, not with the figure, whatever it was, moving toward me again. I pulled the hypodermic out, threw it away from myself, and scrambled to my feet as quickly as I could, hopping on my other leg.

"What's the big idea?" I barked. I tried to sound like a tough guy, though I felt like anything but that. I glanced at my car. Should I make a dash for it? It was locked now. Would I be able to unlock it and jump in before whoever this was attacked again?

Taking another step toward me, the hooded figure stuck the gun into the belt of the robe. It continued to hiss, but this time with words beginning to emerge from the hisses. "... *hiss* ... *hisssth* ... understand *hiss* now? I mean you no harm."

"No harm, huh? You call shooting someone with a tranquilizer dart no harm?"

"Good. You understand me now. It was not a tranquilizer. You're fine. You are Gabriel Lake, correct?" The voice was cool, detached. I couldn't get a read on whether it was male or female.

"What do you mean, am I Gabriel Lake? Man, talk about 'shoot first and ask questions later!' So this isn't some random attack then? You were planning on shooting me. And if it isn't a tranquilizer, then what is it?"

"Don't worry about it."

"Don't worry about it? Don't worry about it? Sure, why should I worry about a hypodermic? It's not like you could have injected me with anything harmful, like a toxin or a virus."

"I have a business proposal for you."

So this was a potential client? Two in one day. At least the trucking company guy didn't hiss at me and inject me with God knows what.

"You could have just sent me an email," I said, rubbing my sore thigh.

"I need you to help with a missing person case."

"What do you mean? Like a database of missing persons or something?"

"No. I need you to help me find a missing person."

"Look … whoever you are … I'm a computer programmer. I don't find missing persons. That isn't what I do."

"I have seen your file, Gabriel Lake. You are the leading expert in this locality on crime solving."

"What? No, I'm not. I've never solved a crime in my life."

The figure was silent for a few seconds.

"You *are* Gabriel Lake, right?"

"Yes. We agree on that one."

"I know you have studied crime extensively." The hooded figure pulled out a phone-sized device and tapped it a few times. "*The Maltese Falcon, The Murder of Roger Ackroyd, Murder on the Orient Express, If Death Ever Slept.* The list goes on. You have been identified as an expert on crime."

"Those are all novels, mysteries, detective stories. They're fiction. Rex Stout, Dashiell Hammett, Agatha Christie."

"And you have studied them, correct?"

"I have read them, yes. For fun."

A car turned down the street. My attacker's head was buried too deep inside the hood for the headlights to illuminate the face. But the light did catch a reflection in the eyes, an eerie reflection of yellow, like an animal's eyes. It gave me the creeps. Who was this? What was this?

"And these books were about crime, correct?"

"Well, yeah. But I—"

"We need your considerable knowledge about crime on this … in this locality."

"I've been trying to tell you. I don't have any considerable knowledge of crime in this locality or any locality. Not in real life. And those stories weren't even about crime in this locality. They were set in Los Angeles, New York, England."

"I meant locality in a somewhat larger sense."

"What larger sense?"

"Earth. But whatever knowledge you have will suffice. It is a simple missing person case. I was told to bring you."

"Who told you to bring me?"

"My employer did. He wants you for the job. He wants to meet with you. Can you come right now?"

"No, I will not come right now. Depending on what you injected into me, I may need to go to the hospital right now." My hands clenched into fists. I would not go willingly off into the night with some hooded figure who had just shot me full of something. Some green-skinned hooded figure. Though surely, I thought to myself, that was a trick of the light, right?

"Tomorrow afternoon then. My employer will make it worth your while, even if you decide not to take the case."

I didn't have any big systems I was working on at present. And the bank balance was running a bit low. A missing person case would be kind of like stepping into one of my detective novels. Maybe I owed it to myself to at least give it a listen. It might be fun. Besides, it didn't sound as if this hooded figure was going to take no for an answer.

"All right, all right. I'll come. I'll come. Where do I go?"

She, or he, or whatever it was, reached into a pocket of the robe, pulled out a card, and held it out to me. "This has the time and location."

The fingers holding the card appeared rough and leathery and had that same olive cast. I stared at the hand for a second before hesitantly reaching out to take the card. It said:

2:00 p.m.
39.7837035 -86.1367679

"What are these numbers?"

"The time and location, as I told you."

I stared back at the strange numbers in bafflement. Then it dawned on me. "Are those GPS coordinates?"

"What else would they be?" the figure hissed.

"So how do I find your employer once I get there?"

"Look for me."

"I may not recognize you. I can barely see you in the dark with that hood on."

The leathery hands reached up and pulled back the hood. I gulped. When I was a kid, I had a pet Australian Water Dragon named Harriet. Harriet had two crested ridges on her head, one on each side. The head I now saw before me in the dying light was similar. She — for some reason, maybe it was because of Harriet or maybe it was something in the glinting, yellow eyes, but I now thought of this odd person as female — was hairless. The scaly olive-toned head and face were definitely reptilian. And five ridges swept back across her head starting where the hairline should have been, one crested ridge in the center and two on each side. I took a step back in shock.

"Will you recognize me now?" she asked with a cold-blooded smile.

I nodded my head, unable to form words to answer. Yeah, I would recognize her. I wouldn't soon forget that face, even if I tried.

"Tomorrow then," she said. She raised her hood again and began walking down the street. At the bottom of the robe, something was twitching. Did she have a tail?

"Wait." My voice came out raspy. I cleared my throat.

She half turned back to face me.

"You never told me what the deal was with the hypodermic."

"That, Gabriel Lake, is what is allowing you to understand me."

"What do you mean?"

"You can ask my employer about it. All your questions will be answered tomorrow." She turned away again.

All my questions? I had *a lot* of questions. I had so very many questions.

"What's your name?" I had to raise my voice as she was a good twenty feet away by now.

"Zastra," she hissed over her shoulder.

At least I could take a parting shot. "Cool name. Is that French?"

Chapter 3

Coffee Time

Our more-or-less every Friday coffee meet-up was a chance to hang out with two other technology friends to share information and help each other with problems. Or at least that's how I justified it when I deducted the lattes as a business expense. We did actually help each other with problems. But most of the time was spent shooting the breeze and joking around.

I had met Adam Campbell when we worked together at a software startup. When the startup eventually went belly up, I moved into freelance work, and Adam moved to a corporate job as a network engineer. We began meeting for coffee as a way to keep in touch. He was ten or fifteen years older than me, but we were like brothers. We had a similar solid work ethic, and we shared the same off-beat sense of humor.

The third member of our group, Sarah Gallo, had been meeting with us for a couple of years now. She had been brought in as a contract web designer to work with Adam on an overhaul of his employer's website. Adam said he invited her to our coffee group because she was smart and because of one amazingly hilarious joke she told him. But I've always suspected he was also trying to set Sarah and me up. Not that I would have minded. Only a year or two younger than me, she was clever, funny, and pretty. And I eventually found out that she and I enjoyed some of the same old movies. But we soon became such good friends that I didn't want to risk the relationship with dating. That's how I thought of the situation. To be honest, I didn't know what she thought.

When I got to the Buzz House that morning, Adam was sitting at a table with his laptop open, writing something. I said hi and swept on past to get in line and place my order. When I came back with my coffee a couple of minutes later, he nodded at me, typed a bit more, tapped the Enter key, and then closed the laptop.

He took a sip of his Americano and closed his eyes. "Ah, I needed that. I was up most of the night upgrading a server."

"Didn't go well?" I asked.

"Does it ever?"

"There's always something, right?"

"Hey, guys!" Sarah bounced past us on the way to the counter, fresh and enthusiastic.

"She looks full of energy today," I said. "I don't think she even needs coffee."

"Yeah," said Adam. "It makes me feel even more tired."

We sipped our coffees and let the conversation lag while we waited for Sarah to be served and join us. I took the opportunity to check out the new artwork on the walls. The Buzz House was a locally owned coffee shop and hung works by local artists. It had a small stage in one corner where local musicians would play on Friday nights. Its unique vibe was an oasis in a society full of chain-store corporate sameness.

When Sarah joined us, she placed a plate of three pastries on the table. "My treat, guys. I'm having a fantastic morning. I got emails confirming two new jobs. And both of them will be pretty lucrative and kind of high-profile. And best of all, they came from word-of-mouth referrals. My satisfied clients have been talking me up!"

"Well, sure," Adam said. "You do an amazing job."

"Don't lay it on too thick," I cautioned him. "We still have to live with her."

Sarah punched my arm playfully. "I need to get started on those projects this weekend. Gabe, remember you promised to hang out with Lucas tomorrow?"

"Yeah. I'm looking forward to it." Lucas was Sarah's five-year-old son. Since she was a single mom, I tried to help out whenever I could. And Lucas was a great kid.

"What are your plans?" she asked.

"You always ask that. Don't you trust me?"

"Not after you showed him *The Day the Earth Stood Still*, and he had nightmares about murderous robots for a week."

I held up an index finger. "That was one time. And I think you're exaggerating about him having them for a week. Look, if the weather is warm enough and windy enough, we might fly a kite. If not, we'll play in the park and watch cartoons and make pizza. Is that okay?"

"That is fine," she said. "So how are things going with you guys?"

"Same ole, same ole for me," Adam said, taking a sip. "Most of my time is spent trying to keep the users from clicking on phishing emails and then cleaning up the mess after they do. Thirteen years 'til I retire."

"You're not fooling me," Sarah said. "I know you love it there."

"I don't love all the meetings," he shot back. "I like computers better than people."

"Boy, you're in a mood today," I said.

"I'm just short on sleep."

"Yeah," I agreed, "at your age, you're probably used to hitting the hay about nine o'clock."

"You're hilarious," Adam replied in a deadpan voice.

"And what's up with you, Gabe?" Sarah asked.

I told them about how the other day I fixed a software bug that another programmer had left in the code. IT people love stories about other IT people messing up.

"And yesterday I drove out to Plainfield to see a guy about a trucking app."

"How did that go?" Adam asked.

"It didn't. Wasn't a good fit. I didn't fit with his budget, and he didn't fit with my mental health. Then when I got home ..." I paused. The encounter with Zastra had been on my mind all night. I had even had fitful dreams about talking reptiles. But what could I tell them about the strange lizard person without sounding insane?

"What?" Sarah asked. "What happened when you got home?"

I had to tell them something.

"Nothing ... much. It was ... I don't know ... unusual. Someone was waiting on my porch. Real strange. They wanted to hire me to do an investigation on a missing person case."

"You mean like a web search or database analysis or something?" Adam asked. "Or like a private investigator?"

"More like a private investigator, I think. This ... um ... this person didn't say much. Just set up an appointment for me to meet with their boss this afternoon."

"You're not going, are you?" asked Sarah. "This sounds like underworld stuff. What did this person look like?"

"I couldn't see much. It was getting dark, and he ... or she wore a hoodie."

"Yup, sounds like criminals," Sarah said. "You shouldn't get mixed up in this. Besides, don't you need a license to be an investigator?"

I shrugged. "Beats me. Not Miss Marple or Angela Lansbury."

"You do understand the difference between fiction and reality, right?"

"I thought it wouldn't hurt to at least listen to what they have to say. I don't have much else going on currently. Besides, what's the point of working for yourself if you don't take an oddball gig every now and then?"

"Well, drive for Uber or something. This sounds suspicious. If you go to this meeting and then try to get out, you may end up wearing cement overshoes."

Adam looked at her over the tops of his glasses. "Cement overshoes? C'mon, Sarah. You've been watching too many old B movies. Gabe's a grown-up. He'll be okay. Where's the meeting?"

"Some industrial park east of downtown. They gave me the address in GPS coordinates. Did you realize you can just type those into Google Maps?"

"Sure," Sarah said. "There's this game where you search for clues and do math to come up with a longitude and latitude to find a prize. But that's not the point here—"

Adam raised a hand and interrupted her. "You know, it might be fun. I can sure understand wanting a change of pace."

"Thank you," I said.

Sarah shot Adam a look. I wondered what was with all these motherly feelings of trying to keep me protected.

Chapter 4

The Galactic Detective Agency

The GPS coordinates Zastra had given me led to an empty warehouse in an industrial park. An overhead door on the warehouse was open, pulled up about head height. I parked my car and walked in. Everything was steel and concrete. And dirt. The place was filthy. A line of skylights in the ceiling admitted a dim light. In the far corner, Zastra was standing in front of something the size of a small house covered with a tarp. I walked toward her down through the line of concrete support columns, my footsteps echoing in the empty space. I walked past a rusted-out forklift, past a stack of empty pallets, past rusting barrels, past a pile of trash, past more pallets, more trash. It was a really long warehouse.

Zastra wore the same robe she had the night before, but this time the hood was off her head. The scaly olive skin and crested ridges looked as they had the previous evening. I had half convinced myself I had made that part up in my dreams. I kept gazing at those crests."

"What are you staring at?" Zastra said gruffly. "My eyes are down here."

"Sorry. I've just never seen anyone like you?"

"You've never seen a Srathan?"

"If I had, I think I would remember it. What did you say again?"

"A Srathan, someone from the planet Sratha."

"You're from another ... planet? Well, that explains why I've never seen anyone like you at Applebee's."

"Where did you think I was from? Canada?"

"We don't get a lot of people from other planets around here. So where is Sthr ... Sthr ... Sthratha?" My tongue was stumbling on the word.

"It's Sratha."

"Srr ... Srra ... Sratha. Sratha. Is that it?"

"Close enough. It's about twenty light-years away if that means anything to you."

"Not really. And just for the record, are you male or female or something else?"

"I am female. But not every species in the galaxy even has gender ... or just those two. What about you, Gabriel Lake?"

"You can call me Gabriel. I'm male. From Earth. A human man."

"Male. Are you sure? I would have guessed female."

"What? Couldn't you tell from my muscular physique?" I made a mental note to work out more, or at least grow a beard. "Anyway, so I'm supposed to meet your employer?"

"Yes."

She stepped back and pulled the tarp to the floor. It had not been covering a small house. It had been covering what looked to be a spaceship. It was shaped like an egg lying on its side, a red egg with small wings, a black ring running horizontally around its middle, and a low dome on top. Landing struts were holding it off the warehouse floor. As I stood staring at it, a ramp began to lower with a *whir* from the side of the egg. A line of red lights ran up the ramp into the ship.

"Follow me." She turned and walked up the ramp.

I placed a foot at the bottom of the ramp, then hesitated. What was I getting myself into? This was like being swept away into Oz. This was taking the red pill. This was stepping into a new, unknown world. Each step was—

"Gabriel," Zastra called from inside the ship, interrupting my train of thought. "I said to follow."

I followed. The ramp led to a curved corridor that seemed to circle around the ship ... or rather ovaled around it since the ship was egg shaped, with doors along the corridor. Directly in front of the ramp was an opening leading to a large vertical shaft. The shaft had two ladders on opposite sides leading down and up. Zastra swung herself onto one ladder and motioned me to the other.

"We're going to the office," she said. "Climb."

I climbed up after her. The corridor I had first entered resembled how a spaceship is often portrayed in the movies with gleaming white metal. The office we climbed into was entirely different. Everything was wood and natural materials. The walls were a deep hunter green with works of art hanging on them

— paintings, sculptures. One of the pieces appeared to be a 3D model of the galaxy.

A view screen hung on one wall, with a half dozen red leather chairs arranged in a semi-circle around it. Two wooden desks stood against another wall, each with a chair and what looked like some kind of computer terminal on top. Zastra sat down at one of the desks and motioned me toward the other. I sat. A large, domed porthole was above me. It was currently affording a view of the dingy warehouse ceiling, but in space I was sure it would show the stars. Across the room, a birdcage hung from a hook. Inside it two birds with bright yellow feathers were giving me appraising stares.

The view screen flashed to life, and a face appeared. It was a human face. In fact, it was the face of Dwayne "The Rock" Johnson.

"Good afternoon, Gabriel Lake," said the face. "My name is Oren Vilkas."

"Hello," I said. "So you're not Dwayne Johnson? You know, you look just like Dwayne Johnson, the Rock. I bet you get that a lot."

"No, Gabriel Lake, I have simply taken a form that you would be accustomed to. If you do not like this one, I can change it." The screen began flipping through different faces at a rapid pace. Tom Hanks, Richard Nixon, Helen Mirren, Bill Gates, Mahatma Gandhi, Morgan Freeman, Abraham Lincoln, George Clooney, Taylor Swift, Angelina Jolie, Steve Jobs.

"Wait. Stop," I said. "You're giving me a headache. Just use your normal appearance, whatever your body really looks like. I can take it."

"I don't have a body. Not anymore." The faces continued to shift, though at a slower rate. He was now trying old sitcom characters — Urkel, Kramer, Ron Swanson, Lucy, Fonzie, Aunt Bee. "I once had a body, of course. But at the end of my life, I had my consciousness digitized and uploaded. Now I exist inside this ship's computer. I can appear on the screen taking any form I like. Or as a hologram. Or I can be downloaded, at least in part, onto mobile devices."

"Wait. You did what now?"

"I assume you are asking about digitizing my consciousness."

"Yeah. How the heck does that work?"

"First, scientists had to map the structure of the brain. From that, they were able to develop software to emulate that structure. Then it was simply a matter of taking a data snapshot of my brain at the time of my physical death and uploading that to the software."

"Wow! I'm a computer programmer. I'd love to have a glance at that code."

"Not a chance, Gabriel Lake. You have never seen a computer like this. You might … break something."

"Fine. I wouldn't want to break you. So how do you make a decision like that, to upload your consciousness?"

"It was simple. I was not ready to die."

"If you say so. It seems unnatural somehow."

"Does it seem unnatural to you for people on Earth to continue living with the aid of artificial hearts or for them to walk with artificial hips?"

"Okay. Okay." I raised my hands to concede the point. "I guess I'm simply not accustomed to it. So what did you use to look like? Why don't you just appear that way?"

"I don't particularly like my former appearance. I was overweight then."

The faces were now sequencing through alien species. There was one like Zastra. Others were furry or feathery and one looked surprisingly like E.T.

"So how would you like me to appear to you, Gabriel Lake?"

"Just go back to Dwayne Johnson." The face settled into the Rock wearing a suit with an open shirt collar.

"Now, how should I address you, Gabriel Lake?" the Rock, or rather Oren Vilkas, asked me.

"You can call me Gabriel."

"Satisfactory. You may call me Oren. All this is obviously a lot for you to take in. I will allow you time to ask any other questions you have before we begin talking business."

"Okay. I take it you're an alien, too, like Zastra?"

"I dislike that term. I do not think of myself as an alien. To me, you are the alien. But it is true, I am not from Earth. But neither am I from Sratha, like Zastra. I am from a planet called Rheged Prime."

"Are there a lot of planets with intelligent life?" I was struggling to wrap my head around all this.

"Thousands of them. Possibly hundreds of thousands in this galaxy alone."

"And you came to Earth in this?" I waved my hands around the cabin. "This is your spaceship?"

"Yes."

"And you … you live inside a computer."

"That is correct, more or less."

"If I can ask, what's that like? You mentioned you were transferred at your physical death. How long has it been?"

"About four hundred twenty Earth years."

"Wow. So how do you like it? Is it boring or fun?"

"I do miss some things from having a physical body. The scent of a flower, the taste of food, the touch of another person. I do have simulators that can give me those experiences. But, in truth, it is not quite the same thing. All I really have is an intellectual life. But I have found that extremely rewarding. I have read the great works of literature from every known world other than Earth. I can think deeply and quickly. I am not distracted. And I have my work."

"So what was the deal with the hypodermic dart last night?"

"Ah, yes," said Oren. "Are you familiar with nanites? Do you know what they are?"

"I've heard of them on sci-fi shows. They're microscopic robots."

"Correct. The hypodermic needle injected nanites called translator bots into your bloodstream."

"You put robots inside me?"

"Let me assure you, they are quite helpful and mostly harmless."

"*Mostly* harmless?"

He waved a hand. "Only minor side effects. Upon injection, some of the translator bots began scanning your mind to determine your native language. Others moved to attach to the auditory cortex of your brain. There they intercept the sounds coming from your ears and translate it into your native speech."

"These bots translate language?"

"Yes. I am not speaking English to you now. The translator bots translate what I am saying in my language into English for you. You can now travel to any country on Earth or any planet in the known galaxy and understand what they are saying. You should also be able to understand dolphins, elephants, and dogs, though their language is limited."

"So I guess I wasted two years in high school Spanish. I suppose you have these bots, too. Is that how you are understanding me?"

"Precisely. Zastra has them implanted in her, and they are built into my sound-processing software. Every space-faring race in the galaxy is using them."

"Except humans," I pointed out.

"Correct. Earth is currently quarantined."

"Quarantined? Why are we quarantined?"

He chuckled. "Seriously, Gabriel? Do you follow the news on your planet?"

"Yeah, okay. I get it. But I hate feeling like we're the outcasts of the galaxy."

"Yours is not the only quarantined planet. And if it helps, Earth's status is scheduled for a re-evaluation."

"That's not so bad, then. When will that happen?"

"It's in about five hundred twenty-five of your years."

"Oh. Guess I won't put that on my calendar. But wait, that means you are violating the quarantine."

"Yes, we are. But I'm trying to earn a substantial fee. It is worth the risk."

"The missing person case."

"Precisely. Queen Scythia of the planet Diere has hired us to find her daughter, the crown princess and heir to the throne. Her Royal Highness has run off with her boyfriend, a male from a different planet called Cunedda."

"The boyfriend is named Cunedda?"

"No. His home planet is Cunedda. His name is Tam Elam. He is from a noble family. However, he is considered an unsuitable match by the palace because he is not Dieren."

"Is this like a Romeo and Juliet situation?" I asked. "Diere and Cunedda are bitter enemies, but these two star-crossed lovers have found each other despite the rivalry between their worlds?"

"I do not know what you mean by Romeo and Juliet," Oren said.

"You don't? It's Shakespeare. Terrific writer. Some of the best literature written by anyone on Earth. You should read it sometime."

"Earth literature is also subject to the quarantine. It is feared that is how Earthlings spread their terrible ideas. But to your point, Diere and Cunedda are not enemies. They are in the same star system and have been on friendly terms for centuries. Indeed, there has been a fair amount of intermarriage between their people, but not in the royal line. Their constitution stipulates that the ruler must have Dieren parents."

"I see."

"We have been hired to locate the princess and bring her back to Diere, with or without the boyfriend. We have reason to believe they are hiding on Earth. With the quarantine, Earth would be an excellent place to stay under the radar."

"Hey, you said 'under the radar.' So that's a term in your language, too?" I asked.

"It is not. That would be the translator bots paraphrasing my words into English parlance."

"Oh. So where on Earth do you think this princess is?"

"Very near this location. Our information places her in a town called Potato."

"Wait. What? A town called Potato?"

"Yes. Doubtless, you are familiar with it, Gabriel. It is not far from here."

"I have never heard of a town called Potato in my life." I was going to say I couldn't imagine someone naming a town Potato, but I've seen some weird town names — Bread Loaf, Boogertown, Buttzville. "How is it spelled?"

Two words appeared on the view screen like a caption below the face of Dwayne Johnson — *Port Otto.*

"Oh," I said. "Port Otto. You mean Port Otto."

"Isn't that what I said?"

"You said Potato. It's Port Otto."

"Sorry. It must be a glitch in the translator bots. It happens occasionally."

"Yeah, well you know the old saying, 'You say potato, I say Port Otto.' Anyhow, that little burg isn't too far from here. So what do you need from me?"

"Obviously, neither Zastra nor I can go to Potato and inquire. I do not have a body, and hers is ... we might say ... uncommon in these parts."

"Yes, we might say that."

"I, therefore, require local talent."

"So you want me to just go to Potato ... I mean Port Otto ... and ask if anybody new has come around?"

"Correct. They should not be difficult to find. The boyfriend, Tam Elan, appears vaguely human except he has a flat nose and horns on his head."

"Yeah, that should make him stand out," I said.

"Agreed. And Princess Ralph has green skin and is twenty feet tall. Any questions?"

"Yes! I have a ton of questions. Starting with ... what? She's twenty feet tall? And her name is Ralph?"

"What is so surprising about her name? It is considered a lovely name for girls on Diere."

"Well, not so much here. But the thing is, like I told Zastra, I don't actually do detective work. I just read detective novels. I'm a computer programmer by trade. Now if you need an application for recording your cases or something, then I might be able to help."

"I know what you do for a living," Oren said. "Allow me to ask you a question. Suppose there was a room, a typical room on Earth, and you wanted to discover if someone comes along after you and enters the room and searches it. What would you do to make sure you find that out?"

"I don't know. I wasn't prepared for a quiz today." I thought for a moment. "I suppose if it had a desk or a dresser, I might position all the items on it to point to something across the room. That way I would know if they had been moved. Or wait, another thing would be to take a hair and close the door with the hair between the door and the doorframe. If I come back and the hair is gone, then obviously someone had opened the door and let it fall." I remembered Archie Goodwin doing something like that in a Nero Wolfe book.

Dwayne Johnson's face beamed. "See, Gabriel. Your experience reading, even of fiction, has made you an excellent Earth operative."

I admit I was tempted. It sounded like fun.

"When would you want me to do this?" I asked.

"As soon as possible. How about tomorrow morning? I can pay you well. I understand that gold is of some value here on Earth."

"That it is. But I'm tied up tomorrow morning."

"We need it done tomorrow morning, Gabriel."

"Sorry. I'm taking care of a friend's kid tomorrow morning."

"The child can come along with us. There should be no danger to it. You simply need to verify the location of the runaway princess. We'll take care of the rest."

"You're coming too?"

"Yes. Zastra will download as much of me as can fit onto her tablet and bring me along in an advisory capacity."

"And Zastra's coming?"

"Yes, along with Buad and Blan." Dwayne Johnson's head nodded toward the birdcage.

"You mean the birds?"

"Hey, who you callin' birds, buddy?" I jumped in surprise. It was one of the birds talking.

Oren said, "Buad and Blan are my associates from the planet Avan. It is an ancient and very advanced culture. As you can imagine, they are excellent at reconnaissance and surveillance. They are part of the Galactic Detective Agency team, as you will be, temporarily at least."

"Galactic Detective Agency. That's quite a name." I kind of liked the sound of it. But I could only imagine what Sarah would say if I dragged Lucas along on an adventure with Oren's menagerie of associates.

"Sorry," I said. "It's a hard pass. My friend would not want her little boy going on an adventure with Zastra and talking birds."

"We ain't birds, mister," one of them shrieked. "We're Avanians. Are you dumb or something?"

"Well, you're in a cage," I shot back.

"Cage! This ain't no cage. It's a habitat. Let me at him. This guy needs a good pecking."

Dwayne Johnson's face remained still until the Avanians quieted down. "As you wish, Gabriel. Zastra, erase his memory and drop him off at his house."

"Wait a minute," I stammered. "What's this about erasing my memory?"

"It's because of the quarantine. We can't let you remember us. We'll erase everything since Zastra approached you last night … more or less."

"And by *more or less* what exactly do you mean?"

"Memory erasing is an inexact art, Gabriel. Let's say, since last night plus or minus one Earth year."

"I can't afford to forget everything in the last year!"

"No?"

"You have me, don't you?"

"I believe so." Dwayne Johnson's face wore a definite smirk.

"Fine. Fine. I'll do it. I'll take the kid with me. Only … Zastra, keep your hood up, and you … Avanians, don't talk to him."

Chapter 5

Going to Potato

Saturday morning dawned sunny and mild, which was an encouraging change from the gray days we had lived with through most of January and February. Still, I was worried as I drove to Sarah's apartment. I wondered if I could juggle both Lucas and the Galactic Detective Agency at the same time. Could I show Lucas a good time without him discovering that Zastra and the others came from alien worlds?

Sarah met me at the door. She called back into the apartment, "Lucas, Gabe is here." She pulled off her glasses and cleaned them while we waited for him to appear. "Thanks for doing this."

"No problem. He's an awesome kid."

Lucas loped to the door with a grin on his face. "What are we doing today, Gabe?"

"Well, this morning, we are taking a little drive down to Port Otto with some friends of mine. There's an awesome donut shop in town I think you'll like. The afternoon depends on how long we spend in Port Otto. But it looks like a lovely day to go to the park."

"Friends?" Sarah raised her eyebrows. "I didn't know you had any friends other than Adam and me."

"Very funny. It's a client, and we have to go check out something." It wasn't technically a lie.

Sarah's lips swerved to one side in a look of disappointment.

I said, "Sorry. I couldn't get out of it. But don't worry. It shouldn't take long. And Lucas will be my first priority."

She wagged a finger at me. "He had better be."

I held up two fingers in my old Cub Scout sign. "Scouts honor."

Lucas and I walked to my car in the parking lot. I pulled the car seat I always kept for him from the trunk and fixed it in the back seat. He climbed in, and we drove off.

I had agreed to drive everyone to Port Otto since I was the only one with a valid Indiana driver's license. Lucas and I headed toward the warehouse where I had met Oren the day before. I stopped the car in front of the door.

"What are we doing here?" Lucas asked.

"This is where I'm picking up my client. Sorry it won't be just you and me, but I think this will be fun. I hope so anyway."

Zastra came out carrying a tablet device in one hand and the birdcage … correction, the Avanian habitat … in the other hand. Placing the cage in the back seat beside Lucas, she climbed in the front. Thankfully, she didn't turn around and hiss a hello at him.

Since Lucas hadn't been injected with translator bots, Oren, Zastra, Buad, and Blan could talk to me without him understanding them. But I had to be careful about what I said back to them. I didn't want Lucas to find out he was in the presence of extraterrestrials. We pulled out of the industrial park and hopped on Interstate 65 heading south.

"I have been trying to learn about Earth," Zastra said as we drove. "So this vehicle is called a truck?"

"No. It's called an automobile, or a car. Trucks are bigger and boxy."

"What did you say?" Lucas asked.

"Oh, nothing. Just … um … talking to myself."

"Why is your friend hissing like that?" Lucas said.

"She … um … has a cold," I replied. I leaned over to Zastra and muttered, "Keep your voice low."

"How long will it take to get there?" Zastra whispered.

I decided the best course of action would be to phrase my answers as a conversation with Lucas. "It's about thirty or forty minutes to the donut shop, Lucas. Hang loose and look out the window."

Oren's face, or rather Dwayne Johnson's face, flashed onto the tablet. "How will this donut shop assist us in our search?"

"What's that noise?" asked Lucas.

'Um … my car started making that sound. I need to have it checked. You know, buddy, this place is called the Donut Dive. I stopped by there once a few years ago. It's a regular Port Otto institution, the place where everybody goes. My friend here and I need to talk to a couple of people in Port Otto, and I think going to the donut shop will help us find them."

"Acceptable," said Oren.

We passed out of Indianapolis into the open countryside of rural Indiana. We drove through rolling hills and small towns. We passed woods and pastures and fields awaiting the spring planting.

"Can we play a game while we drive?" Lucas asked.

"Sure, buddy. What do you want to play?"

"How about I Spy?"

"Okay. You can go first."

"What are donuts?" asked Zastra.

I held up a hand to indicate she should wait.

"I spy something with my little eye, and it is … green," Lucas said.

"Green, huh? Is it a green donut? How would you like to eat a green donut? That would be yummy!"

"No, silly. There aren't any green donuts. What would they be made of? Broccoli? Spinach? Yuck! Besides, we can't even see the donuts yet. It has to be something we see right now."

"So donuts are food?" Zastra asked.

"Uh-huh," I said. "I had a pistachio donut once, and it was green. It tasted amazing, too. But something we can see right now. Hmm. Is it the grass along the road?"

"Yup," said Lucas. "You got it. That was an easy one. Now it's your turn."

"Okay. I spy something with my little eye, and it is—"

"What are those animals out in that field?" Zastra asked.

I nodded at her. "Brown."

"Yes, those brown animals," said Zastra. "What are they?"

"Brown. Brown," said Lucas. "Is it the dirt on that truck?"

"Nope. That's not it," I said. "Hurry, we're almost past it."

"The trees?"

"Not the trees."

"The cows!"

"That's it," I said. "Those brown animals are called cows. It's where milk comes from."

"I see," said Zastra.

Lucas said, "I know they're called cows, and they give milk. I'm not a baby. Okay, I spy something with my little eye, and it is yellow."

"Is it the sun?" I asked.

"No, not the sun."

"How about the birds in the seat beside you?"

"Again with the birds!" said Buad or Blan. I couldn't yet tell them apart, so I didn't know which one said it. "We ain't birds, you knucklehead."

"Yup, it's the birds," said Lucas. "Why are we bringing these birds along?"

"They below to my friend here," I said.

"Belong! Belong!" the Avanians squawked. "We belong to ourselves, thank you very much."

"Sorry," I said. "It's easier to explain it that way."

"Who are you talking to?" asked Lucas.

"Hmm? Oh, I was just talking to myself. I work at home all alone, you know. So I talk to myself a lot. It's my turn now, right?"

"Pick that red truck up there," said Zastra. I gazed at her. A gleam had crept into her yellow eyes. She seemed to be getting into the game.

"Okay. I spy something with my little eye, and it is red." I glanced at Zastra. A tiny smile was sneaking across her face. Who would have thought it?

"Red," said Lucas. "Is it the light on the dashboard?"

I quickly checked the dash. Did I have a warning light on? No. The only red was the little indicator that told me I was in drive. "Not the light," I said.

"There's red on this old fast-food bag on the floor back here," Lucas said.

"Yeah, but I can't see that. By the way, remind me of that when we get to the Donut Dive. I'll throw it away."

"Oh! Is it the red delivery truck up there?"

"That's it, buddy. That's it." By now my head was spinning from carrying on multiple conversations at the same time. "Hey, I better quit playing for now and concentrate on my driving. The turn-off isn't too far from here."

"Okay," said Lucas. "I'll watch the birds."

"Somebody better tell this kid we ain't birds," Buad or Blan muttered.

I glanced in the review mirror and glared at the Avanians.

Fifteen minutes later we crested a hill and saw the single stoplight of Port Otto ahead of us. There wasn't a lot to the town, a string of homes, a concrete block firehouse, a gas station mini-mart, one fast food joint, and a little church with white clapboards. There were a couple of other buildings that used to be something but weren't anymore. On the right was a small, square building made of painted concrete blocks with a big sign on top reading: *Donut Dive*. I slowed and pulled into the parking lot.

"Is this the town called Potato?" Zastra asked.

"Welcome to Potato," I said to Lucas. "I mean Port Otto."

"Potato!" Lucas giggled. "That's funny. A town called Potato. Do they build houses out of French fries instead of boards?"

I parked the car and turned to Zastra. "Do you want to stay in the car while Lucas and I go in?" I dropped my voice to a whisper. "Nod your head forward and back. Don't say anything."

Zastra nodded.

"Okay. We'll bring you back something."

"Bring us something, too," sang one of the Avanians.

I walked around the car and opened Lucas's door. He already had his seat belt unbuckled and jumped out.

The Donut Dive was a tiny hole-in-the-wall kind of place, but it was packed with people that Saturday morning. There were families with kids, older couples, middle-aged men in cycling shorts who had ridden here on their bikes. Everyone was crowded around tiny tables, talking and laughing and eating donuts.

Lucas and I weaved through the crowd to the long glass counter. Lucas stared wide-eyed at the huge variety of donuts on display.

"I'll have a regular yeast donut," I told the kid behind the counter. "Wait. Is that bacon on those over there?"

"Yeah, those are maple bacon donuts."

"I'll have one of those!"

"Instead of the yeast?"

"No, the yeast is for a friend out in the car. Make that two yeasts," I added, remembering the Avanians. "And a cup of coffee. Lucas, have you made up your mind?"

"I want this one with sprinkles," he said, pointing at the display case. "Gabe, can I have two?"

"Why not, buddy?" I answered.

"Thanks! I'll take a chocolate one also. And some chocolate milk?"

"Sure." I nodded at the clerk. "That's the order then. Did you catch all that?"

"Two yeasts, one maple bacon, one yeast with sprinkles, one chocolate cake, one coffee, one chocolate milk."

26

I paid the toll with a credit card, and we moved to the end of the display case to wait for our order to be pulled together. An older couple was sitting at a table nearby, sipping coffee and watching the crowd. They looked like they might be the kind of people to keep track of what was going on around town. There were two empty chairs at their table.

"Hi, folks," I said. "Mind if we sit here while they fill our order? We got it to go. It'll only be a minute."

"Help yourself," the man said with a chuckle.

"Thanks. We're here looking at houses this morning. We might be moving into the community. Would you call this a friendly place?"

"Sure," the man said. "We've lived here forty-two years."

"We're very proud of our little town," said the woman. "Of course, we don't have all the amenities of Indianapolis, but at least you know all your neighbors here."

"Sound pleasant," I said. "Are a lot of other people moving here?"

"I don't know about that," the man said.

"Well, do you know of anyone who has moved in recently?"

"I don't think so," he said.

The woman said, "Kitty told me the Holtz place just got rented. But I haven't met the folks. Neither had Kitty, for that matter. She thought the man was kinda stand-off-ish."

"Any idea when they moved in?" I asked.

"Couldn't have been that long ago. Less than a month."

"I might try to look them up while I'm here. You know, try to find out what other people found attractive about the town."

The kid behind the counter called out, "Order for Lake."

"Pick that up, would you, Lucas?" I said. "So where's this Holtz place? Just in case, I want to chat with the folks."

"Go west at the stoplight a couple miles," said the man. "Turn left on Beanblossom Road and go, I don't know, maybe three miles. The place has a round barn. You can't miss it."

"Thank you so much." I stood to my feet. Lucas slipped beside me holding the bag. "Let's go, buddy."

Lucas and I left the crowded shop. There were tables outside on a patio, and the day was becoming genuinely pleasant.

"Let's sit over here," I said.

"Gabe, did you tell a lie in there? You aren't moving here, are you?"

"Oh! No, I'm not moving, buddy. Sorry about the fib. It was a little white lie. Nothing that hurts those people. It was just a quick way to get an answer to a question. More like playing pretend. But you should talk to your mom about that. I don't want to be a bad influence."

I led Lucas to a table and got him set up with his donuts and chocolate milk. I sat down my coffee. "I'll run these other donuts over to my friend in the car."

"Isn't she going to come over here and join us?"

"Probably not."

I walked over to the passenger side window of the car, opened the door, and handed Zastra the bag. "Here are two donuts. You can have one, and Buad and Blan can split the other."

She opened the bag and sniffed at it. "This is not meat," she said frowning at the donuts. Evidently, she was a carnivore.

"No," I answered. "Mainly sugar ... and a few other things."

"And this is an Earth delicacy?"

"Oh yeah. You could say that." I shut the door and walked back to the table where Lucas was struggling to open his chocolate milk.

"Want some help with that, buddy?"

"Nah. I've got it." He gave it one more twist and got it open, looking proud at his accomplishment. "Your friend is kinda scary."

I wondered how much he had actually seen of Zastra. "Scary how?"

"All hidden away in that hoodie where I can't see her. And hissing all the time."

"Like I said, she has a cold. It's down in her throat, that's all. So how's kindergarten going?" I asked, trying to change the subject.

"School is okay, I guess. It's boring sometimes." He bit into his first donut, and his eyes lit up.

"Boring?"

He held up an index finger and waited to answer until he had swallowed the bite. This kid was getting raised right.

"Yeah. It's all baby stuff. I learned all that in pre-school."

He was a smart one, for sure, just like his mom.

I tried a bite of my maple bacon. "Oh," I said.

"Oh what?" asked Lucas.

"Oh my, this is delicious."

Chapter 6

Princess Ralph

The guy in the Donut Dive was mistaken. I *could* miss it and did the first time. But after retracing the route, we found the round barn sitting further back from the road than I had expected.

The farmhouse wasn't what I would have expected either. Instead of being a grand old two-story frame house with a broad porch, built along with the barn in the late 1800s, it was a shabby A-frame, no doubt built during that style's short heyday in the 1970s. Between the A-frame house and the round barn and a square shed in the corner of the yard, the farmstead looked less like a traditional farm and more like a find-the-shapes toy for toddlers.

I told Lucas to stay in the car. Zastra, carrying Oren's tablet, and I went to the door.

"Should I kick the door in?" Zastra asked.

"What? No!" I said. "We aren't sure these are the right people. Let me make the approach."

I knocked on the door. A minute later it opened a crack, the door chain stretched across the opening. Half of a man's face stared out at me through the narrow gap. It appeared human enough.

"Hello, sir," I said. "We're from the county welcome wagon. We are looking for a Mr. Tam Elam, whom we understand is a new resident of our community. We have a lovely welcome basket for him and his family."

"Never heard of him," the half face said.

The door started to close. I slid my foot into the crack, immediately wishing I had worn something more substantial than sneakers.

"Excuse me, I couldn't hear you. Would you repeat that?" I asked.

"I said I don't know anybody by that name."

"I'm sorry. My hearing is starting to go. Must have been my early days in a rock band. Would you mind opening the door more fully, so I can hear you?"

The eyes in the half face rolled, but I saw a hand slide back the chain. The door opened enough to show the full person. He still appeared human. He was about my height, dark eyes, thin. Oren had said Tam had a flat nose and horns on his head. An Indianapolis Colts ball cap covered his scalp, so if there were horns, I couldn't see them. His nose looked human, but the skin on it was a shade darker than the rest of his face. Could it be a fake nose?

He spoke slowly, "I said there's nobody here by that name. Did you hear me this time? This isn't going to work, Earth man. You don't have translator bots. When are you going to take the hint that I'm speaking a different language?"

I rubbed a spot at the side of my mouth with my finger while pointing at his face with the other hand. "You've got a little sumpin there." I reached forward and then quickly flipped my hand up, knocking off his cap. Two horns extended an inch above his hair.

Zastra pushed me aside and stepped forward. She threw back her hood, exposing her full lizard-like head. I glanced back at the car, hoping Lucas wasn't watching.

"We are not Earthlings," she said. "Well, he is, but pay no attention to him."

"Hey!" I said. "I thought I was part of the team."

Zastra held up the tablet. I couldn't see Oren's face, but I heard his voice say, "Tam Elam, I am Oren Vilkas. I am here representing Queen Scythia. Her Majesty has an offer to make to the princess. May we come in?"

Tam sighed and opened the door wide.

"Before I come in," I said, "I have a kid in the car. Could he play in your backyard? I noticed a swing set back there." I lowered my voice. "He doesn't know that you're ... um ... space aliens ... no offense or anything."

"None taken," said Tam.

"Thank you. All in all, I'd like to keep it that way. Fewer questions. You understand, right?"

Tam waved an arm, which I took to mean he was granting permission. I started toward the car. Oren called after me, "Gabriel, bring Buad and Blan."

I opened the car door beside Lucas. "Hey, sport. We're gonna be inside a few minutes. Why don't you go play on the swing set in the backyard? Don't come to the door. Just play out there. I'll get you when we're done."

"Okay." Lucas hopped out and streaked to the backyard, no doubt still under the influence of donuts.

I returned to the front door carrying the cage and let myself in. The door opened directly into a great room that extended all the way up the tall A-frame. Tam and Zastra were sitting in chairs. The tablet holding Oren was leaning against a lamp on a table. Oren wore a different appearance now. His face was thin, had a protracted forehead, and was sage green.

Over in a corner lounging on an oversized couch was a young woman whom I assumed was Princess Ralph. She was a lovely girl. That is if you weren't put off by her being twenty feet tall. Her skin was sage green like Oren's, and on her head, she wore a tiara the size of a basketball hoop.

"Ah," said Oren. "May I present our associate from Earth, Mr. Gabriel Lake. Bow to Her Royal Highness, Gabriel. Also, my Avanian associates, Buad and Blan."

I bowed, too dumbstruck by her size to say anything. Meanwhile, Buad and Blan were making birdly bows inside the cage.

"Please be seated, Mr. Lake," Ralph said.

I sat in a chair next to Zastra, setting the cage on the floor between us.

Princess Ralph said, "First we must offer our guests refreshment." She called out, "Oh, Khan."

A man appeared in the doorway to the kitchen. He was regular size, by which I mean human size, though he was sage green and had a tall forehead similar to the way Oren was appearing on the screen.

"This is Khan, my personal butler. Khan, our guests are Zastra, Oren Vilkas there on the tablet, and Gabriel Lake. Oh, and Buad and Blan in the habitat. Would you bring them some drinks?"

"Very good, m'lady," Khan said with an infinitesimal bow of his head.

Oren bowed his head on the screen. "Nothing for me, thanks. I'm digital."

"As you wish, sir," Khan disappeared back into the kitchen.

"Excuse me, Your Highness," I said.

"Your Royal Highness," Zastra muttered.

"Your Royal Highness," I continued. "If I may ask, is it usual on your planet to bring your butler along when you run off with a man?"

"Oh, Khan has been with me since I was born," she said. "I wouldn't go anywhere without him. He sang me to sleep when I was little. He taught me to read. I don't know how many times he has kept me out of trouble. Khan is absolutely essential and the most loyal companion anyone could ever have."

"Plus, he is discreet," Tam added. "He made himself scarce during the honeymoon. He would disappear for hours at a time."

"Honeymoon, you say," said Oren. "So you two have gotten married since you left Diere?"

Tam said, "I thought we should wait until we could have an official Dieren wedding, but Ralph insisted."

"Mummy forbade us to marry on Diere," Ralph pouted. "She and the entire council of elders and that vile Commander Woad. They insisted I marry a Dieren. No off-worlders in the royal family tree, they said. So old-fashioned! So we eloped here. We got married in a city called Las Vegas."

"Really!" I said. I pictured the two of them, Tam with the horns and Ralph twenty feet tall being married by an Elvis impersonator. "And you didn't encounter any problem with that?"

"No. I'm told that quickie marriages are standard business in Las Vegas."

"So I've heard," I said. "But I mean with you being green and, let's say, taller than the average human. No problems with that?"

"No," she beamed. "No problem at all. The couple before us were blue. I think they said they were dressed as smurfs."

"Well, that's Vegas for you," I said.

Khan glided back into the room carrying a tray of cups. He served Ralph first with a deep bow, then brought the tray to Tam, Zastra, and me. He had two tiny cups for Buad and Blan.

He seemed like such a stuffed shirt. I thought I would have a little fun with him. When he got to me, I said, "You know, the name Khan is quite famous on Earth."

"Is it indeed, sir?"

"Yes, there was a conqueror by that name. He conquered most of Asia and a fair bit of Europe. It was quite a while ago."

"I see, sir."

Zastra snapped at me, "It isn't proper for you to talk to the butler in front of the princess."

"Oh, go right ahead," said Ralph. "This is fascinating. Well, except that none of it is about me."

"His name was Genghis Khan," I said.

"I do not believe he was any relation," Khan said.

"Well, I wouldn't have thought so. So do you have a second name, or is Khan the whole thing?"

"My last name is Krete, sir."

"Wait! So your name is Khan Krete? Khan Krete? Ha!"

"Is that somehow humorous, sir?"

"Well, see, on Earth we have a building material called concrete, so …" I let the sentence hang.

"I see, sir. So my name makes a play on words, as it were. I suppose one might find it humorous that your last name means a body of water. Not that I would find such a thing amusing, of course."

"Oh, well, point taken. And then there was also a Khan who was a bad guy in a space movie."

"Will that be all, sir?"

"Sure."

Khan disappeared through the kitchen doorway, and I realized everyone was staring at me. I guess I had been talking a lot. But how often do you mean space aliens?

"I mean, Khan was the best Star Trek villain ever," I said.

"What are you going on about?" hissed Zastra.

"You've never seen it? It's an awesome movie. You know, KAAAHN!" I shook my fists.

Khan appeared again at the kitchen door. "You bellowed, sir?"

"Oh, sorry," I said meekly. "Nothing. Just a movie quote."

"Very good, sir." Khan turned and disappeared.

All their eyes were still on me, so I turned my attention to the cup in my hand. I was unfamiliar with the beverage. It looked like hot tea, but when I got it close to my face it smelled more like a landfill on an August afternoon. I clamped my lips shut and tilted the cup, letting some of it splash on my upper lip without going into my mouth. Even so, the smell nearly caused me to have a second pass at my donut.

The others sipped their drinks and talked about the weather. It apparently fell to the princess to bring up business because nothing of substance was discussed until she finally said, "So, Mr. Vilkas, you said you come with an offer from Mummy?"

"I do, Your Royal Highness. However, the offer may have changed slightly in light of your recent marriage. I had been instructed to offer you significant inducements to abandon your relationship and come home again to take up your royal duties. But the queen told me that if you had married, I was to make a different offer."

"And what offer would that be?" Ralph asked.

"Your mother believes the most important thing is to have you back on Diere as heir apparent. Without you, the planet would face a political crisis when the time eventually comes for her to pass."

"May it be in the distant future," chanted Ralph. "Long live the queen."

"Certainly," said Oren. "But it is a wise regent who plans for eventualities. The queen is prepared to accept Tam as her son-in-law."

"She is? And the council of elders agrees to this?" Ralph asked.

"There is one proviso."

"Oh, there is, is there?" Ralph's eyes narrowed.

"Tam will be accepted as your prince consort and a member of the royal household, provided you agree to also take a Dieren as a second husband."

"What!" Tam yelped. "A second husband?"

"Interesting," said Ralph, tapping a huge finger to the side of her cheek.

"I am told there is precedent for such a thing in the royal household," Oren said, "though it has not been practiced for several centuries. And, of course, your royal heir must come from your Dieren husband."

"Do I get to pick the Dieren," Ralph asked, "or does it have to be the choice of those old women on the council?"

"Her Majesty assured me the decision is yours and yours alone."

Tam stood. "I don't want to share her!"

"But Tam darling," Ralph said, "this way we can be together, don't you see? Mummy will accept you. And I can still serve my people."

"But what about the other man?" Tam protested.

"Don't worry about him," she assured him with a glimmer in her eye. "It will be solely for politics, a marriage of convenience." She made a pouty face. "I truly do want to go home, baby. And this way you can come with me! Oh, Khan."

The butler glided into the room again. "Yes, m'lady?"

"Khan, please contact Yorbah, and see when she can come and take us back to Diere."

"As you wish, m'lady." Khan glided away again as unobtrusively as he had appeared.

Princess Ralph turned to us, "Yorbah is the private pilot who flew us here. We may as well have her take us back. Her service was … well it was adequate. Frankly, it was cramped. But I have already paid her an exorbitant amount for her silence. Which reminds me, Mr. Vilkas, how were you able to track me down?"

Oren cocked his head modestly. "Oh, I have my ways."

"I'm sure you do," she replied. "Now, Mr. Vilkas, may we talk in private? I want to make sure all my stipulations are fully understood."

"We may indeed, Your Royal Highness. Is there another room to which we can adjourn?"

"There is not another room in this house where … I fit. But I'm sure the others would be glad to move to another room. Khan," she called, "would you show our guests into the kitchen?"

Zastra, Tam, Buad, Blan, and I crowded into the tiny kitchen with Khan. Zastra, Tam, and I found seats at a dingy little table that had seen better days. A plate was still on the table from an earlier meal. The sink was piled with dishes and pans.

I leaned over to Tam. "I sure don't want to yuck your yum, dude, but I'm surprised you would go for a woman that much bigger than you. Not that there's anything wrong with that. But I mean, how do you … how do you even kiss?"

Tam replied with a wink. "Oh, we manage it. More to love, man. More to love." But even as he said it, his face fell. The idea of a second man was clearly bothering him.

I tried to be encouraging. "Hey, don't worry about the other guy. Remember, she loved you enough to run off to a whole different planet. That has to mean something right?"

He gave me a weak smile.

* * *

Oren and Ralph finished up their business quickly, and soon we were in the car heading back to Indianapolis. Lucas fell asleep on the drive back and didn't even wake up when I dropped off the others.

"Your help was quite satisfactory, Gabriel," Oren said. "Zastra?"

The lizard lady told me, "Wait here."

She disappeared into the warehouse, returning a couple of minutes later with a briefcase. She handed it to me. It almost dropped out of my hand, it was so heavy.

"What's this?" I asked.

"Gold," she said. "Your payment." She turned and began walking back into the warehouse. So this was it.

"Thanks," I called after her. "It was a pleasure meeting you, I guess."

As I got back into the car, Lucas was waking up. "Are we back? What are we doing now? I'm hungry."

"It is about lunchtime. And you were great this morning, pal. Let's go out to eat. You can even pick the place." I figured I could afford any place he wanted. After all, I had a briefcase full of gold.

Being a five-year-old, Lucas picked the place with the golden arches. We ate our burgers and told each other dumb jokes. After we ate, we hung out in Garfield Park for a while. Then we went back to my place and found an animated kids' movie on a streaming service. During the movie I texted Sarah:

Watching a movie. When do you want him home?

A couple of minutes later I got a response.

Want to eat dinner with us? What movie BTW?

I texted back.

Yes on Dinner THX. What time? Movie is Friday the 13th. He's loving it.

Moments later I got:

6P and you better be lying about the movie.

* * *

Sarah's apartment smelled wonderful with the aroma of the coming meal.

"Did you have a nice day, slugger?" she asked Lucas.

"Yeah!" Lucas said. "We went to this donut shop, and I got one with sprinkles and one that was chocolate. And Gabe's friend was this weird hissing lady who brought two birds along. She was sick, and her face was green, really green, Mom. And then I played outside at this house while Gabe went inside, and there was this guy inside with horns on his head. And somebody was in the barn looking at the house. They didn't think I saw them, but I did. And we ate at McDonald's.

And Gabe's house is kinda messy. I gotta go to the bathroom. Bye, Gabe!" He ran off up the stairs of the townhouse.

"I didn't get all of that," Sarah said.

I chuckled. "Yeah, five-year-olds and their imagination." I hoped that let Sarah ignore the parts about green faces and horns. But what was that he had said about somebody watching from the barn?

Chapter 7

A Gruesome Discovery

So I had met aliens. I had been part of an investigation, an interstellar woman hunt even. But now it was behind me. It was time to return to my comfortable and slightly boring regular life. Or so I thought.

On Sundays during NFL season, I watch the Colts, but this was March, and football was over. Or if the weather cooperates, I take a bike ride, except this Sunday the weather was a cold drizzle. So this was a day for reading … and picking up the house a little since Lucas had tattled on my messiness.

I had finished Raymond Chandler and moved on to Rex Stout's *The Second Confession*, in which Nero Wolfe takes on a job to investigate the boyfriend of a millionaire's daughter. But the case soon turns into a murder investigation. With these sorts of books, no matter how they start, they always seem to find their way to murder.

I stretched out on the living room couch to read. It was a delightful book. But this was a lazy, rainy Sunday, and I found myself dozing off. I didn't fight it. There are few pleasures in life better than reading and drifting off to sleep on a Sunday afternoon. The only thing that would have made it better would be if this were June, and I was outside in my hammock.

Tap-tap-tap. Tap-tap-tap.

I was dreaming I was Archie Goodwin, Nero Wolfe's assistant and the narrator of all his cases. I was sitting at Archie's desk, listening to a suspect tell Wolfe his version of the events when a tapping sound began echoing from somewhere else in Wolfe's New York brownstone.

Tap-tap-tap. Tap-tap-tap.

In the dream, the suspect stopped talking. He and Wolfe both looked at me. Wolfe said, "Archie." I got up to investigate the tapping. I moved to the hallway.

Tap-tap-tap. Tap-tap-tap.

It was the sound of tapping on glass. I went to the front room and gazed out the window. Nothing there. I moved to the kitchen and found Fritz, Wolfe's chef, tapping his finger against the windowpane. Three taps and a pause. Three taps and a pause.

Tap-tap-tap. Tap-tap-tap.

I started to ask Fritz why he was tapping on the window. But even as I was doing so, my mind began climbing back up into consciousness. I realized the tapping wasn't in the dream. It was in real life, and it was waking me up. My eyes fluttered open.

Tap-tap-tap. Tap-tap-tap.

I sat up and looked around. My eye caught movement at the living room window where a bird was sitting on the windowsill. I pulled myself up from the couch and moved to the window waving my arms to shoo it away.

Tap-tap-tap. Tap-tap-tap.

I knocked on the glass to scare the bird, but the bird merely tapped back. That's when I recognized it. This was one of the Avanians from the ship. I reached up, thumbed open the window lock, and raised the sash a few inches. The Avanian hopped inside, bobbing his head around to take in the surroundings.

"Wake up sleepy head. The boss needs you."

"What for?" I asked, rubbing my eyes "I thought he got everything sorted with Her Royal Highness."

"Well, something came up."

"What?"

"The boss would rather tell you himself. Come to the warehouse."

"Okay. When?"

"When do you think, you bonehead? A week from Thursday? No, now! He wants you now."

"Okay. Okay. Don't ruffle your feathers. I have to put shoes on. Then I'll be on my way. Um … Which one are you, by the way?"

"Which one what?

"Buad or Blan."

"I'm Blan. Can't tell us apart!" He shook his head in disgust.

"Okay, You're Blan. So is there an easy way to tell?"

"Yeah. See this black spot here on the end of my beak? Buad doesn't have that."

"Thanks. Black spot on Blan. Black Blan Got it. So is Buad your mate or spouse or whatever you call it?"

"Mate? Spouse? Dude, you are a dumbbell, aren't you? Buad's my brother. We're brothers, him and me. Get it, dimwit? We were eggs together."

"Okay. Okay. Don't get sore. This is all new to me."

"Yeah, sure. You're just a dumb Earthling who's never met anybody from another planet. So are you coming to see the boss or not?"

"I'm coming. I'm coming. I have to find shoes."

"Don't dawdle. The boss doesn't like it when people dawdle."

"I won't dawdle. Now fly away so I can close the window."

Blan disappeared out the window, and I shut it. I got my shoes on, picked up the car keys, and set off for the warehouse. I wondered what it was that had come up.

I parked my car outside the warehouse and walked in. The spaceship had been moved. It was now closer to the door. The ramp was open as before.

I stepped on the ramp and rapped on the side of the ship with my knuckles. "Hello. Anybody home?"

Nothing. I walked up the ramp and into the corridor. I called out again, "Hello. This is Gabe. You sent for me?"

Oren's voice came from around the corridor. "Gabriel, room six."

I looked at the doors. Each was marked with a symbol in an alien language. I had no idea what the symbols meant.

"How am I supposed to know which room is six?"

"Keep looking at the markings on the doors," Oren called back. "Focus on them."

"I studied the symbol on the nearest door. The lines of the symbol began to dissolve and rearrange themselves into a number three.

"Well, I'll be," I called. "Is that the translator bots doing that?"

"Yes. They work on both your visual and auditory nerves."

"You didn't mention that part the other day."

"You had a lot to take in the other day. Why overload you? But now that you have activated the visual matrix, it will now work much faster. You won't even notice it happening. Now come to room six."

I followed the corridor, staring at the symbols on the doors until I came to six. As I approached the door, it opened automatically like doors in spaceships on TV. I stepped inside. Oren was on a screen built into the back wall. A table stood in the middle of the room. On the table was the body of Tam Elam. He was lying there face up, and it didn't take a detective to figure out he was as dead as disco. A carving knife was sticking out of his chest so straight, so vertical it reminded me of the flagpole down in the neighborhood schoolyard. Blood, which was yellowish rather than red, had coagulated around the blade of the knife and down the side of his chest. The day before I had noticed his nose was a different skin tone from the rest of his face and had wondered if it was fake. Now I knew it was. The nose was half torn off and lying to one side, revealing a flat, much more alien nose underneath.

"Poor guy," I said. "He flies light-years across the galaxy to visit Earth only to end up facing the pointy end of a dagger. That can't be good for Earth's interstellar Yelp rating. I take it this is the something that came up?"

"Yes," said Oren. "We flew back there this morning to work out the timing of when they would return to Diere. We found Tam here on the kitchen floor and no sign of either Princess Ralph or Khan."

"And you brought the body back? It's against the law here to tamper with evidence."

"Really, Gabriel? Do you believe we should have left the body of someone from another planet there for the local police to discover? What kind of red flags would that have raised? The whole area would have been cordoned off and crawling with every kind of law enforcement and military. No, we need to investigate this, if for no other reason than to locate the princess and again persuade her to return to Diere, so I can collect my fee."

"Do you figure it was one of them, Khan or Ralph, who did this?"

"It might be. It might also be someone else."

"Someone else from Earth?"

"Possibly. Or someone not from Earth."

"You didn't happen to tell the Dieren palace they were on Earth, did you?"

"I most certainly did not. But they might have tracked us somehow. We need to find out what happened to the princess and Khan. Are they dead too, and their bodies moved? Or did they escape? Or did one of them commit the murder?"

"Those are all excellent questions. So what do we do?"

"We investigate. I would like you to fly with us back to Potato this afternoon. As a human, you will be our point person for the investigation. Obviously, I can't send Zastra in to talk to people."

"How long will it take?"

"Probably just today, two days perhaps."

I thought about what I had on my to-do list. It wasn't much. I could spare a day or two. Not to mention that Oren paid quite well.

"Okay. Let's do it," I said. "But I should run home to grab some clothes and other things."

"Satisfactory. But hurry. It is already afternoon. We need to begin the investigation today. When you return put your things in room eight. Then come up to the office."

I turned to go, then stopped and turned back to Oren. "By the way, Lucas said something last night about seeing someone in the barn who was watching the house. That might be relevant."

"It might indeed. Hurry back."

As I drove home, I thought about if there was someone I should contact. I didn't think so. Nobody would miss me if I disappeared for a couple of days. If clients needed something, they would email or text me. I would have my phone with me, and I would take my laptop too in case I needed to work on something. I doubted that Oren's ship had Wi-Fi. Why would an alien ship be fitted with Earth technology? But surely I could find Wi-Fi somewhere.

I packed a few things and headed back toward the warehouse, taking a city bus so I wouldn't have to leave my car in the industrial park overnight. The closest bus stop was a good four blocks from the warehouse. But by then the drizzle had finally dried up, so the walk was fine. I found room eight on the ship. It was about the size of room six, except it had a bunk, built-in dresser drawers, a cockpit lounge chair that looked pretty comfy, and a small bathroom walled off in the corner. And as in room six, it had a screen on the back wall. I hoped Oren didn't just pop up unannounced whenever he felt like it. I dropped off my things, headed to the central shaft, and climbed up to the office.

Buad and Blan were back in their habitat. "Hello, Buad, Blan," I said, pointing at each of them as I said their names to indicate I now knew which was which. Zastra was sitting at her desk. I nodded and greeted her, too. Another person I didn't know was standing beside her. He was stocky and short, probably about five feet tall. He had light blue skin, a broad nose, and black hair. He wore a charcoal-colored jumpsuit.

"So you are Gabriel," he said, extending his hand. "This is the Earth custom, right? Shaking hands? I am Jace Gilead. Call me Jace."

"Nice to meet you," I replied, shaking the outstretched hand. "I didn't see you the other day. I take it you're part of the team, too."

"I'm the ship's engineer. I usually hang out in the bowels of the ship. I hear you'll be flying with us today. Welcome to the *Shaymus*."

"The who?" I asked.

"The *Shaymus*. That's the name of the ship."

"You're kidding me, right?"

"No. Why would I kid about the name of the ship?"

"It's just that shamus is an old Earth slang term for a detective. Like PI, gumshoe, private eye. And, well … that's what Oren does."

"Well, on my planet Shaymus is the name of a beautiful mountain overlooking the sea. That's a picture of it over there." He pointed to a painting of an impossibly tall rocky peak towering over boulders that rose from the water far below.

"Wow! And what planet is that? There's so much I don't know about things off Earth. Everything actually."

"He's got that right," Blan interjected from across the room.

"I'm from Rheged Prime, same as Oren," Jace said.

"So you are what people from Rheged Prime look like."

"Um, yeah. I suppose."

"When Oren had a body, he would have looked like you?"

"Well, that was before my time. I have no idea what he originally looked like. But, yeah, I assume it would have been more or less like this."

Oren came on the screen, looking again like Dwayne Johnson. "Are we about ready to go, Jace?"

"Yes, sir."

"So, Oren," I said. "Now that I'm clued in on what a Rhegedian looks like, how about you blue yourself up a little?"

"I decide how I appear, Gabriel. That's one of the advantages of being digital. But if it appeals to you …" Dwayne Johnson's face took on a bluish tint.

"Sweet. Thanks!"

Oren's screen flashed off.

"Well, I need to get to work," Jace said. He moved toward the shaft.

"So you fly this thing?"

"No." He turned back to face me. "I just make sure it can fly. We have an AI pilot. You'll meet her. Come see me sometime, and I'll show you around the ship. Climb down the shaft instead of up. I'm down there in the engine room … or what we call the sherlock."

"Now you're kidding me."

He started grinning.

"You *are* kidding me," I said.

"Yeah, even I know about Earth's greatest consulting detective. Oren came across him in researching Earth and mentioned him to me."

I was going to like this guy.

Jace disappeared down the shaft.

"Better sit down," Zastra said.

I sat at the desk opposite hers. "So how come you even have a second desk here?" I asked. "This wasn't brought in just for me, was it?"

"There used to be another guy."

"What happened to him?"

"You don't want to know."

I started to say that I did want to know, but I realized she might be right.

While I was still thinking about that, a well-modulated female voice came over the speakers. "Prepare for take-off."

"Is that the AI pilot?" I asked Zastra.

"You may address me directly, Gabriel Lake," said the voice. "Yes, I am the piloting AI. My name is Kah-Rehn."

"Karen?"

"No, Kah-Rehn. The emphasis is on the first syllable and pronounced with more of an 'ah' sound. Kah-Rehn."

"Right. Karen."

"Kah-Rehn."

"Sure. But can I call you Karen? I have an Aunt Karen. Really nice lady."

"I'd rather you not, Gabriel Lake. It is Kah-Rehn."

Clamps extended from the floor and locked down my desk chair. The chair tilted back. A five-point harness snaked itself out of the chair and fastened me in. The same thing was happening to Zastra's chair. I glanced across the room. Clamps were rising from the floor to take hold of the red leather chairs. Bars descended from the ceiling like stalactites to hold in place Buad and Blan's habitat. The screen at the front of the office came on, showing the interior of the warehouse.

"We are taking off," Kah-Rehn said.

The engine roared. I felt the *Shaymus* lift off and watched the image on the view screen move up the warehouse walls. We moved forward slowly through the warehouse door to the outside. The screen displayed a view of the other warehouse buildings around us. The dome above showed the cloudy March sky.

"Commencing climb to avoid alien detection," Kah-Rehn said.

I commented to Zastra, "I suppose by alien she means Earthlings. We are going to climb so that nobody— Holy..."

I never finished the sentence because the g-force of sudden acceleration had pinned me to my chair.

Chapter 8

Investigation in Potato

In seconds we must have shot up ten thousand feet, maybe twenty thousand feet. The g-force felt like an elephant sitting on my chest. I managed to roll an eyeball toward the view screen where a tiny Indianapolis, looking like the model of a city in a museum, was getting smaller with each passing second. Then it turned into a blur as we began moving forward. At this rate, I figured we would be over Port Otto in minutes.

And we were. I had barely gotten my stomach back under control when Kah-Rehn announced, "Preparing to land."

The *Shaymus* began to descend like an elevator in free fall. The view screen showed the ground rushing toward us. It was like the wildest roller coaster ride ever, and I had to work to suppress a shriek. I had always loved roller coasters until that day, but that short flight was thrill ride enough to last me the rest of my life.

We landed. The harness straps unbuckled and disappeared back into my chair. I sat there breathing heavily, my eyes bulging and my hands still gripping the arms of the chair for dear life.

Oren's voice came to me. "Gabriel, are you all right?"

I stood shakily. "I'm fine … except for my stomach … and maybe my head … and my knees. So what's the plan?"

"The plan is for you to investigate, ask questions. I have opened a communications connection with your translator bots. I will be able to talk to you. I will also be able to hear what you hear and see what you see."

"Sure. That's not intrusive at all. By the way, I meant that sarcastically in case you didn't know. Do you have sarcasm on your planet?"

"No, Gabriel," he said in a sarcastic tone. "Earthlings are the only species in the galaxy who understand the nuances of sarcasm."

46

"No need to get snippy," I said.

They lowered the ramp for me, and I walked out. We had landed on the back side of the round barn — if round objects even have sides, that is. Let's just say the barn was shielding the ship from view from the house and the road.

As I approached the A-frame, I could hear the sound of a vacuum cleaner roaring inside. I knocked on the door, but when no one came and the vacuum kept running, I walked on in. The sweeper was being operated by a woman with short gray hair whose glasses were working their way down her nose. I waved to get her attention before stepping toward her. She switched off the machine and straightened up with difficulty.

"If you're interested in renting the place, it'll be a few days," she said, shaking her head. "The other guy just moved out, and he left a heck of a mess. A lot more than what the damage deposit will cover."

"I was actually looking for the guy who moved out. I take it you're the cleaning lady?"

"I'm the whole shebang. Cleaning lady, rental agent, and landlord all rolled into one. My name's Mildred Rawlings, by the way." She wiped her hand on her apron and extended it to shake mine.

"Gregory Lane." I sometimes used that as a fake name with restaurant reservations just for the fun of it. I shook her hand.

"So does Matt owe you money, too?" she asked.

"Matt?"

"Matt. The guy who lived here."

It took me a second, but I got it. Tam — Mat. He just turned it around.

"Oh, Matt. Sorry, see um … I knew him as Matthew. No, he doesn't owe me money. I need to return something to him, a tool I borrowed."

"Well, I don't know where you can find him. He just up and disappeared. I came by this morning because the rent was due, and he was packed up and gone."

"Maybe he went out to eat or something," I suggested.

"The place is cleaned out. Look around. Does this look like somebody just stepped out? Besides, it's been six hours so far, and no sign of him. Anyways, I'm cleaning. And if he does come back, I'm hitting him with the cleaning bill in addition to the rent."

Oren was in my ear. "Did she only know of Tam? Not the others?"

"So it was only the one guy renting the place?" I asked.

47

"That's what he told me. But this place was messy enough for seven. And would you look at that couch over there? The frame's broke and the springs are shot. It's like a rhino was lyin' on it."

"Well, that's a bit unkind toward Her Royal Highness," I muttered.

"Indeed," said Oren.

"And get a load of this kitchen, that mess by the table. They must have spilled a whole bottle of mustard and just left it."

I walked to the kitchen door and stared at the yellow-brown ooze on the floor. I remembered the yellow coagulation around Tam's knife wound. This wasn't mustard, but I wasn't telling her that.

"Dierens have green blood," Oren said. "Ask her if she found any green stains like that. This morning I didn't let Zastra take the time for a thorough investigation."

"Did you find any other stains? For instance … um … pesto spills?"

"Nope, thank God for small favors."

"Did you find any damage to the doors or windows?"

Oren whispered, "Insightful question. You are checking for signs of forced entry, aren't you?"

"Nah," she said. "But I got ninety-nine other problems. It looks like that rhino used the toilet too 'cause that's all plugged up six ways from Sunday."

I decided I wouldn't investigate that.

"Have you found anything missing?"

"You sure ask a lot of questions, son."

"Oh, just making conversation. I thought if I caught up with Matt then I could do you a favor and tell him about anything he had taken by mistake."

"Hmm. If you say so. You can tell him one of the good carving knives is gone."

I nodded. I knew right where it was.

"Do you know if he made any friends around here? Um … I'd really like to return that tool to him. Maybe they'd have an idea where he is."

"Well, you might talk to Henry Koster. He lives the next place over. I own that one too. One day when I stopped by, Matt was over there hanging out with Henry. But honestly, I hardly knew the guy. We conducted all our business in writing."

"I'm not surprised," I said, thinking of the need for translator bots to communicate verbally. "Anything else, Oren?"

"Pardon? Speak up, son," she said.

"That will do," said Oren.

"I said thanks, Ms. Rawlings. You've been super helpful."

I nodded and backed away. I walked out of the A-frame, doing a thorough examination of the door lock on the way out. As she had said, there was no damage, no sign of forced entry. I gazed across the farmstead. A pasture stretched from the edge of the round barn over to a low brick ranch-style house just beyond.

"That must be Henry Koster's house," I said to Oren. "I'll walk over there."

A wire fence with a strand of barbed wire on top separated the farmstead from the pasture. I scanned the pasture for bulls or other livestock before crossing but didn't see anything. I climbed the fence at a post, being careful with the barbed wire, and jumped down on the other side. The pasture was uneven and thick with grass only now beginning to turn from brown to green in the early spring. There was another strand of barbed wire on the other side of the pasture. I climbed over it into Henry Koster's driveway. The garage door was open. A man was inside, moving around stacks of boxes that filled the garage from one end to the other and from floor to ceiling.

"Hi," I called to him.

The man turned and looked me over. He wore cargo shorts, Crocs, and a baggy T-shirt with enough holes to qualify as Swiss cheese. He looked like the punchline to a joke, a picture in an Internet meme.

"Where'd you come from?" he asked suspiciously. He blew a bubble gum bubble, popped it, and sucked the gum back into his mouth.

I pointed toward the A-frame. "I understand you knew Matt. I'm trying to find him."

"Why?"

"I owe him twenty bucks."

"Well, he comes by every few days. You can leave it with me."

"Are you Henry Koster?"

"Yeah, who told you?"

"Mildred Rawlings."

"She would," Henry said, popping the gum.

"What's with all the boxes?"

"That's my business."

"No need to get huffy. I was just asking."

"No," Henry chuckled. "I mean the boxes are *for* my business." He blew another bubble.

"Wow. That's a lot of inventory."

"My business is all inventory. I buy overstock stuff. Or look for things in short supply. Or guess the next must-have Christmas toy and go around and buy it all up. Then I sell it online. Sometimes I can mark it up a thousand percent. During the pandemic, this place was stacked with toilet paper."

"I've read about people doing that." And I didn't think much of it, but I decided to keep my opinions to myself in the interest of the investigation.

"Right now, I'm looking for more St. Patrick's Day stuff and Easter stuff. I've been selling a ton of it this week." He moved a box from one stack to another and opened the one that had been under it. "Bingo!" He held up a pair of fake green glasses with lenses shaped like shamrocks. "I got an order for these."

"Good for you." I started walking through the grass toward the garage.

"Be careful walking through there. I got stung by a bee or somethin' a few weeks ago. Come to think of it, it was the very day Matt first came over to talk."

I figured that had not been a bee. Most likely it was a dart full of translator bots.

Koster continued rummaging through the boxes. "Matt went on a couple of buying runs with me. But mostly when he came over, we just shot hoops."

Oren spoke in my ear, "They went hunting? That's interesting."

"Shooting hoops, as in playing basketball," I said to explain it to Oren.

"Duh," said Koster. "What else would I mean? Man, that dude can jump."

Oren said, "The gravity on Cunedda is twice that of Earth. Being used to that g-force, he would have excelled at jumping here."

"Interesting," I said.

"Yeah, you oughta see it." Koster opened another box and held up a headband with bunny ears attached. "Here we go. Easter!"

I said, "So Matt called me last night. He said there was some kind of trouble, but he didn't have time to explain. Any ideas what that would be?"

"He had a peculiar living situation. He said he and his old lady had just gotten married. But they also had this other guy living with him, an old friend of her family, I guess. The whole thing sounded weird."

"You're telling me. Did you ever see this other guy or Matt's wife?"

He didn't respond right away. "No. I would have liked to. Matt said his wife was quite the looker. Never saw the other guy, either. But from what Matt said, he sounded creepy."

"Creepy in what way?"

"Matt thought the guy was trying to push him and his wife apart. Nothing obvious, but subtle digs. Like he didn't approve of the marriage."

"Did anything seem odd or off about Matt the last time you saw him?"

Henry stopped messing with the boxes and turned to face me. "I tell you what, everything about the guy is odd."

"How so?"

"Well, he says weird stuff, like he doesn't quite get how English works. And those implants. Did you know about those?"

"What implants?"

"Okay. We were playing basketball one day, and he was wearing his hat like he always does. I put up my arm to block his shot. My arm hits his hat, and it goes flying off his head. And … turns out the dude had horns. Horns like the devil or something. I've read about things like that, subdural implants I think they're called, but to see them in real life … it kinda creeped me out. I mean, I've got some ink on my body. But that implant stuff's crazy. And from what I hear, you can forget about ever getting an MRI with 'em."

Koster was staring at me hard now as if he were watching for my reaction. I wondered what he supposed I knew about it. I tried to act surprised.

"What did Matt say about it, the horns?"

"Nothing. He put his hat back on and kept playing."

"So what about last night? Did you hear or see anything unusual?"

"Come to think of it, I did hear arguing last night."

"What time?"

"I don't know. I was in bed. Maybe midnight?"

"Male voices? Male and female? Was one Matt?"

Henry stared up and away, sticking his tongue into one cheek so it protruded. "Male voices. Both the voices were men … I think."

"Could you make anything out?"

"Dude, I try not to listen in on people's fights."

"No. Of course not."

"Well, that's about all I know of the situation," Koster said. "Soooo … I need to place these things online."

"Sure. Sure. Thanks for your time."

"So you wanna leave that twenty bucks with me?"

I smiled. "Nah. I've got a hunch where I can find him."

I decided not to risk climbing the barbed wire again. I walked to the end of the driveway and took the county road back to the round barn. The ramp to the *Shaymus* was open when I got there. I climbed up to the office. Oren was on the screen, still looking like a blue Dwayne Johnson.

"How'd I do, boss?"

"Satisfactory. What have we established?"

"It appears Khan and Tam didn't get along," I said.

"That's understandable," said Zastra. "Khan was part of the palace staff. He would have been against the marriage, like the queen and the council were."

Oren nodded. "Yes. But would his dislike of Tam extend to murder, especially after we had worked out an arrangement acceptable to the queen?"

"Or perhaps Henry Koster was lying about the argument," said Zastra. "We have only his word for it. I think he might be a suspect."

"Possibly," Oren said. "When he was telling about Tam's horns, he looked suspicious. If he had an inkling Tam was from another planet, he might conceivably have attacked and murdered him. I understand Earthlings can be like that."

"I suppose," I said. "But he didn't quite seem like the murdering type. So what's our next move?"

"We were hired to bring the princess back. I thought that assignment was wrapped up, but now it is not. It doesn't appear she was attacked, but we can't be sure. It is possible she was kidnapped by whoever killed Tam Elam. Or she and Khan may have run off in fear. In either case, we need to follow the trail. Would you like to be part of that, Gabriel?"

"You mean, follow the trail off into space?"

"Precisely. Given Princess Ralph's size and Khan's green skin, they could not remain on Earth by themselves. I know I prepared you to spend a few days here in Potato, but I don't see that helping us now. So I propose we investigate away from Earth. If you don't want to come along, Zastra can handle things. But you have been involved so far, and I thought you might like to finish what you have started."

My heart was a firm yes. I would be the first human to fly out in the stars, though it would have to remain my secret. My stomach, however, was voting no, especially after this afternoon's flight. I was weighing the pros and cons when my heart threw a left hook at my stomach and knocked it to the mat. Heart won by a knock-out.

"Sure. Count me in. Beam me up, Scotty."

"I am unfamiliar with that idiom," said Oren. "But I'll take it as a yes. Jace?"

Jace's voice came over the speakers. "Yes, sir."

"We will stay here until darkness falls and then fly back to the city. Prepare to leave Earth the next evening. Gabriel, can you be ready in one day?"

"Will we be gone a long time? I should pay ahead on my rent and utilities. And I'll need to inform my clients."

"That won't be necessary," assured Oren.

"Really?"

"Really. You'll see. And, Gabriel, I don't have to tell you to reveal none of this to anyone. It would cause a frenzy for which your civilization is not prepared."

"That's for sure. But I do have one request."

"What is that?"

"Can we take it a bit slower on our way back into town?"

Chapter 9

So Long, Indy

While waiting for dark I decided to wander around the *Shaymus*. Some of the doors on the middle level, where my quarters were, would not open automatically. I assumed it was because they were personal areas for Jace and Zastra. One door that did open led into something that looked like a galley. It had a long table running down the middle of the room. Around the walls were control panels, appliances, and a small round sink. I wondered what they ate and what I would be eating on my voyage with them.

I returned to the central shaft and this time climbed down to the lower level. I found Jace there surrounded by controls and going over a checklist on a tablet device.

"Hi, Gabe," he said. "I think we'll be getting underway in a few minutes."

"Speaking of that," I said. "On the trip down here, my stomach attempted to leave my body. I think it would have made it, too, if only it could decide whether to exit through my mouth or out the other end. I don't suppose you have any tips for surviving these flights, do you?"

He shrugged while flipping some more switches. "I can have Kah-Rehn dial it back a bit. But most people adjust to it after a few trips."

"That makes me feel better."

"Fifty or a hundred trips, maybe."

"I'm sorry. What?"

His grin told me he was probably kidding but wasn't going to say anything more. I would have to wait and find out.

"So do you just mind the ship while the detectives do all the detecting?"

"I mind the ship. Somebody has to be here to open the door for them."

"How did you get the job?"

"You could say I came with the place. I used to own the *Shaymus*. I ran it as a luxury ferry service between Rheged Prime and Rheged Minor. That's a colony planet in our system. Anyhow, one day I was transporting Oren and Zastra and your predecessor, may he rest in peace, and—"

"What's that now?"

"Your predecessor. The guy before you in the job."

"Yeah. I got that part. I meant the *rest in peace* thing. What happened to him?"

Jace shook his head. "Not my story to tell. You want to hear my story or not?"

"Fine, tell your story." I made a mental note to rethink my decision to go on this adventure.

"Actually, I guess there's not much more to my story. Oren liked the ship and the service. He made me an offer to sell him the ship and come work for him, jumping all around the galaxy on his cases. Oren had the ship retrofitted with the chrono drive engine for traveling between star systems and remodeled the observation deck into the office. And here we are. I tell you what, it gives me a lot more variety in life compared to making the same ferry run over and over."

"I know what you mean. Sometimes my job can become a little repetitive, too."

"They all do. Hey, would you like to play cards sometime? Buad and Blan don't have hands, as you know, so they can't hold cards. And Oren, since he's digitized, works on a whole different level. And Zastra, well she's a bit too intense."

"I can imagine."

"No pressure. But if you're looking for some diversion sometime."

"Sounds great to me. I imagine there are lots of long hours, long weeks even, in space travel."

"And you would be wrong. See with the chrono drive—"

But he didn't have a chance to explain, because Oren's voice came over the speakers. "It is sufficiently dark now. Let's get underway."

"Guess I'll tell you about the chrono drive later," Jace said.

The flight back to Indy wasn't quite as bad as the flight out. This time I didn't think I was going to die. I merely thought I *might* die. But even that small improvement was offset by Buad and Blan anticipating my discomfort and mocking me the whole time.

"Check him out, Buad," Blan said. "He's gonna hurl."

"Yup, here it comes," said Buad. "He's turning as green as a Dieren."

I put on a fake smile and thought happy thoughts. "I'm fine," I sneered back at them. "Cut the chatter."

They chirped in laughter.

They landed in the warehouse, and I left the ship, resisting the urge to kiss the ground. City buses weren't running on Sunday night, so I called Adam and hit him up for a ride home. Since I was coming back the next night, I left all my stuff on the *Shaymus* except for my laptop. I almost always keep it with me in case something comes up with a client.

"So why exactly were you down here in an industrial park at night?" Adam asked when I climbed into his car.

"It's all part of my new gig as a private eye." I grinned, trying to make it sound cool.

"So you took the job, huh?"

"I took the job."

"What's the case, Sherlock?"

"Um … I can't tell you. It's all very hush-hush." He wouldn't have believed me anyway.

"Fine," Adam said. "I was going to volunteer to be your Watson, write it up to make you look like the Miss Marple of the twenty-first century. But have it your way."

"First of all, I don't want to be the Miss Marple of any century."

"Nancy Drew?"

I shot him a look. "Sam Spade maybe. But I'm sworn to secrecy. Let's just say it's out of this world."

When I got back to my bungalow, I realized most of my conversation with Adam had been false bravado. I kept having this sinking feeling that I was in way over my head. What was it I was getting myself into? What was flying off into space going to be like? How long would I be gone? How dangerous was this going to be?

I tossed and turned most of the night. I always keep a bedside novel to read as I'm falling asleep. Most nights I only make it four or five pages before I find myself drifting off. But that night I started in rereading Sue Grafton's *A is for Alibi* for about the fifth time and read through two whole chapters. I closed the book and tried to sleep. Twenty minutes later I turned the light back on and read another chapter. It went on like that for hours. I finally called it at 4:00 a.m., got up, and put on a pot of coffee. I went over my to-do list from my Earth-bound clients — a revision here, something to examine in the data there. I knocked them all out by 7:30, then took a shower. I went to brush my teeth but remembered my toothbrush was still on the *Shaymus*. I used my finger to do the job.

At 9:30 I tracked down Sarah at the Buzz House where she sometimes goes to do her work. As a programmer, I need the silence I have at home to concentrate. But as a web designer, she somehow works better amid all the hum and energy of the coffee shop. She was focused on her laptop, bouncing her head to whatever she was listening to in her earbuds, and didn't even see me until I sat down opposite her with my cup of tea. Tea was all my stomach could handle after downing most of a pot of coffee in the wee hours.

"Well, hey, Gabriel," she said, pulling the earbuds out. "Let me just save what I'm doing … and … and … done." She shut her laptop and reached for her latte. "What's up?"

What could I tell her? That I thought I would check in before flying off into space? Probably not.

"I wanted to let you know I have to go out of town on business."

"Okay. How long will you be gone?"

"I can't be sure. I might not be back in time for coffee on Friday."

"That's too bad. It's not the same without the whole gang. Where are you going?"

"Well … I honestly don't know."

She cocked her head. "You're telling me you don't know where you're going? How do you not know where you're going?"

"The client is calling the shots."

"Right," she said skeptically. "What's this really about?"

"Just business," I shrugged.

"It is not just business." She squinted at me over her glasses like a schoolteacher catching a kid doing something wrong. "When was the last time you had to go out of town on business anyway? You normally sit at home where you can remote in to any computer in the world. This isn't a programming job, is it? This is about that investigation, am I right?"

Wow! She should be the detective. "Yeah." I flashed her a smile. "It's pretty cool."

"Is it dangerous?"

"Nah. Shouldn't be." That was at best stretching the truth. I was flying off into the hostile vacuum of space. One person had been murdered. Another guy who used to work with Oren had died in some way no one wanted to talk about. "Not much, anyway. Possibly a bit more dangerous than writing software."

"Don't make me have to tell Lucas you're dead."

"Nah. Look, this probably isn't any more dangerous than riding a bicycle on the city streets. You don't worry about me when I do that, do you?"

"As a matter of fact, I do."

"You worry about me? I never knew that."

"Well." She stared into her coffee as she said it instead of making eye contact. "Now you do."

"Wow. That's … that's kinda nice to know. But I already have a mother. Speaking of which, I should probably call my mother."

"So will you be careful?" Her eyes flashed back up at me.

"Of course."

"I mean it. Be careful."

"Okay. Okay." I raised my hands in surrender.

"When do you leave?"

"This evening."

She ran a hand over her ear, tucking a lock of blonde hair behind it. "Then spend the day with me."

"What?"

"C'mon. Let's do something."

I had my work caught up. Oren said I didn't need to worry about upcoming bills. I did have packing to do, though I had no idea of what to pack.

"Sure. Why not? What do you have in mind? A movie?"

"No. Something where we can talk. Hey, I need to buy some new towels. I know, I know, not that exciting. But it would be fun to do together. And there's an amazing Mexican place near the store. My treat. Then how about we go to Broad Ripple and feed the ducks on the canal?"

"Sounds like a plan." I hadn't realized until she suggested those things how much I would enjoy doing something normal after the weirdness of the last few days.

So we did. We bought some towels and browsed the household gadgets at the store. We ate tacos and then stopped by a fudge shop. We fed the ducks and were practically attacked by them. We picked Lucas up after school, and I went with them back to their apartment where Lucas and I watched a cartoon together. It was a *Looney Tunes* that took me back to my own childhood. Bugs was taking on a couple of gangsters with his usual wisecracks and mayhem. At one point when one of the gangsters pulled a gun on him, Bugs stomped on his toes. The gangster dropped the gun and grabbed his foot, cartoon pain lines shooting from the throbbing toes. Lucas laughed and laughed. When the cartoon finished, I noticed the sun was starting to drop toward the horizon.

"I need to go, sport," I said.

"Already? Can't you stay for dinner? This is meatloaf Monday."

Sarah called from the kitchen. "It's meatless Monday. We're having mac and cheese."

Lucas grinned. "That's even better!"

"Thanks for the offer, but I have places I have to be." I tousled his hair and stood up.

Sarah walked me to the door. "Remember, you promised to be careful."

"I'll be careful. I'll be careful. Nothing to worry about."

"Can you call me when you get there?"

"I doubt it. But I'll call you when I come back."

She stood in the doorway as I drove away.

I got back to the bungalow and tried to think through packing. My travel bag was already on the *Shaymus* with a couple of shirts in it. I didn't know what else I would need to pack or even how I was going to carry it. I ended up dumping a spare pair of jeans, pajama pants, a sweater, and a couple of other T-shirts into an old cloth laundry bag. I tossed in an Agatha Christie whodunit and slung the bag over my shoulder.

I was ready to head out the door when my phone beeped. It was an email from a client. Something had gone wrong with their application. Why did these things always happen at the least convenient times?

I opened my laptop and went to their in-house website using the admin login. I checked the log and noticed that a process to import data from their user website had started but not completed because of an oddball connectivity issue. I reset the process pointer to force it to start again. This time it ran without a hitch. I emailed the client back and told her it was fixed.

Computers are supposed to be logical and predictable, and most of the time they are. But then weird stuff happens. I hoped nothing weird happened to my clients' systems while I was gone. And come to think of it, I hoped nothing weird happened to me either. But then, this whole thing was weird, so very weird.

See this was the problem with flying off into space. I had clients who depended on me to be there. Seemingly Sarah and Lucas needed me too. I didn't want to let anybody down. But a murder had been committed. A princess was missing. And I wanted to see this through.

I knew I wouldn't be able to remotely connect from another planet even if something came up. So I slid my laptop into a drawer for safekeeping. I picked up my laundry bag and locked the door behind me.

The warehouse was only about three miles from my house. The thought struck me that I could walk it in about an hour, which appealed to me. I could take the time to take one last look at Indy. Who knew when I would see it again? Plus, I could think about what I was walking into.

When I was a kid, I loved all things related to space. I followed all the NASA launches. I watched all the sci-fi shows old and new. I perfected the Shatner roll where you roll on your shoulders, rise to a kneel, and squeeze off a shot with a phaser. I once took an old busy board I had had as a baby — it had all kinds of knobs and buttons and levers and stuff — and I built it into what I called my spaceship console. Under the blankets of my bed or inside a big cardboard box I would press those buttons and spin those knobs and fly off into space in my imagination. I dreamed of what it would be like to go to outer space, to visit another planet and meet another species.

Now all those things were going to get checked off my bucket list. And though the grownup me kept thinking about all the bad things that might happen, the nine-year-old in me was thrilled. I smiled and cocked a finger gun at a passing car.

Pew Pew Pew

I picked up a stick from the ground and began a lightsaber dual with an invisible adversary.

Whum whum whum pchouch whum whum fvsih!

Yeah, I guess you could say I was excited.

All that laser fighting worked up an appetite. I diverted to Yats on Mass Ave. for an awesome last supper on Earth of Chicken Creole.

Chapter 10

The Final Frontier

I reached the *Shaymus* and found the entrance ramp closed, leaving me wondering how I was supposed to get in this time.

I called out, "Hello! Hello! It's Gabriel, Gabriel Lake." I tried knocking on the side of the egg.

Jace's voice sounded through a tinny speaker. "Hey, Gabe. Your voiceprint has been added to the command interface. Just say, 'open ramp' and that will do it."

"So you were kidding about you having to open the door for people?"

He chuckled. "Guilty as charged."

"Okay, I'll try it," I said. "Open ramp."

Whoosh! The ramp began to descend. I had to jump out of the way to avoid getting hit by it. I boarded and went to my quarters to drop off the laundry bag.

"Oren, I'm here," I said. "Can you hear me if I just say your name?"

"Yes, I can," Oren's voice said.

"Okay. Again, not creepy at all."

I returned to the corridor and climbed down the shaft to the engine room. Jace was there, working on a small red device.

"Welcome back," he said.

"Thanks. What's the do-hickey? Some super high-tech space gadget?"

"Not so much. This is a water pump for the galley sink."

"Oh. Well, that's disappointing. I was hoping it would be something you could reverse the polarity on."

"Do what?" He set down the pump. "Hey, do you want to grab a cup of coffee?"

"You can get coffee on board this ship? Wait. The other day Khan served some disgusting substance disguised as a drink. Is this real Earth coffee or something that smells like the cat died?"

He winked. "Let's go find out."

We climbed up the shaft to the crew level. He led me to the galley I had found earlier. "Do you want creme and sugar?" he asked as he approached a panel.

"Black is fine," I answered.

"Coffee black," he said to the panel.

With a low hum, a ceramic mug materialized on the counter below the panel. It contained a dark, steaming liquid.

"Take a drink," Jace said.

I picked up the mug tentatively. It felt solid and real enough, even though I had just seen it materialize right in front of my eyes. I sniffed the drink inside. It smelled like coffee. I tried a sip. The taste was like coffee, like really excellent coffee.

"So that's like a food replicator?" I asked.

"Exactly."

"How does it work?"

"See, any food, any material, in fact, is just a specific arrangement of quarks and electrons. The replicator takes other quarks and electrons and re-arranges them into what you want."

"How did it know how to make coffee?"

"Yesterday, after I knew you would be coming with us, I tapped into what you call the Internet and searched for the favorite foods and drinks of Earth."

"Wow! What else do you have in here?" I ran over to the replicator and said, "Apple pie,"

Absolutely nothing happened.

"Cinnamon rolls," I tried again.

Nothing again happened.

Jace shrugged. "I made a whole list of Earth foods — hamburgers, tacos, grilled salmon, sugar creme pie, pizza, wine, lemonade. But the replicator needs a sample of the food to deconstruct, so it can learn how to make it. The only sample I managed to obtain was some coffee. I put on a disguise and went to a diner this morning before the sun came up."

"Well, at least I have coffee. Have you tried it?"

"Yeah." His voice sounded skeptical. "The first time I thought it was awful. But I think it's starting to grow on me." He turned back to the panel and said, "Coffee with cream and two sugars."

"Baby steps." I chuckled as his drink appeared.

"What's that mean?"

"Only that most people start off drinking coffee with a lot of creme and sugar. Eventually, some start paring it back as they get used to it until they start drinking it black."

"I think I'm a long way from that. How about you try a Rhegedian favorite food?" He turned to the replicator and said, "Poosha." A bread-like loaf appeared on the counter. "I'll need to grab a knife to cut you a slice."

He pulled a knife out of a drawer, and we both sat down at one end of the long galley table.

"Couldn't you just have the replicator make it already sliced?" I asked.

Jace looked up, his blue face creased like he was thinking. "Pre-sliced bread. I've never thought about that. I don't think anyone has ever thought about it."

"You're kidding me. They've been making sliced bread on Earth since ... well, I don't know for how long, but definitely for a while now. And it's great. You know how great it is? It's so great that every other great thing is compared to it. They always say something is the best thing *since* sliced bread."

I wondered how an advanced civilization with food replicators and interstellar travel and digitized consciousnesses could have missed the part about inventing sliced bread. How did they do sandwiches? How did they make toast?

"Bread must be important in your culture," Jace said.

"Is it? Yeah, I guess it is. Especially if you add a little sugar to make cookies or cake or donuts."

I took a moment to sip my coffee and take a bite of poosha. The taste was a bit like a coffee cake. "Hey, this is good. So do you know where we're going?"

"The first stop will be the Girsu Space Port."

"What's that?"

"It's a space port built on a moon called Girsu, hence the name. It's a stopping point on several different star routes. I guess Oren is trying to track down the pilot Princess Ralph used."

I nodded. "Yorbah, I think she said, apparently a female. So how does this work, this interstellar space travel? Do we jump into hyperspace or something?"

"Hyperspace? No. What's hyperspace?"

"Hyperspace? It's … it's um … hyperspace is how you go real fast in a spaceship … isn't it? You know, stars go streaming past you in streaks of light."

"Nope."

"Then what do we do? Engage the warp drive?"

He laughed. "No. Warp drives are theoretically possible, but they take way too much energy to be practical."

"So we don't go really fast?"

"Oh, we go fast, Gabriel. Astoundingly fast." His blue face beamed with pride.

"So how do you do it?"

"Hmm. Let's see. How to explain it to a novice, to someone whose planet has never worked it all out? So, you know how the universe is expanding, right?"

"I wouldn't say I do, but I'll take your word for it. I mean, aren't we all expanding once we reach a certain age?" I patted my stomach.

"Speak for yourself. But anyhow, if the universe is expanding, then that means it used to be much smaller. Stands to reason, right?"

"Sure, like a Twenty-eight slim."

"What's that?"

"It's a pants size. I'm picturing expanding waistlines here."

"If you insist. Generally, we explain it with a balloon getting blown up, but I suppose we can use pants. Now don't get the idea the universe held less stuff back then when it was small. Everything we have today existed in some form then, but it was all just a soup of electrons and quarks all compressed together."

"Sounds sticky."

"Not that kind of soup. So imagine this ship is like an ant on the waistline of your pants."

"Can we make it a ladybug? Ants bite."

"See, that's why the balloon analogy works better. But sure, a ladybug. So if you've put on weight and gotten a bigger waistline, it might take this ant—"

"This ladybug," I corrected.

"It might take this ladybug, let's say, two minutes to walk around your waistline."

"Ooh. If the ladybug had a tiny bicycle, it would be the Tour de Pants."

"What?"

"Never mind."

Jace shook his head. "But suppose the ladybug traveled back in time to when you wore the eighty-two slim—"

"Twenty-eight slim."

"Sorry. I'm not familiar with Earth pants sizes. The point is, with those smaller pants, the ladybug might possibly travel around your waistline in just one minute."

"I think I'm with you. You're saying that a ladybug on my pants back when I was in high school would be able to move around my waist faster than a ladybug on my pants today, just because the trip is now longer."

"Exactly!"

"But how does that apply to space travel?"

"This ship is the ladybug. We want to go to the Girsu Space Port. But that moon is about twenty-five light-years from here. That's a long way around the waistline. With normal ion propulsion, it would take, oh, about eighty-four Earth years."

"Yikes!"

"Yikes, indeed. But with the chrono drive engine, we just travel back in time thirteen billion years to when the universe was tiny. Then we travel using conventional engines to the point in space where Girsu Space Port, or any planet or moon we are heading toward, will form in the future. And then we travel back to the present time. It would be like the ladybug traveling on your slim high school pants instead of your current fat pants."

"For the record, my pants are *not* fat. They're relaxed fit."

"The point is that it saves time. It saves gobs of time. We can travel those twenty-five light-years in minutes. Make sense?"

"Not in the least. I mean, yes, all of those words make sense ... individually, but ... well, how do you travel through time?"

"Ah, well let me see if I can come up with an analogy for that one. Hmm. Something you would understand." He rubbed his chin for a minute. "Nope, don't have one. You wouldn't understand it unless you studied for an advanced degree in temporal physics."

"Well, that's probably not gonna happen."

"There you go then. I guess you'll just have to trust me." He waved his hands around in circles and said in a spooky voice, "It all just works." Switching to his normal voice, he added, "But the calculations for a jump like that are amazingly complicated. Stupendously complicated. Which is why we have Kah-Rehn to fly the ship. You would be crazy to try chrono drive travel without an AI. You wouldn't want to hit a planet, would you? Or end up inside the corona of a star or a black hole?"

"I'm gonna say no."

He pointed at me. "And you would be right."

"But this Yorbah is a person pilot, not an AI, right?"

"She might actually be an AI," Jace said. "Some AIs are pilots for hire. But some people like to fly the ships themselves and use an AI only for chrono drive calculations and difficult maneuvers."

Kah-Rehn's voice came over the speaker. "Prepare for takeoff. All crew please strap in."

"We can't stay in here," Jace said. "These seats aren't equipped with straps. I have to go down to the engine room. You'd better go up to the office."

"How about my bunk?" I asked. I thought if flying from Indy to Port Otto was almost more than I could take, what would traveling thirteen billion years do to me? I didn't want to face Buad and Blan mocking me.

Jace grinned. "The bunk would work, but the chair in your quarters would be better."

I gulped down the rest of my coffee. Jace showed me where to dump the cup so that its quarks and electrons would be recycled back into the replicator. I returned to room eight. As I sat down in the chair, a five-point harness appeared from it and fastened itself snugly around me.

Kah-Rehn's voice came over the speaker. "Ready for take-off."

"Say, Karen," I called.

"Yes, Gabriel Lake, and it's Kah-Rehn by the way." You wouldn't think an AI would sigh, but I swear she did.

"Right. While we're flying can you show me on the view screen what's happening?"

"Of course, Gabriel Lake."

The engine roared into life. The view screen switched on, showing the warehouse. The spaceship whizzed out the door and out into the Indianapolis night. The camera shifted to a view from the bottom of the ship. The landing struts had retracted, making us an egg with wings flying higher and higher up into the atmosphere. This time my stomach pretty much stayed inside my body. Maybe I *was* getting used to it.

The lights of Indianapolis receded. I recognized Chicago, Cincinnati, and St. Louis as splotches of light connected by arteries of light along the interstate highways. I began to feel weightless. Now only my straps were holding me into my seat. Across the cabin, the laundry bag and all the other things I had casually dropped on the floor rose up and started floating around the room. I hoped none of them bumped into something important, like my head or some button that ejected my chair out into space. As we began to orbit the Earth, the engine roar became silent in the vacuum of space. The continents passed under me from darkness into morning light into afternoon and back into darkness again.

Then a different sound started up. It was kind of a buzz vibrating through the ship. The lights of Earth dimmed and then flickered out. I wondered what caused it. Then I remembered the chrono drive engine was traveling back in time. We had passed out of the twenty-first century, through the twentieth, and back into the pre-electrification era.

We must have picked up speed through time because next I began to see the continents move and shift. The atmosphere clouded up until I could no longer see through it, then it turned red. The Earth seemed to deform and dissolve into dust. The stars began moving faster and faster. I witnessed stars melt into nebulae and the nebulae compress back into stars. The universe became a thick, red glowing soup of something. Something I couldn't name, but I knew would eventually become everything and everyone I could name.

The buzzing of the chrono engine stopped, and I felt the ship begin moving through the physical space of the red soup. We seemed to be swimming in this primordial mass of particles. We inched forward slowly and pitched to one side and down. We moved for a minute or so. Then we stopped, and the buzz of the chrono engine started up again. Now the red soup cooled to purple, to blue, then to black. I observed as globs of dust combined and spun and orbited each other. Stars coalesced. Planets and moons came together. Solar systems and galaxies appeared. Stars formed, burned for a time, and then exploded in brilliant flashes.

I saw a planet appear near us, gathering dust and debris and growing in size. A comet zipped into view, passed close to the planet, and seemed to get caught in its orbit. The comet became a moon, grew a thin atmosphere of its own. Spaceships launched from the planet and came to the moon. More came, and then more. Buildings popped up on the moon's surface below us, and a steady stream of spaceships began coming and going. This had to be Girsu Space Port. We drew closer to the moon's surface and began flying through the thin atmosphere over the cratered surface. I felt partial gravity return and all my things that had been floating crashed to the floor with a thud.

Oren's voice came over the speaker. "What was that noise?"

"Nothing," I said. "It's all good. Sorry."

Chapter 11

Girsu Space Port

"Approaching Girsu Space Port," Kah-Rehn announced over the speakers. I watched on my view screen as the *Shaymus* swept low across a barren, rocky landscape. A yellowish sky lent an amber cast to everything on the ground.

"Karen, what's it like outside there?" I asked.

"Again, my name is Kah-Rehn," the AI harrumphed. "The temperature outside in Earth units is negative eighty degrees Celsius or one hundred twelve degrees below zero Fahrenheit. The atmosphere is composed of ninety percent carbon dioxide, seven percent nitrogen, plus other trace elements, none of which are oxygen. The air pressure is five point two millibars."

"Is that a lot of millibars?"

"I measured the air pressure in Indianapolis at nine hundred eighty-two millibars. So no, Gabriel Lake, Girsu does not have a lot of millibars, almost no air pressure, in fact. Without a spacesuit, the low pressure would pull all the air from your lungs. And even if it didn't, you couldn't breathe what air there is."

"Not to mention freezing to death in that cold."

"No, you would not freeze to death," Kah-Rehn corrected.

"I wouldn't?"

"No. You would asphyxiate long before the cold killed you."

"Okay then. So I guess I'll stay inside."

"That would be for the best."

We slowed as we flew over a sprawling structure of steel, concrete, and glass, which I assumed was the space port. On the screen, I saw the roof doors of a hanger open beneath us. The ship dropped into the hangar and touched down. My straps shrank back into my chair, and I stood. I felt lighter. I hopped on the balls of my feet. I jumped and touched the ceiling of the cabin. I rebounded out into the corridor and bounced up the shaft ladder, skipping several rungs with each hop.

I bounded into the office. "I'm as light as a feather! I can fly like you guys," I said to Buad and Blan.

"I'd like to see you try," said Buad.

"Oh, there he is," said Blan. "Where were you hiding out during the flight?"

"I was in my cabin. And I wasn't hiding. I just wanted to watch everything on my screen without being heckled."

"Yeah, sure," scoffed Buad. "He was hiding."

"And probably hurling," said Blan. They both laughed.

"Girsu has only about one-third the gravity you're used to," said Oren, flashing on the screen. "This will be a new experience for you, Gabriel."

I kept bouncing. "I think I'm starting to get used to it." But my next bounce brought me down at an odd angle into the arm of my chair, and I boomeranged — or is it boomerung? — into the side of my desk and fell. Zastra rolled her yellow eyes.

"So what's the program?" I asked when I stood up again.

"It is possible Princess Ralph is here," Oren replied. "That is unlikely, but you can ask around. What is more likely is that the pilot, Yorbah, is here or has come through here, and you can pick up a lead on her. You and Zastra will go out together to ask around."

"I don't really need him," said Zastra.

"You might," Oren said.

"C'mon, let's go," I said. "This is my first space port." I moved toward the central shaft.

"Not so fast," she replied. "They have to finish re-pressurizing the hangar first. Unless you want your insides sucked out to your outsides."

"Ah, good idea," I said. "We'll wait."

"Sit at your desk," she commanded. "There's an informational video about the space port you should watch so you don't accidentally walk out of an airlock or something."

I sat.

Fifteen minutes later we were walking down the ramp into the hangar. I was trying hard to keep from bouncing and skipping like a small child, but it wasn't easy.

Zastra said, "It's nice to finally be able to walk around with my hood off. Your planet was so annoying."

"Yeah, but Earth has its charms, don't you think? Like green grass. Did you wiggle your toes in the grass?"

"I did not."

"Maybe it's a little early in the season, but it's a delightful feeling."

As we approached the hangar wall, a door slid open. We passed through it into a corridor. An arrow painted on the wall directed us to the right. The corridor passed other hangar doors and eventually opened up into a large circular glass-domed mall filled with people of all types. I gazed up through the glass into the yellow sky. A small red sun glared down like an angry eye from high overhead. A few stars were shining through the thin atmosphere even during the day.

Dotted through the mall and lined along the outside wall were shops, rough-looking restaurants, and rougher-looking saloons. Music was emanating from some of them, odd music with sounds I had never heard before. Passing through the middle of the mall were more kinds of aliens than I can describe. Green skin, blue skin, red skin, gray skin. Aliens with scales, aliens with feathers, aliens with fur. I saw aliens who appeared almost human and some that resembled insects or fish or birds. Some had fangs, some had horns, some had tentacles, some had claws.

"You're staring," Zastra scolded.

"I ... I've never seen anything like this."

"Staring can get you killed. Some cultures consider it extremely rude."

"Oh." I shook it off. "Okay, where do we start? Do we stop and ask people walking by?"

"Not the ones who will kill you just for talking to them."

"Maybe you should take the lead on this."

"I was planning to."

Zastra approached an alien who looked like a cross between a polar bear, a walrus, and a platypus who was sitting on a nearby bench.

"Greetings," Zastra said. "We have become separated from our party, two Dierens. Perhaps you have seen them?"

"You couldn't miss the woman," I added. "She's about three times my height."

Zastra scowled at me. "I already said they were Dierens. All Dieren women are that size."

"Seriously? All of them? I thought it was like a queen bee thing. And all the men are regular sized like Khan? Dude!"

The alien spoke in a kind of growl, the words struggling to make their way out through his long tusks. "I haffe theeen no Dierens."

Zastra bowed her head. "Thank you for your time."

As we moved on, she approached a lizard-like creature who looked a lot like her and was standing in the mall with a confused expression. "May I help you, friend?" Zastra asked.

The lizard alien flicked out its tongue. "Thank you, sister. I was looking for the bookstore."

"I believe it is in hallway four," Zastra said. "And perhaps you can help us. This creature," she nodded at me, "is the slave of Princess Ralph of Diere. I was to meet her here to present it to her. Have you seen her?"

"I have not. I would know the princess," the alien said, flicking its tongue again. "I am sorry I am not able to help."

"Thank you all the same."

We walked away.

"This could take all day," she said to me.

"Did you have to call me a slave?"

"The only Earthlings most of them have ever seen are slaves."

"How's that?"

"The Thomians sometimes break the quarantine and kidnap Earthlings for the slave market."

"What? That's horrible! Show me a Thomian. I want to give him a piece of my mind."

"There are no Thomians here now. You'd notice them. They're built like gorillas ... except bigger."

"*Bigger*? Than gorillas? How much bigger?"

"So much bigger. If I see one, I'll point him out so you can give him a dressing down."

"Or ... perhaps I could send a strongly worded email."

"Yeah, that might work," she said.

"Say, I don't suppose this place has a public toilet anywhere, does it?"

She glared at me. "You should have thought of that before we left the ship."

"Thanks for the advice, Mom. But seriously, is there a bathroom? I sincerely need one."

Zastra scanned the mall. "Over there." She pointed to a sign that looked like an alien in silhouette. "You go. I'll wait here and keep asking around."

I made my way through the crowd and went through the door beneath the sign. It opened into a short hallway. I expected to see the normal two doors. Instead, there were five, each door marked by an image with a different alien silhouette on it. None of them were shaped like a human.

I finally picked a door at random and went in, hoping for the best. The walls inside were lined with various sizes and shapes of devices at heights ranging from down at my ankles to way above my head. Some had basins. Some had hoses. Some had holes that were round, square, or triangular. I stared at them, trying to figure out how to make it work. I had finally picked one of the basins and was doing my business when a feather-covered alien hopped in.

"Whoa!" the alien squawked at me. "Don't do it in the sink!"

"Sorry. Sorry," I said. "I'm new around here." I figured out how to wash my hands and left as quickly as I could.

When I rejoined Zastra she said, "Asking around isn't working. We need to find someone we can bribe. Come with me."

She led me over to a little shop that sold weapons. Huge axes and knives hung on the wall. A collection of blaster pistols and other smaller items were displayed in cases under a glass counter.

"Buy a knife," she whispered to me.

"I don't have any space money," I whispered back.

"You don't need it. Oren has an account with the space port."

I stepped up to the counter. "I need a knife. A small one I can keep in my boot."

The shopkeeper had a yellow head the size of a beach ball and no nose. His two huge black eyes glanced down quizzically at my sneakers.

I smiled. "And boots are going to be my next purchase."

The shopkeeper shrugged and pulled out a tray containing small knives.

"May I touch them?" I asked.

The shopkeeper nodded silently. He appeared to be a man of few words. Or possibly no words at all.

I pulled out a knife and inspected it. The serrated blade was about three inches long and attached to an ornate grip.

Zastra said, "He needs it for an assignment. We will be guarding Princess Ralph of Diere. We were supposed to meet her here on Girsu. Have you seen her?"

The huge head shook left and right.

"Her pilot was named Yorbah," I remarked. "Is Yorbah around here?"

Again, a head shake.

"How much for the knife?" Zastra asked.

The shopkeeper held up fifteen fingers, which surprisingly were all on one hand.

"Does it come with a sheath?" I asked.

The shopkeeper nodded, reached below the counter, and pulled out a sheath with a clip to go on the side of the boot I wasn't wearing.

Zastra said, "Put this on the account for Oren Vilkas."

The shopkeeper picked up a tablet and tapped on it.

"Put it down for twenty if you can tell us where to find the princess," Zastra said.

The shopkeeper shrugged.

"Or Yorbah," I said.

The shopkeeper stared at us and blinked, his eyelids coming in from the sides of his eyes.

"Twenty-five," said Zastra.

The shopkeeper nodded and tapped on the tablet, then pointed a long bony finger across the mall at a drinking establishment.

"Thank you," Zastra said.

The shopkeeper slid the knife into the sheath, bowed, and handed it to me. I stuffed it into a side pocket of my jeans as we strode across the mall toward the saloon.

The place was dark. A circular bar sat in the middle of the room with tables and booths positioned around it and tucked away into corners.

Zastra walked up to the bar and nodded to the bartender. "Two fuisces."

The bartender, a bald alien with gray skin and a trunk like an elephant, brought over two small glasses and a bottle. He poured our drinks. I watched Zastra down hers in one gulp. I followed suit and felt my tonsils try to jump out of my throat. I smiled and nodded while struggling to breathe.

"Again," said Zastra.

The barkeep poured again. We chugged again. My eyes popped out, and I felt flush.

Zastra said, "We're supposed to meet a pilot here about a job. Yorbah."

The bartender slyly pointed with his trunk to our right. I leaned back to gaze around the curve of the bar, and there she was. She was leaning back against the counter, dressed in blacks and grays, one foot crossed over the other. Leather gauntlets extended up her arms to her elbows. Above the gauntlets were the kind of biceps you don't get by accident. In one gloved hand, she held her glass. Her other hand was resting on some kind of pistol strapped to her thigh. Except for the thin, pointed elf-like ears poking out of her dark hair, she looked just like a human woman. An attractive human woman. A tough, no-nonsense human woman.

I moved to her, Zastra on my heels. "Yorbah?" I asked. "We have a few questions."

She casually glanced my way and flashed me a wry smile. The glass dropped from her hand. My eyes followed it down. As it shattered on the floor, she punched me in the gut. I bent over, wheezing out all the air from my body. She grabbed my shoulders and pushed hard, propelling me back into Zastra and sending us both tumbling to the floor. She planted a booted foot on my back as she leaped over us and sped toward the door.

"Idiot," Zastra hissed at me as we struggled to our feet. "You spooked her." She pointed toward Yorbah's back receding across the crowded mall. "After her."

I was already running, my strides mutating into wild leaps in the low gravity. I sprung with each step, soaring high and covering fifteen feet or more with each stride. I was catching up to Yorbah with each leap, though knocking into people and causing a general ruckus. Zastra, meanwhile, was leaping lizard-like off the roofs of kiosks dotted across the mall floor.

Yorbah ducked down a hangar corridor identical to the one we had entered on. I figured she was making for her ship. I needed to stop her, but in the low corridor, I had to constrain my leaps lest I crash into the ceiling. I was still gaining on her, though. She was a mere few feet ahead of me now. I sprung hard with my knees, sailed above her, and landed on her back.

Yorbah and I tumbled to the floor, landing with our combined weight on the side of my left leg. I flinched in pain as the sheathed knife in my pocket ground into my thigh. We rolled across the floor, our faces close to each other. She ended up on top and sat on my chest, punching me in the face. I reached up, grabbed her arms, and managed to keep the punches at bay. As we grappled, I saw Zastra flit along the corridor, leap, and knock Yorbah off me.

The two of them rolled on down the corridor while I rose shakily to one knee. Zastra and Yorbah stood and faced off, circling each other. Zastra threw a punch that hit Yorbah in the mouth. Yorbah stumbled backward, then charged back with her own left hook to the face. Zastra's head spun to one side, and she took a step back to regain her balance. Yorbah leaned back, lifted one knee high into the air, and flicked a kick, catching Zastra in the chin with the toe of her boot. Zastra landed hard on the floor as Yorbah turned and ran down the corridor.

I jumped up and limped after her. She turned into a hanger as the door slid open. I came racing after her. Across the hanger stood a ship, but I didn't see Yorbah anywhere. She shouldn't have been able to dash to the ship that quickly. I swung around just in time to see some kind of steel tool in her arms coming down toward my head. Then everything went dark.

Chapter 12

Space Port Security

I opened my eyes slowly and winced at a bank of lights glaring down on me from a concrete ceiling. I seemed to be lying on some kind of narrow bench. Images of the fight with Yorbah flashed back through my mind, especially the sight of that hunk of steel swinging toward me. I groaned and rolled onto my side. My leg hurt. My gut hurt. My head really hurt. I raised a hand and touched my forehead, then pulled it quickly away because of the pain. A goose egg sat above my left eye, and it stung sharply when I touched it.

"I gotcha a good one, didn't I?" someone said. The voice was smooth and warm, like butter on grandma's dinner rolls. I raised my head to see.

I found myself looking at Yorbah, who was sitting on the bench beside my head. I recoiled from her, which brought more pain. I pulled myself up to a sitting position and looked around. Zastra was sitting at the other end of the bench with her arms crossed, her eyes straight ahead, and an annoyed look on her face. We were in a small concrete room. A wall of bars made up one whole side of the room. We were in a cell.

"What happened?" I asked, holding my head.

"She got behind you and knocked you out," Zastra said without looking at me.

"Yeah, I kinda remember that."

"Then I came up behind her and placed my blaster in her back. I was ready to escort her to the *Shaymus* and call Jace to come collect you when the space port security showed up and arrested us all. It appears they don't like brawls."

"So they'll sort this out, right?" I asked. "I mean, she's the murderer, and we apprehended her. We're the good guys here."

Yorbah and Zastra both started talking at the same time. It was like stereo speakers on each side of my head turned up way too loud.

76

Zastra said, "I apprehended her. You were unconscious. And we wouldn't be here if you hadn't spooked her."

Yorbah said, "I didn't murder anyone. What are you talking about?" Who am I supposed to have murdered?"

I waved the arm that wasn't holding my head to get them to quiet down. I turned to Yorbah. She had a fat lip and a tear in her shirt. "We're talking about Tam Elam. He's dead. Somebody murdered him."

"I didn't do it. What possible motive could I have to murder him?"

"Oh yeah? Well, if you didn't murder him, why did you run from us?" I asked.

"I had a dispute with a client recently. I delivered some goods, and there weren't as many of them as the client thought there should be. They blamed me. I assumed you were from them. You never identified yourself."

"Likely story," Zastra muttered.

"Listen," said Yorbah. "When I got there on Earth, Tam was already dead. The princess was freaking out, and the butler was trying to calm her down. All I could do is load them on my ship and take them away."

"Why didn't you take the body with you?" Zastra asked.

"Like I said, she was going nuts. We needed to get her away from the body."

"Where did you take Khan and Princess Ralph?" I asked.

She stared at me. "That information will cost you."

"It already has," I said, gingerly touching the bump on my head again.

"We'll get the information out of you," Zastra said, "once we get out of here."

"Getting out of here may be easier said than done, sister," Yorbah jeered. "You ever had a run-in with Girsu security?"

"No, why?"

She chuckled. "You'll see."

We waited. Then we waited some more. That was followed by more waiting. After a while I stood to stretch and limped around the cell, trying to loosen up my sore muscles. Then I sat back down and waited some more.

"So what's the drill here?" I finally asked. "Are they ever going to come and talk to us, or do they just wait until we die of old age?"

"They'll come when they're good and ready," Yorbah said. "They are Donovians, very meticulous people. They probably have to fill out seventeen forms before they can even interview us. And they'll fill them out in detail."

"Great," I said glumly.

"While we're waiting here, what's your story?" Yorbah asked. "Are you an Earthling? That's what you look like."

"Yeah. I'm an Earthling. We like to call ourselves human."

"Fine by me, human. Do you have a name?"

"Gabriel."

"Gabriel. I like it." She nodded her head toward Zastra. "So did she kidnap you or something? Is that how you got off planet?"

"Does that happen a lot? No. We're both working for the same employer, the Galactic Detective Agency."

"A detective. I'm impressed." She gave me an approving nod.

"Yeah? Well, I still think you're a murderer."

"So what bad guys have you caught, Gabriel?"

"This is his first case," Zastra growled. "Maybe his only case after this fiasco."

"This is just a momentary setback," I insisted. "They'll get this ironed out soon enough."

The conversation lagged, and we continued waiting. I ran over the scene in Port Otto in my mind. Yorbah stood and stretched, extending her arms and arching her back. She wandered over to the bars and leaned against them.

"When did you arrive in Port Otto?" I asked her.

"The first time or the second time?"

"After the murder."

"It was right before sunrise."

"And where was the body then?"

"On the kitchen floor."

"That's where you found it, right?" I asked Zastra.

"Yes," she replied.

"And where were the others, Yorbah?"

"The princess was in the big room. I think it was the only room she really fit in. She was crying and babbling about the guy being dead. The butler was in the doorway to the kitchen."

"Doing what?" I asked.

"He was just standing in the doorway. He had the knife in his hand."

"THE knife? When I saw Tam's body the knife was still in his chest."

Yorbah ran a hand through her hair. "You're right. It couldn't have been the murder weapon. I followed the butler into the kitchen to talk to him, and there was the knife in the body."

"So what knife did Khan have in his hand?"

"Beats me," she shrugged. "Some other knife, I guess. I suppose he was cleaning up. He stuck it back into this wooden block thing with a bunch of other knives. That's what butlers do, right? They clean up."

I thought back to the messy kitchen table I had seen there. This butler didn't seem to clean up very much.

A metal door creaked from somewhere down the hall, and the sound of footsteps approached the cell. A uniformed guard and a man in a suit came into view. They were short, about the height of an aged great-grandmother. They had thin, stick-like arms and legs and large purple heads with eyes like ping-pong balls sitting on top. They seemed more comical than threatening.

"Right," said the guy in the suit. "Who wants to go first?"

"Go where?" Zastra grunted.

"We'd like to ask a few questions to understand what this altercation was all about."

Zastra's yellow eyes were slits of anger. I was afraid she might do or say something to make the situation worse. And I figured Yorbah would lie and pin everything on us. "I'll go first," I said.

"Fine," the suit guy said. He nodded toward the guard, who withdrew a plastic disc from a pocket and waved it in front of the bars. Several of the bars lowered into the floor. I limped out through the opening.

The interrogation room where they took me could have been taken from any Hollywood movie or cop show on TV. Harsh lighting, concrete walls, a metal table with metal chairs on opposite sides, even a mirror on one wall that was undoubtedly two-way. The alien in the suit nodded his huge purple head toward a chair, and I sat. He sat down on the other side of the table. The guard left and locked us in.

"My name is Lieutenant Xox." He pulled a tablet device from a pocket. "Name and species?"

"Me? My name is Gabriel Lake. I'm a human."

"Thank you, Gabrielake. Home planet?"

"Earth."

"Earth?" His ping-pong eyes widened and wobbled around. "The quarantined planet?"

"That's what I hear."

"Eyes?"

"Brown."

"Don't be a wise guy," Xox said. He glanced up from the tablet to look me over. "One, Two. That's the answer I was looking for. You have two eyes."

I guessed two wasn't standard issue all across the galaxy.

He tapped on the tablet for a minute then asked, "How did you get off Earth?"

I hesitated to bring Oren into this, not knowing how it all worked. But I hoped name-dropping might help. "I'm investigating a missing person case for the royal house of Diere."

"A private investigator." Xox's eyes rolled around.

"That's right."

He gazed up from the tablet. "To be frank, Gabrielake, I don't like private investigators. In my experience, they get in the way of law enforcement and operate way too much in the legal gray areas."

"Sorry." I shrugged.

"Are you working the case by yourself?"

"The lizard person in there is my partner. Zastra."

"I take it you are referring to the Srathan."

"Yeah. Sorry, I had forgotten the name of her species. We only met a few days ago."

"She brought you from Earth?"

"We came together. This isn't a kidnapping situation if that's what you mean. We're associates."

"Seems unlikely, but I'll put it down." He tapped in my answer. "Now, Gabrielake, what was the cause of this disturbance for which you were arrested?"

"We were attempting to interview Yorbah. She's the other person in the cell. She's a pilot who transported the missing persons we are seeking. During the interrogation, she sucker-punched me and fled."

"If she was the aggressor, why did she run?"

"You'd have to ask her that."

"I will. And how do you know this Yorbah?"

"I don't know her! We only got her name in connection with our investigation."

"But you knew she would be here and came here looking for her."

"We didn't know for sure. It was a hunch. A lot of pilots come through here, right? Look, the story is not complicated. I spoke to her. She attacked me and then ran. We pursued and caught her."

"While knocking down several visitors, causing damage to vendor establishments, and creating general mayhem," Xox said, all the while typing in my statement with his eyes on the tablet.

"I'm sure we can provide restitution. But you should know there was a murder connected to the missing person case. It is likely Yorbah is the murderer."

Xox looked up with shock on his face. "Was this murder committed on Girsu?"

"No. On Earth."

He shrugged it off. "Then we are not concerned." His eyes went back to the tablet.

"But the point is we apprehended a dangerous criminal."

"Did you, though? Yorbah is a frequent visitor to Girsu. We have never had a bit of trouble from her. You, on the other hand, come here once and look what happens."

"What do you want from me? Do you want us to leave? Fine. Release Yorbah into our custody, and we'll go. Do you want to banish me forever from your little space port here? I don't have a problem with that."

We had an investigation to conduct. We had a princess to find and a murder to solve. And this guy was only concerned with the equivalent of a cleanup on aisle five. It was just like in the books. Nero Wolfe had Inspector Cramer giving him grief on every case. Holmes had Lestrade. Poirot had to deal with Inspector Japp. Now I had this guy, this bureaucratic twit Xox.

He tapped some more on the pad. He sighed and scrolled back through the text, nodding his giant purple head at what he read there. Finally, he looked up and turned the pad toward me. "What I want from you, Gabrielake, is for you to sign this confession. Then I can process it and move on to other things."

I studied the tablet. It was a report of what it termed "an incident." It worked in my answers but was heavily slanted toward making Zastra and me the guilty parties.

"This isn't exactly the story as I told it," I said.

"It is my report, though."

"If I sign this, is there a fine or something I have to pay?"

"There is no fine, Gabrielake."

"Oh. Then that's okay. How do I sign? Do I just use my finger?"

"Just use your finger."

I raised my finger toward the tablet. "And then I'll be free to go? Can I take Zastra and Yorbah with me?"

"Oh no, Gabrielake," he laughed. "You won't be free to go. You will have to serve your sentence."

I had touched my finger to the tablet and had started the first swirl in Gabriel. I pulled my hand back from the tablet like I had touched a hot stove. "What sentence?"

"See the notation there above where you sign. Your translator bots should convert it to Earth time units for you."

I looked. Then I gawped. It said five years!

"Five years! Five years in jail for a bar fight?"

"And destruction through the mall, and along a corridor, and into a hanger. Let me assure you, Gabrielake, we take these kinds of altercations very seriously. It is for everyone's protection. It is for your own protection."

"Then protect me a little less! I'm not signing this."

Xox smiled at me. "Well, we'll see. Perhaps you are not familiar with our court system."

A knock sounded on the door. It opened, and the guard stuck in his head.

"Excuse me, sir," said the guard. "The commander would like a word with you."

"The commander?" The smile dropped from Xox's face.

He stood, his metal chair shrieking across the concrete floor. He left the room and closed the door. Muffled voices were coming from the other side, animated voices, voices that sounded just this side of shouting. The commander, assuming that was the one voice, seemed to be giving Xox orders, and Xox was protesting. The conversation went back and forth, the volume ebbing and flowing. Finally, the voices died away. Xox came back in and stood in the doorway.

"Well, Gabrielake, it appears your story about working for the royal house of Diere is true."

"Duh," I said.

"Of course, Diere has no real authority over Girsu, but as a gesture of goodwill, Girsu Space Port has agreed to ..." He stopped to swallow. "... to assist your investigation ... by releasing you and ..." He consulted his tablet. "... Zastra, and releasing the pilot into your custody."

"Thank you," I said with a bow of my head. I couldn't help grinning. Somehow Oren had found out about our arrest and had called in the big guns. Xox had been forced to back down. I stood and limped toward the door.

Xox stepped aside but stuck his skinny arm across the door before I passed, blocking me. "But, Gabrielake," he pointed a long twig of a purple finger in my face, "If you ever come back to my space port, I will be keeping a close watch on you. Do not step out of line."

"I wouldn't dream of it," I grinned at him.

Xox led me down a hall to a foyer where Zastra and Yorbah were picking up our weapons, which had been confiscated. Buad was perched on Zastra's shoulder. Presumably, Oren had sent Buad to investigate, and he had gotten the ball rolling. I nodded toward him in thanks. He stretched his wings and cackled.

I turned toward Yorbah. "Are you going to come with us quietly this time?"

She shot me a smile. "As long as you aren't working for my last client or my ex-husband, I'll go wherever you want. And sorry about smacking you with the spanner. You'll forgive me, won't you?" She reached up and touched the goose egg on my forehead. I pulled away. It still hurt.

"Aw," cackled Buad, "you two are so cute."

"Let's just get back to the ship," I said.

Buad flew off. We followed on foot.

Chapter 13

Yorbah's Ship

"Report," Oren said.

We were back in the office on the *Shaymus*. Zastra and I were at our desks. Buad and Blan were perched inside their habitat. Yorbah slouched on one of the red leather chairs, with her legs crossed casually and smiling at the screen where Oren had sprouted elf ears in honor of her visit.

"You mean about the fight?" I asked.

Oren shook his head. "I don't care about the fight. Tell me about your conversation with Yorbah. Clearly, you had time to talk while you were being detained."

I scratched my head and tried to remember the conversation. It always seemed so easy in the books when Archie Goodwin reported things word-for-word to Nero Wolfe. But I couldn't remember anyone's exact words or even the order in which the conversation flowed. Of course, in my defense, I had probably been concussed from getting hit in the head. I managed to report the highlights with Zastra and Yorbah both correcting me as I went along.

Oren turned to Yorbah. "You transported Princess Ralph and Khan off Earth?"

"Yes."

"And they were both uninjured?"

"They were fine. Physically, at least. The princess was hysterical."

"And what did they tell you about the attack?"

"Nothing. I don't think they saw it. They just found the body."

"All right. What will it cost for you to tell us where you took Princess Ralph?"

Yorbah smiled. "I assume the queen is paying you generously to recover her little girl. I want a share of that."

Oren nodded. "Very well. One-seventh of the fee for truthful information, which leads to finding the princess and returning her alive to Diere."

"I was thinking more like one-third."

"Nonsense. There are six of us in this room plus our ship's engineer. That's seven. I am being generous at that. All you are providing is information."

"Crucial information. But fine. Pay me one-seventh now. I'll give you the location and be on my way."

"I think not. I'll pay you after I am paid, after a successful conclusion."

"Then I'm tagging along," she said. "Not that I don't trust you or anything."

"Very well."

"What about my ship? Should I leave it on Girsu until we return?"

"Why don't you dock onto the *Shaymus*? I think it might be helpful to have my team inspect your ship. Just to get a sense of how you transported the princess and her party."

She glanced over at me. "I'll agree to it as long as it's Gabriel who does the inspecting."

"That is satisfactory," Oren said.

I raised a hand. "Shouldn't I have a say?"

"Yorbah is our partner now," Oren said. "We can grant her some reasonable requests."

"For all we know, she murdered Tam," I said.

"Reasonable requests," repeated Oren. "We will, however, take precautions. Yorbah, you may fly your ship here to this hanger where we will dock and then take off. I assume you won't object to Gabriel going with you for that short flight, simply as a precaution."

"Of course not," she smiled.

Another of Oren's precautions was for Yorbah to leave all her weapons on the *Shaymus*. Zastra patted her down and removed two blaster pistols and three knives. Of course, she could still throw a heckuva punch, but I'd have to take my chances with that. Yorbah and I set off through the space port mall for her ship.

"So how long have you been a pilot?" I asked, trying to make conversation.

"Five years."

"How did you get into it?"

"I used to be married to a pilot. When the marriage fell apart, I got to keep the ship, and he got to keep his four-armed, feathered girlfriend. My husband was a jerk, but he taught me to fly. So I became a pilot, and I did what I had to do to make ends meet. I've been all over this quadrant."

We left the hangar corridor and started across the mall. The place was still filled with aliens of all kinds. I was afraid she'd try to give me the slip, so I moved closer to her.

"What kind of jobs do you take?"

"I take whatever jobs I can find. Carrying cargo, smuggling sometimes, ferrying people."

"Like the princess."

"Yeah. And like the princess, most of them are running from something — debts, spouses, the law."

I must have made a face because she asked, "Does that shock you? Listen, a girl's gotta eat. This life has toughened me up. And I think I kinda like myself better tough."

She was tough all right, I thought. My gut still hurt from her punch. We moved into the corridor leading to her hangar. Custodians were there cleaning up after the fight we had had a few hours before. They shot us side-eye glowers as we passed.

The hangar door slid open, and we stepped into the large bay. Her ship was smaller than the *Shaymus*, and it looked like some kind of grasshopper. It had a cylindrical body, a globe-shaped cockpit in the front, and long landing struts that hinged in the middle and swept back past the end of the ship like a grasshopper's back legs.

"There she is," Yorbah said. "The *Falcon*."

"Your ship is called the *Falcon*? Wait, is it just THE *Falcon*? Or is that short for a longer name, maybe, you know, with another word in there?"

"THE *Falcon*. That's the entire name. Why? Should it have another word?"

"No. No. It's just ... well, there's this awesome spaceship in the movies ... But ... no, the *Falcon* is a good name."

She pressed a button built into one of her gauntlets. A *chirp* sounded, and a cargo ramp descended from the back of the ship. We walked up the ramp.

Oren's ship, the *Shaymus*, was shiny, clean, and bright. The *Falcon* was a contrast, dark and disordered. The ramp led to a small cargo bay strewn with crates. If Ralph had been quartered in here during their flight — and this had to be the largest space on the ship — then Her Royal Highness would have been pretty cramped.

Yorbah headed for a door in the front of the bay, but I said, "Wait up. Oren wanted me to inspect the ship."

"Inspect away, by all means."

I wandered around the cargo bay. I stomped on the floor and knocked on some of the bulkheads.

"What are you doing?" Yorbah asked.

"Looking for secret compartments. Don't smugglers always have secret compartments?"

"Well, if I told you about them, it wouldn't be a secret."

I finished my tour of the cargo bay and nodded. "Okay, lead on."

We passed through a door into a little hallway with two doors on the left, one on the right, and one at the end. She pressed a button on a keypad beside the first door on the left. The door slid open to reveal a tight compartment with a bed and some built-in drawers. It wasn't as large as my quarters on the *Shaymus*. I wasn't sure it was as large as my bedroom closet back in Indy.

Yorbah opened the door on the right to a slightly larger compartment. "Sorry. My room's a mess." She was right about that. The room was carpeted with clothes. The drawers were hanging open with more clothes draped out of them. "The bed's comfortable, though."

I pulled my head back into the corridor and pointed toward the other door on the left. "What's behind door number three?"

"Toilet and sonic shower. Wanna see?"

"Why not? I paid for the whole tour."

She opened the door. It was as tiny as the bathroom on an airliner.

At the end of the hallway, a door slid open to the cockpit. I followed her in. There was only one seat, which she slid into.

"It's a short flight," she said. "You can stand here behind the seat."

She flipped a series of switches.

A deep manly voice came over the speakers. "What is our destination, Yorbah?"

"We're only going to a different terminal, Dylan," she answered. "I'll fly this one myself until we get to the docking part."

"Whatever you want," Dylan said.

"So I take it you can choose the voice of your AI?" I asked. "Ours sounds female."

"You sure can," she said. "I spend a lot of time here alone. I figure I should have a voice that keeps me company."

The engine started up, and the hangar door in the roof opened. The small red sun was hanging near the horizon now, and the sky had darkened from yellow to gold. As we rose, I viewed the five terminals of Girsu Space Port extending out from the circular mall like tentacles. We merely had to hop over the dome and come down into the hangar where the *Shaymus* was parked.

As we approached the other terminal, a hangar door opened ahead of us. The *Shaymus* was nestled inside. Yorbah worked the yoke to gently position the spacecraft and start to descend.

"How does this docking procedure work?" I asked.

"Carefully. Otherwise, we wreck both ships" She flipped a switch, and the screen in front of us showed the egg shape of the *Shaymus* below us gradually getting closer. "You see the dome on the top there?"

"Yeah, that's the office."

"Right. So a bit behind it is a hatch. See it?"

"Uh-huh."

"I've got a hatch like that on the bottom of the *Falcon*. Those things are mostly a universal size and shape. A few species, who are much larger or much smaller than you and I are, use different sizes, but we have adaptors for those. My job is to line up the hatches."

"Is that difficult? It looks difficult."

"It ain't easy. That's why I let Dylan do it." She flipped another switch.

"Docking program activated," Dylan said. "Docking in ten, nine, eight …"

When the countdown reached zero there was a gentle *screech* of metal on metal as the docking connections met followed by a *whump* as hydraulic clamps were engaged.

"Docking completed," Dylan said.

Yorbah switched off the engine. "The hatch is right here in the cockpit, just aft of the seat. Better watch your feet."

I looked down. I had been standing on a circular manhole cover this whole time. It was a good thing she hadn't opened it yet. I stepped forward as she leaned across to flip a switch. As she sat up again, I turned around to see the hatch spinning open. I gazed down the tube at Jace smiling up at us from below.

The docking hatch led down to an access closet on the crew level of the *Shaymus*. To reach the office we had to climb down the hatch, then step around the corridor to the main shaft and climb up.

"Welcome back," Oren said from the screen as we climbed into the office.

"Do you want me to report on her ship now?" I asked.

"No need. I activated the connection with your translator bots, so I saw everything you did."

"You know, I would appreciate it if you tell me before you do that."

"Duly noted. Now, Yorbah, will you tell me where you took the princess so we can lay in a course?"

"Donovio," she answered.

"Donovio. Donovio," I said. "Why does that sound familiar?"

Zastra said, "That mall cop Xox was Donovian."

"Oh great," I groused. "The most annoying people in the galaxy."

"Correction," Zastra said. "The most annoying people in the galaxy you've met so far. There are some very annoying people out there."

That didn't sound encouraging.

"Fortunately," said Oren, "Donovio is a neighboring planet in this star system. We can travel there with the ion engine. "Kah-Rehn, please plot a course to Donovio."

"Already plotted." Kah-Rehn's voice came through the speakers. "Take your seats, please."

"Yorbah, you can take my seat at the desk," I said. "I'll go to my cabin."

"Yeah, he prefers to——" Buad started in on a jibe, but I raised my eyebrows at him to silence him.

"I climbed down the shaft to my room. Remembering the problem with my things floating around last time, I stowed everything in drawers. I was getting strapped into my seat as Kah-Rehn said, "Ready for take-off. Gabriel Lake, would you like your screen to show the flight again?"

"Yes, I would," I replied. "Thanks for thinking of it. You're the best, Karen."

"Seriously? Still Karen?"

The ion engine rumbled to life, and we lifted off from the space port. It was now night on Girsu. Millions of stars were shining across the sky. I wondered if one of them was my sun with Earth and all my friends orbiting around it. It took but moments to climb through the moon's thin atmosphere and enter orbit. I felt my body drift up weightlessly against the straps of the chair. Then the engine accelerated away from the moon, and I was pushed back hard into my seat. After a few moments of feeling my cheeks trying to slide into my ears, the thrusters cut out and the g-force subsided.

Kah-Rehn's voice came over the speakers. "You are free to move about the ship. Be aware that you are now weightless. Flight time to Donovio will be three hours."

"Karen, you mean I can float around?"

"Absolutely, Gabriel Lake. Try it. I'll release your harness."

The straps around me slipped away and I began hovering above my chair.

I tried doing a butterfly stroke like I was swimming, but that got me nowhere.

"How do I move?"

"Push off from something, Gabriel Lake."

"Thanks. And you can call me Gabriel."

"All right. I have updated my record. And you can call me Kah-Rehn."

"Nice try, Karen."

I extended a leg down to the seat of the chair and pushed off. I went sailing up to the ceiling. I used my hands to keep from bumping my head and pushed off. I shot back down to the floor. I bent my knees, sprang against the floor, and found myself sailing through the cabin door out into the corridor where I slammed into the opposite wall. I ricocheted down the corridor like a pinball until I reached the central shaft. This time instead of climbing the rungs, I bounced off the first rung and flew up into the office. The others were still strapped in. Buad and Blan were floating upside down inside their cage. Through the ceiling dome, I saw a zillion stars shining out through the blackness of space.

"Hey, guys," I said. "This is awesome!"

Zastra rolled her eyes. "Traveling with you is like being with a hatchling."

But Yorbah grinned at me. "First time, Earth man?"

"You bet. This is amazing!"

"Release straps," she said.

Her straps retracted. She floated up and pushed off toward me. Taking my hands, we floated in circles together in a dance of weightlessness.

Chapter 14

Searching for a Princess

We reached Donovio and dropped into orbit. The view screen showed it as a planet with thick swirling clouds in reds and purples. Before landing I had to head back to the chair in my cabin to strap in. It took me a moment at the central shaft to figure out how to go down in weightless conditions. I finally realized that there is no "down" in weightlessness. I could propel myself through the shaft in either direction by simply pushing off the rungs of the ladder. I bounced back into my cabin and got myself strapped in.

I watched on the view screen as we descended through the dense atmosphere. It was like moving through a red fog, and it seemed to last forever. Finally, the ground appeared below us, a rocky landscape with roads and fences laid out in a precise grid. The *Shaymus* landed a few hundred feet from a group of buildings all painted white.

I got unstrapped and moved to the corridor where I met Zastra and Yorbah standing beside the ramp as it descended. Yorbah had her pistol strapped on her thigh again. Evidently, Oren had allowed her to rearm herself.

"She's going to show us where to find the princess," Zastra said to me with a nod toward Yorbah.

As we walked down the ramp a wave of hot, damp air enveloped us. It was like being slapped in the face with an invisible hot moist towel.

"Ugh," I said. "I can hardly breathe."

"Welcome to Donovio," Zastra said. "Personally, I kind of like it."

Yorbah pointed toward one of the buildings. "That's where I deposited them."

I suppose you might call it a hut because it was made of some kind of mud or adobe clay material and consisted of a single dome. But unlike any hut I had ever seen the dome stretched up as tall as a two-story house on Earth, and it was as wide as a three-car garage. It looked like Ralph would fit inside it better than she did in the Port Otto A-frame.

We walked to the building. Zastra knocked on the circular hatch, which seemed to be the front door. We waited, but no one answered. Zastra knocked again, and we waited again. Still no one came.

"Let's just go in," Yorbah said. She pressed a blue button on the keypad mounted beside the hatch. Nothing happened. She pressed a red button on it. Nothing continued to happen.

"Allow me," said Zastra. She pulled her blaster out of its holster and shot. A pulse of blue laser light streamed from the barrel, and the keypad exploded in sparks. She re-holstered the pistol while the hatch rolled open.

We stepped inside to a large single room that seemed to take up nearly the whole interior space of the building. It was empty.

I called out, "Hello. Princess Ralph. Khan." But I knew no one would answer.

Zastra wheeled on Yorbah and grabbed her by the collar, lifting her inches above the floor. "You lied to us!"

"I didn't. I didn't," Yorbah choked out.

I saw Yorbah reaching for the blaster holstered on her thigh. This didn't look like it would end well. I swung my arm and knocked the pistol out of her hand as she pulled it out.

"Cut it out!" I yelled. "Zastra, put her down."

"Taking her side?" Zastra hissed at me.

"I just don't want to see anybody get killed," I said. "Let's talk this out."

Zastra released Yorbah. I kept my eye on her as she reached for the pistol and re-holstered it.

"Ah-hem." The voice came from behind us. We turned to find an alien with a large purple head and ping-pong eyes like Xox. "May I help you?" the Donovian asked.

"We're trying to track down the people who were here," said Yorbah. "Tell my associates they were here a few days ago."

"Yes," the Donovian said, "People were here, and then they were gone. But I must say, I thought I heard a blaster shot. Weapons are not allowed on Donovio, you know."

"We'll be leaving soon," said Zastra. "Now these people who were here, describe them."

'Well, let me see, let me see. They were Dieren, I think. A man and a woman."

"Told you," Yorbah said.

"Was the woman like twenty feet tall?" I asked.

"Oh indeed," said the Donovian. "She was quite tall. I remember saying to her, 'My, you are quite tall,' and she replied, 'Uh-huh.' Yes, those were her exact words. 'Uh-huh,' she said. I couldn't get much else out of her. The man was a bit more talkative. He was asking about where to obtain food, and I told him—"

Zastra interrupted him. "When did you last see them?"

"Hmm. When did I last see them? Hmm. What do I remember? Let's see. I took a walk yesterday, and I don't remember seeing them then. So they may have been gone by then, but of course, I can't be sure. They might have been inside. Or they might have been out shopping or visiting. There is a charming little market in town. So I don't know where they were yesterday, but they clearly were not here, or I would have seen them."

"When *did* you see them?" Zastra hissed impatiently.

"Well, I do believe it was the day before. Yes, the day before yesterday, I was straightening the rocks along my path. You wouldn't think rocks would move, but let me tell you, they do. People kick them by accident. Some children even move them on purpose, which I think is disgraceful."

"And that's when you noticed the people who were here?" Zastra prompted.

"Yes. I was getting ready to say that. In any case, the woman was outside. I don't believe we said anything to each other. She wasn't much of a talker. We waved though. Yes, I remember distinctly waving to her, and she waved back."

"How did they leave the planet?" asked Yorbah.

"Well, I'm sure I would have no idea. There is a daily ferry to Girsu Space Port. Most likely they took that. And from there, well, from there they could have gone anywhere."

Zastra turned to stare down Yorbah.

Yorbah said, "I swear, I did not see them on Girsu. There are any number of pilots and ships for hire around Girsu at any time. Even commercial flights to most planets."

Zastra said, "We'll go back to the *Shaymus* and hear what Oren has to say." She glared at Yorbah. "If you are lying, Oren will find out. Then you will be sorry."

"I'm not lying, all right?" Yorbah turned to the Donovian. "Thank you. You have been most helpful."

The Donovian bowed deeply. "It is our duty to be helpful."

"Is it?" I muttered. "Tell that to Xox next time you see him."

"Oh!" The Donovian sounded thrilled. "Do you know my cousin Xox? He is an important person at the Girsu Space Port."

"Yeah, we've met," I said flatly. "If you see him, tell him Gabriel Lake says hi. He'll enjoy that."

We started walking back across the bare, mucky terrain toward the *Shaymus*. As we reached it a small red lizard creature darted from under the ramp and shot up into the air on purple wings. I jumped back in surprise.

"Zastra, is that a relative of yours?" I asked with a grin.

"I would claim it. The creature is majestic. When we get back to Earth, why don't you take me to see your cousins the orangutans? From what I hear they are almost exactly like you."

"Okay. Point taken. No more biology jokes."

When we got back into the office, Oren came on the screen. "Did you find them?"

"They were here, but they've flown the coop," I said.

Zastra said, "Yorbah may know where they are."

"I don't," Yorbah protested. "I dropped them off here on Donovio, and that was the last I've seen of them."

Oren frowned. "Accusations will get us nowhere. Perhaps we can deduce where they went. It is possible they have returned to Diere. But in that case, we would lose any claim to a fee, so that does me no good. They would not go back to Earth after the murder. Perhaps the princess is frightened for her own life and wanted to cover her tracks even from Yorbah, who, as we have seen, can be induced to betray a confidence."

I glanced at Yorbah who was wearing a hard look on her face.

"Kah-Rehn," said Oren. "Plot a course to Astrid."

"Plotting course," came Kah-Rehn's voice.

"Why Astrid?" asked Zastra.

Oren said, "If Princess Ralph is running for her life, she would want to go someplace she could blend in. Given her size, that eliminates many planets. But where better for a twenty-foot-tall woman to hide than on a planet of fifty-foot-tall people? She would seem to be a child, and no one would take any notice."

I gaped. "The people are how tall you say? We're going to a planet where the people make Princess Ralph seem small?"

"Calm down," said Yorbah. "It's a great place. Fabulous nightlife."

"Oh really? You go out dancing with people as tall as trees?"

"There are plenty of off-worlders there," Yorbah replied. "As you can imagine, people that big eat quite a lot. The food import business is huge."

"Course plotted to Astrid," said Kah-Rehn. "Astrid is in the Kahari star system. We will be using the chrono drive. Please strap in."

I returned to my cabin and slipped into my chair.

"Karen, I have a question," I said.

"It is Kah-Rehn, remember?"

"I'm sure it is. Anyway, Jace explained to me that the ion drive we used to go from Girsu to Donovio is gobs faster than any kind of rocket Earth has yet invented."

"This is true, Gabriel. The ion drive is approximately one thousand forty-three percent faster than Earth spacecraft."

"That's a lot. So I'm wondering why isn't that fast enough to go to Astrid?"

"You may be underestimating the vast reaches of interstellar space, Gabriel. The Kahari system is forty-three light-years away. As fast as an ion drive is, it would still require one hundred forty-four Earth years to reach it."

"Seriously? One hundred forty-four years?"

"I am always serious, Gabriel."

"Well, we don't have *that* kind of time. I have a dentist appointment in a couple of weeks."

"Then we will use the chrono drive."

We took off, bounced back thirteen billion years to when the space of forty-three light-years was shrunk to walking distance, and came back to the present, landing on the planet at a space port. Oren convened a meeting in the office and briefed us on our orders. Photos of Ralph and Khan had been printed. They showed each of them inside the A-frame in Port Otto. Oren had apparently shot them from the tablet when we visited there.

"Use these photos and ask around for them," Oren said.

"How do we ask around an entire planet?" I said.

"We don't. Kah-Rehn, what is the population of Astrid?"

Kah-Rehn's voice chimed in. "The population of Astrid at its last census was 3.247 billion."

"Wow! Three billion giants," I said. "I hope they watch where they step while we're out there."

"Thank you, Kah-Rehn," said Oren. "Now please show us the planet."

The 3D artwork of the galaxy that hung on the wall sprang into the middle of the office as a hologram. The galaxy appeared as a gigantic uneven disk with a blazing bright center surrounded by long arms of blue clouds studded with stars. The shining center spun slowly with the arms following along behind in huge spirals like some kind of spinning octopus. The outline of a tiny cube appeared along one of the arms, and the model began to zoom in on the cube.

That arm of the galaxy grew in size, the clouds resolving into thousands of individual stars. As it zoomed in more, the vast spaces between the stars became apparent. The model continued to zoom in until the room was filled with an individual solar system that contained five planets. One of the planets spun hurriedly around the star in a close orbit. Two other planets further out resembled blue pearls like Earth. The final two planets were gas giants much further out.

The model zoomed in further to enlarge one of the blue pearls to the size of a large globe spinning in the middle of the office. It had a single large continent shaped like a giant cocktail shrimp sitting alone in the middle of a sea. I stood there slack-jawed. Unable to stop myself, I stepped toward the spinning globe of Astrid and reached out to touch it. My fingers passed right through it.

"It's a hologram, dummy," Buad snickered from the cage.

Oren said, "We can reasonably restrict our search to the city of Tyr." As he spoke, a large area along the shore of the continent lit up. I couldn't be sure of the scale, but the city appeared to be huge.

"Tyr is the only city with a space port," Oren continued. "If Princess Ralph and Khan took commercial transport out of Girsu, they would have come in through that space port, as did we. Kah-Rehn, what is the population of Tyr?"

"The population of Tyr is 2.238 million."

"Thank you, Kah-Rehn. Still a substantial number," said Oren, flipping his hand over. "But it was only a day or two ago. And Princess Ralph and Khan might have stood out with their green skin. Someone may remember them. Zastra and Gabriel, go to the ticket counters, talk to porters, hover-craft rental associates, anywhere they could have made arrangements to leave the space port. Buad and Blan, fly out over the city searching for them. I will monitor your translator bot connections."

"Can I help?" It was Yorbah.

"If you wish," Oren said.

Something in my desk buzzed, and another copy of the two photographs shot out of a slot. Built-in printer. Cool, I thought.

Yorbah took the photos and shoved them in a pocket. "Thanks. Let's go."

We left the ship, walking down to a tarmac outside the space port terminal. Buad and Blan flew off into a pink, cloudless sky. Yorbah, Zastra, and I entered the terminal and split up.

Chapter 15

Feeling Kind of Small

The terminal concourse looked like any Earth airport, all steel and glass and brightly lit signs. Except on this planet, it was a pink sky filtering in through the glass domes over my head. And those domes were way, way above my head.

I stared in amazement at the passersby. The people of Astrid looked much like humans, that is if humans were fifty feet tall. These giants swept past me, stepping fifteen or twenty feet with each stride, seemingly unaware of my presence. I was afraid of being stepped on and walked with my eyes up and continuously scanning all around.

Luckily, inside the terminal, they had moving walkways segregated by body size as an accommodation for off-worlders. Each walkway was marked with an overhead sign set at the appropriate height. If you had to duck to fit under a sign, then that wasn't the walkway for you. I fit in the next-to-the-smallest one.

High over my head, about the height of a ten-story building, was a sign that said: *Rail Connections.*

I thought I would try asking there. I got off the moving walkway and approached a ticket counter towering as high above me as a three-story house.

"Oren, are you seeing this? How do I get up there to ask?"

His voice in my ear said, "There should be some accommodation for smaller species. Look around."

I looked left and right, up and down, and finally spotted a view screen placed at about my waist level. It had a red button beside it. I leaned down and pressed the button. A face appeared on-screen, a woman's face wearing pink cat-eye glasses. It could pass for a human face, but I knew it must be huge.

"Where to?" she asked in a bored voice.

I held up the pictures. "Yes, um … some friends of mine came through here yesterday, possibly the day before. I was supposed to follow them, but I don't know if they took rail or something else. This is what they look like. And they would be small ... to you, at least. They are Dieren. Did you perhaps help them or see them?"

"Where to?" the face repeated slowly.

"To wherever these people went. That is if you remember them."

"Sir, I just sell tickets. Do you want to buy a ticket or not?"

"Well, I do if my friends bought a ticket. Do you remember them?"

The face on the screen gave a cursory glance to the photos. "No. Next please."

"Did you even look?" I asked. "This is a matter of life and death."

"Next please." The screen went blank.

I moved off. Two or three football fields away was a sign that said: *Platforms — Must Show Ticket.*

A skinny attendant in an oversized blue uniform was leaning against the sign. He appeared young. Maybe he was a teenage giant. I thought if the person who sold tickets wouldn't help me, perhaps the person who checked the tickets would.

"Excuse me!" I yelled up at the attendant.

No reaction. The attendant seemed intent on using his tongue to try to extract something from between his teeth.

"Excuse me!" I yelled louder. I waved my arms wildly.

He continued working on whatever was stuck in his teeth but now switched to using a fingernail.

"HELLO! HELLO!" I shouted at the top of my lungs. I jumped up and down and waved.

He startled and began casting around for the source of the sound. He finally spotted me and leaned over in my direction.

"You scared me there, little guy," he said.

"SORRY. I'M WONDERING IF YOU'VE SEEN THESE PEOPLE." I held up the photos.

"SORRY. CAN'T HEAR YOU." He didn't need to yell back at me. His booming giant voice was reverberating in my ears.

"I'M WONDERING IF YOU'VE SEEN THESE PEOPLE." I waved my arm with the photos back and forth.

"STILL CAN'T HEAR YOU. USE THE SCREEN." He pointed toward a pole a few feet from me.

I spotted a video screen like the one I had used for the ticket agent. This time the screen and button were mounted on a pole a few feet above my head. I jumped up to hit the button and missed. I jumped again and missed again. Reluctantly I wrapped my arms and legs around the pole. It felt sticky, and I didn't want to think about why that might be. But I needed to do this. I shinnied up the pole and smacked the button. When the screen came alive with the attendant's face, I jumped back down to the floor. I stood on my tiptoes and stretched my arms up as far as they would go to hold the photos up by the screen.

"These people may have come through a day or two ago. Did you see them?"

His voice came over the speaker. "Oh yeah, I did. I remember the green skin. Little woman and a tiny man, right?"

"That's them. Any idea what train they took?"

He shook his head. "There's no way I'd remember that. You have no idea the number of tickets I see every day! But I'll tell you this, shorty, all these trains here go to the north side of town. Does that help?"

"It does help. Well, except for the *shorty* part. I'll have you know I am average height for my species. Average height. But thank you!"

I turned away and said, "Oren, did you hear that?"

"Yes, north Tyr. Excellent work. Let me put all the communication channels together. Hello, everyone. Gabriel has tracked them to the north side of the city. Buad and Blan, concentrate your search there. The rest of you, move to the north side and ask at every shop that sells food."

"I'm already there." It was Yorbah's voice.

"Yorbah," said Oren, "you were supposed to be asking around at the space port."

"I played a hunch," she said. "When I dropped them off on Earth Her Highness complained a lot about the house. I mean, a lot. As you can imagine, the palace is much fancier than that dingy little place in Potato. I knew the north side of Tyr is the upscale part, so I started there. I've already had a hit. A street musician spotted Khan earlier today."

"You could have reported it. What was the location of the street musician?"

"He was at the corner of Idun and Nord."

"We'll move to that area." It was either Buad or Blan. I still couldn't tell their voices apart.

"I'll grab a taxi and go there," said Zastra.

"Zastra, I'll catch up with you and come too," I said.

100

"Fine," Zastra replied. "But hurry."

"I'm keeping the channel open," said Oren.

I scanned the concourse for signs indicating where the taxis might be. I didn't see anything. It wouldn't be wise to run off in a random direction simply hoping to find them. I turned back and jumped as hard as I could, and this time managed to press the button for the attendant.

His voice came over the speaker. "Need something else, little guy?"

"Again, average height. But which way to the taxis?"

He pointed, and I sped off. I zigged and zagged around gigantic feet, dodged rolling suitcases as tall as two-story buildings, ducked under enormous electric carts. As I skirted around a pet carrier sitting on the floor, growls and howling erupted from it. I glanced over my shoulder to see something like a saber-tooth guinea pig twice my size trying to squeeze through the bars to get at me. I quickened my pace just in case. I spotted a sign that said: *Ground Transportation*.

I headed for it. A moving walkway was heading in that direction. I jumped on the walkway designed for people my size and began to run. Other people were on the walkway. Most of them were walking at normal speed. Some weren't walking at all, just leaning against the side of the walkway and sipping drinks. I wove through them, crying, "Excuse me," "Sorry," "On your left," "On your right," "Pardon me," "I have to catch a taxi." I heard people grumbling behind me as I shot through them.

"Where are you?" Zastra said in my ear.

"Almost there. I think. Wait, I can see the doors."

I passed through enormous doors to the outside and spotted Zastra standing at the top of a set of steps beside the taxi, her lizard lips pursed in impatience.

This wasn't any old taxi. This was a hover car. It floated about ten feet above the pavement, which would have been low for the giants of Astrid. But Zastra and I needed steps to reach it. I shot up the steps, and we both jumped in.

"Idun and Nord," she told the driver. The taxi *whooshed* away from the curb.

I couldn't see over the seat in front of me. All I could make out about the ride came from what little I saw through the side windows and what I felt as the taxi flew along … and also the muttered comments of the driver about traffic and other drivers. I felt us making a curving arc away from the space port and then, judging from glimpses I got of hover vehicles on each side of us, we seemed to merge onto some kind of highway. We swerved into another lane, as horns honked all around us. We zoomed along at what seemed to be a rapid speed for several minutes.

The taxi slowed abruptly, causing me to all but tumble off the seat.

The driver mumbled, "Stupid traffic."

That's when I learned that hover taxis aren't limited to two-dimensional travel like Earth taxis, because without warning we pitched upward and accelerated hard. Zastra and I were thrown back into the seat. My legs slid down into the crack between the back of the seat and the bench, and for a moment I was afraid I was going to get stuck down there along with loose change and the stale French fries or whatever else might be down there. Zastra pulled on my arms, and I managed to crawl out. By then the taxi had slowed, and I glimpsed the roofs of houses out the side window, leading me to conclude that we had left the highway and were now in a residential area.

The driver slowed and stopped. "Here we are, folks. Idun and Nord. That's forty-two bills."

Zastra pulled a device out of a pocket and pressed a few buttons. "There's your payment."

"Got it," the driver said.

The side door slid open, and we had to jump ten feet down to the sidewalk. I hit the pavement and rolled, feeling lucky I didn't break my legs.

"Which way?" I asked.

One of the Avanians answered me. "I've spotted Khan. He came out of a weapons shop. It looks like he's carrying a blaster rifle."

"Blaster rifle!" exclaimed Oren. "What the blazes is he up to?"

"Location?" asked Zastra.

"He is approaching Idun and Ymir heading north."

"Which direction is that from Nord?" Zastra asked.

"Follow the sun."

Zastra glanced up to the sky. "This way."

We dashed up Idun. The area reminded me of Broad Ripple back in Indy, comfortable, well-kept homes interspersed with restaurants and shops. Of course, on Astrid the blocks were built to the size of giants, and each one seemed a good half mile long. It took five minutes to run one block. I wondered how many blocks away Ymir was and if my heart would be able to hold out that long. I mean, I do some bicycling, but I don't manage to get in much running.

Happily, Ymir was the very next street. We made it across to the other side safely, ducking under hover cars and dodging giant scooters. We continued running.

A couple of minutes later I saw Khan up ahead. I spotted Yorbah running toward him from the opposite direction. We were all closing in. I was getting ready to call out to Khan by name when two things happened almost at once. First, Khan turned to walk up a brick sidewalk to a house. Secondly, Yorbah launched herself at him. She flew through the air and tackled him. The blaster rifle he was carrying sailed up into the air, turning end over end. Yorbah and Khan rolled along the sidewalk, coming to a stop at our feet. Zastra snatched the blaster rifle out of the air.

"Khan," I said smiling down at him. "How ya doin', buddy? Imagine running into you in a place like this. What are the odds?"

Chapter 16

A Princess in Hiding

"What's with the blaster rifle, Khan?" Zastra asked as the butler struggled to his feet.

Khan brushed himself off and glared at Yorbah, who had tackled him. "It is for the protection of Princess Ralph, of course. As I assume you know, her husband was murdered. Since then, we have run from planet to planet trying to find a safe place."

He held an arm out, requesting the rifle. Zastra ignored it.

I said, "What makes you think the princess is in danger? Perhaps the murderer was only after Tam."

Khan gave me a withering look. "Do you believe Tam Elam was significant enough a person to attract a murderer? I find that assumption dubious. But even if it were true, my duty is still to see to the princess's protection at all costs."

"Oren wants to talk to her," Zastra said. "She agreed to return to Diere."

He scoffed. "That was before the murder. Her Royal Highness is in danger now. And you want her to return to the one planet in the galaxy where she would constantly be in front of the public?"

"She would have the protection of the entire palace guard," Zastra replied. "But that's not the point. The point is Oren wants to talk to her."

Khan made a face. "Very well. Please come inside."

The house was an Astrid version of a one-story craftsman bungalow like the kind you find on Earth, small footprint, a low-pitched roof, a porch with substantial square columns. It was not so different from my house back in Indy. Except this one had been built for giants. The roof line soared a hundred feet above my head. The steps leading to the porch were nearly as tall as me. Thankfully, someone had placed a board across them that we could use as a ramp.

We crossed the porch, which took almost a full minute, and entered through a huge doggy door. I hoped they didn't have a huge doggy.

"M'lady," Khan called out. "The Galactic Detective Agency has somehow tracked us."

Princess Ralph came around the corner. She still towered over us, though in relation to the house she might have passed for a toddler. Make that a toddler who just had a favorite toy snatched away from them. Her eyes were red and puffy, her lips drawn tight and downturned.

She eyed us suspiciously. "Hello. How did you find us?"

"We work for a genius," Zastra said. She pulled a tablet from her robe. "Oren would like to talk to you." Zastra tapped a button and Oren's face filled the screen. She held the screen in front of her, tilted up toward Ralph.

"Princess Ralph," Oren's voice said. "It is a pleasure to see you again. I was so sorry to learn of the death of Tam Elam. Let me assure you we did not allow his body to fall into the hands of the Earthlings. We will be taking it for burial either to his home planet or to Diere, at your choosing."

"Thank you, Mr. Vilkas," Ralph said, her voice breaking. She pulled a dainty handkerchief the size of a kitchen tablecloth out of a pocket and blew her nose. "I had been worrying about him ... his ... the body."

"Your Highness, we would still like to persuade you to return to Diere. Your mother desires your presence. You ran away to be with Tam. Now that being with him is not possible, why not return and take up your royal duties once more?"

Ralph narrowed her eyes. "How do we know it wasn't someone from Diere who killed poor Tam? You know how the council, even my own mother, was opposed to the marriage. They might have sent an assassin to Earth. And now ... now he's gone. My Tam. My poor Tam." Her voice trailed away to sobs.

"Your Royal Highness, if someone from Diere did have him killed, and let me stress we have absolutely no evidence of that being the case, surely the threat was only to Tam. You yourself should certainly be safe on Diere. You are adored there."

"Ah-ha!" she cried. "But the situation is different now that we are on to them, don't you see? We have seen through their tricks, their charades. And now the only way for them to cover their tracks would be to kill me, too!"

"Preposterous! Are you suggesting that for the purpose of saving the royal family, someone would actually destroy the royal family? It makes no sense."

Ralph knitted her brows. She obviously hadn't thought of it that way. She glanced at Khan for help.

Khan cleared his throat. "Ahem, if I may be so bold, m'lady, it is possible that it was, of course, their intent originally merely to separate you from poor Mr. Elam. But now that it has come to murder and you are on to them, they find themselves in desperate straits. Their backs are against the wall, and they may lash out. I cannot ensure your safety on Diere."

"I have spoken to your mother, the queen," said Oren, "and she will ensure your safety. Commander Woad has said his entire guard would take personal responsibility for your protection."

"Woad!" Ralph scoffed. "He could be the very person behind the murder. He is a shrewd one, that Woad."

"In addition," continued Oren, "you have me. I have inspected the farmhouse on Earth. I am analyzing the clues. My associates and I are uniquely positioned to unmask the murderer, to avenge Tam Elam."

Ralph straightened. She blinked her eyes and sniffled. She blinked her eyes again. "You could bring to justice the villain who killed my Tam, Mr. Vilkas?"

"M'lady ..." began Khan. But she waved him to silence.

Oren raised an eyebrow. "I can, of course, make no guarantees, Your Royal Highness, but I believe I can. As you know we have no small amount of experience in that area."

"Then do so, Mr. Vilkas. Yes. Yes! Leave no stone unturned. Spare no expense. Catch the scoundrel by all means."

"I only ask one thing of you, Your Royal Highness. Return to Diere. In fact, I would be pleased to transport you. That way I can finish the business I have with your mother and then investigate the murder on Diere or wherever the trail leads without worries about your safety. Would you agree to that?"

Ralph paused a moment to consider it. "All right. I agree ... for Tam's sake."

"M'lady," Khan protested.

"No, Khan, I have made up my mind."

"As you wish, m'lady."

"Now, Your Highness, about the murder," said Oren, "May I ask you a few questions?"

"Of course, if it will assist in the investigation."

"It will. Did you see the attacker?"

"No."

"How and when did you learn of the murder?"

"Khan woke me in the morning and told me he found the body."

"Khan," said Oren, "same question."

Khan cleared his throat. "I went into the kitchen to prepare m'lady's breakfast. The body was there on the floor."

"A neighbor said he overheard two people arguing during the night. What can you tell me of that?"

"Nothing," said Ralph. "I was without question not part of any argument. Tam and I never argued."

"But he was less than pleased with the agreement for you to return to Diere and take another husband," Oren said. "Did you have … a conversation about that?"

"No," said Ralph. "Was he unhappy with the agreement? I was unaware of that."

"Did you hear anyone else arguing?"

"No, but I am a very sound sleeper."

Khan was staring at the ceiling. "The neighbor might have overheard Tam and me as we discussed the situation. Tam was against the princess accepting the queen's offer and returning to Diere. I, of course, stood by m'lady's decision. Our talk was certainly no argument, but I am afraid Tam did get animated at times."

"And after this animated conversation?" asked Oren.

"I retired to my room and went to bed."

"And you heard nothing and saw no one until the next morning when you found Tam's body in the kitchen?"

"That is correct."

Oren asked, "Besides the idea that the murderer was an assassin from Diere, can you think of anyone else who might wish ill of Tam Elam?"

"Tam had an ex-girlfriend," said Ralph. "The girl was obsessed with him. After he left her for me, she sent him threatening messages."

"Do you have any of those messages?"

"They went to Tam's personal tablet. I don't have it."

"It was in his pocket," Zastra said. "But we don't have the password."

"I know it," Ralph said. "His password is the numbers one to ten."

Zastra said, "So it's 123456—?"

Ralph interrupted. "No, the numbers one to ten."

"You mean the numbers 1, 2, and 10?"

"No, no. It's not numbers at all. It is the phrase 'the numbers one to ten' written out."

Zastra stood there for a minute, blinking her yellow eyes. "You mean the words for 'the numbers one to ten' spelled out in letters?"

"That's what I said," said Ralph. "It's either that or pi to fifteen digits."

"He knew the value of pi to fifteen digits?"

"No, I mean the words 'pi to fifteen digits.' The phrase, of course."

"Of course." Zastra shook her head. "Got it … I think. We'll try it."

"This ex-girlfriend," said Oren. "What is her name? And what planet is she from?"

"She is from his home planet of Cunedda. Her name is Ex Awoo."

I had to say it. "So she's his ex, and her name is Ex?"

"That is correct," said Ralph.

"Wow! Talk about an unfortunate name. She would be destined to get dumped."

Ralph cocked her head. "I don't know what you mean, Mr. Lake."

Oren didn't give me a chance to explain. "We can send word to Cunedda that we are bringing Tam's body there for burial. That should attract the ex-girlfriend so we can interview her. Is that acceptable?"

"Yes," Ralph said. "Do that."

"Well, thank you both. Your Royal Highness, we should leave for Diere as soon as possible. My associates will accompany you to our ship."

"It may take some time for Khan to gather my things."

"Take the time you need, Your Royal Highness. My associates will wait for you."

Oren's voice whispered in my ear, "Under no circumstances leave them alone. We don't want them flying off to some other corner of the galaxy."

"Khan," said Ralph, "please see to my packing at once. I will be resting in the spare bedroom."

Khan and Ralph both shuffled off, leaving Zastra, Yorbah, and myself alone in the front room.

"So now we just wait?" I asked.

"We wait," said Zastra.

I looked around the room. A couch and chairs loomed over us, the seat cushions high above our heads. It looked like we would need mountain climbing gear to get up there. I sat down on the floor and leaned my back against a table leg. Yorbah sat down beside me.

"Where do you think the flyers went?" she asked.

"You mean Buad and Blan? Beats me. They probably returned to the ship. They would be as tiny as bugs here."

"Oren talked about analyzing the clues. What clues do you have?"

"I don't know. Not much. The night of the murder a neighbor, Henry Koster, heard sounds of men arguing. And I think Koster knows more than he's saying. He caught sight of Tam's horns, so who knows what he thought of that or decided to do about it. Another clue is that there was no sign of forced entry, so presumably the killer was someone they knew or was already in the house. Those two things might point to Khan, or maybe to Princess Ralph herself. Except earlier that day somebody may have been watching from the barn. So that sounds like it was somebody else."

"Interesting. Who was watching from the barn?"

"I don't know. Maybe Koster. You know, there's another thing — the fact that the murder happened the very night after Oren arranged for the princess to return to Diere. Is that merely a coincidence, or could the deal have motivated the killer to strike then?"

"It definitely is a puzzle," Yorbah said.

"Who's this Commander Woad she was talking about?" I asked.

"I don't know him. Sounds like he's in charge of the palace guard. So do you think he could be a suspect?"

"The princess clearly doesn't trust him. We should keep an eye on him when we get there."

Later, Ralph emerged followed by Khan pulling several huge bags on some sort of anti-gravity sled hovering above the ground.

"That's a nifty device," I said. "Saves your back, huh?"

'Hmm," Khan growled.

A hover taxi was hailed to return us to the space port. This one had better accommodations for human-sized species. From the back seat, you could ascend a spiral staircase mounted on the door to an observation deck so you could see out the window. None of the others wanted to look out the window, but I did. I wanted to get a better sense of what Astrid looked like. I need not have bothered. All I saw was the huge city of Tyr stretching out in every direction. It seemed not all that different from an Earth city, other than being built on a colossal scale, of course.

We got back to the space port and made our way through the terminal to the tarmac where the *Shaymus* was parked with the *Falcon* docked on top.

Jace came down the ramp to meet us. "Oren wants to talk to the princess again."

Zastra pulled out the tablet, tapped it, and turned it to face Ralph.

"Your Royal Highness," said Oren, "we should discuss accommodations for the voyage. I believe on your journeys to and from Earth you rode in the cargo hold of Yorbah's ship. You see that ship is docked with us. The hold is available for you if that is satisfactory."

"It is not satisfactory," Ralph said with her nose in the air. "That hold was far too cramped. Crates were jabbing into my back the whole time. There was so little room that poor Tam couldn't even stay with me." Tears came to her eyes at the mention of his name.

"Well, that will not do," said Oren. "Suggestions anyone?"

Jace moved to Zastra, leaned over, and whispered something to the tablet.

Oren nodded. "Very good. Tell them."

Jace turned to the others. "Well, when this ship was used for a ferry service, we had Dierens from time to time. What is now the office was then an observation deck. It is equipped with an inflatable mattress that blows up from the floor. We often used it for Dierens. If that sounds acceptable, we can see to it."

"I believe it does," Ralph said. "Show me."

"This way, Your Royal Highness," Jace said with a bow.

Jace walked up the ramp. Ralph got down on her hands and knees to follow. Inside the ship, we saw Jace climb up the ladder followed by Ralph who just stood up in the shaft. A few minutes passed while Jace must have moved the furniture and rolled up the carpet. We heard a *pssst* sound like an inflatable mattress filling. She pulled her royal personage up into the office and disappeared from view.

A few minutes later, Jace climbed back down the ladder and joined us. "That's sorted. What about the rest of you?"

"Gabriel and I can ride in our cabins," Zastra said.

"I'll ride in my ship," said Yorbah.

"So that leaves you, Khan," said Oren over the tablet. "We have a spare cabin on the *Shaymus.*"

"I am sure it will suffice," Khan said. "I would like to remain near the princess."

"Excellent," Oren said. "Then let's be on our way."

Chapter 17

At the Palace of Diere

The flight to Diere was uneventful, by which I mean my lunch didn't try to jump out of my stomach this time. I seemed to be starting to adjust to space travel and Kah-Rehn's crazy flying. We descended through a blue sky to a planet of sparkling oceans and lush green landscapes.

After the engine shut down, Oren came on-screen in my cabin. "Gabriel, since this is your first visit to Diere, I want to give you two warnings. First, they tell me it is cold there. So wear your heaviest coat."

"Well, that's a problem," I said. "All I brought was a light jacket."

Oren shrugged. "That's a shame. The second thing is this. Keep an eye on Commander Woad. Princess Ralph doesn't trust him, and frankly neither do I. He actively campaigned against the queen hiring us in the first place. His idea was to send military ships across the galaxy looking for the princess. It could have triggered an interstellar incident. Perhaps it was just hubris. But perhaps he was trying to control the investigation because he has something to hide."

"Got it," I said as I scrounged through my clothes to add layers. I found a sweater and pulled it on over my T-shirt before slipping into my jacket.

We had landed on a sprawling courtyard inside the walls of the palace. I didn't know stone and brick could sparkle, but that's what it did all across the palace grounds. Everything was glittery and grand, all pomp and circumstance. A military band struck up a dignified march as the ramp on the *Shaymus* lowered, though they hit a few sour notes when they saw Ralph inelegantly crawl out on her hands and knees out of the *Shaymus*.

The princess struggled to her feet and brushed the dirt off her hands, while Khan, Zastra, Yorbah, and I followed down the ramp. We were welcomed by an array of soldiers wearing bright uniforms and standing in perfectly straight lines. A man wearing a crisp uniform with a bright red sash marched up to the princess.

A bushy brown mustache filled his upper lip and extended way out even beyond the edges of his face. His eyebrows were equally bushy. It all made him look like someone in a kid's cartoon.

He bowed stiffly and said, "Welcome home, Your Royal Highness. We are so glad to see you again. We were saddened to hear of the death of Tam Elam."

"Were you, Woad?" She gazed down at him, her eyes slits of suspicion. "It was you who turned my mother against Tam. You hated him."

"I assure you, Your Royal Highness, I had nothing against the man personally. He had many … um … qualities. It was only that the constitution would not allow for him to be in the royal line. But of course, that is all water under the bridge now. Welcome home."

Ralph turned up her nose, swept past him, and marched toward the palace. Woad moved to Khan, put a hand on his arm, and whispered something in his ear. Khan murmured something back and followed after Ralph. Woad ignored the rest of us completely.

The palace looked like something out of a fairy tale with towers and turrets reaching toward the sky. All along the roofline were carved stone gargoyles with bat-like wings and hideous faces like on a medieval Gothic cathedral. Then I noticed that some of the gargoyles were moving around and taking off into the air. I made a mental note to not go out at night.

Everything in the palace was built to the twenty-foot scale of Dieren women though with allowances made for six-foot Dieren men. The elegant doors, tall enough for the women, contained cut-out doors for human-sized men. Inside, the ornate hallways soared above us. We were ushered into a throne room, which was immense even by the scale of Dieren women. People stood at attention all along the sides. As we entered, a group of trumpeters trumpeted their trumpets.

Queen Scythia sat on a grand throne at the far end of the room looking serene and stern, as if nothing could move her and nobody had better try. Commander Woad skirted past us and took his place beside the throne. Several huge ladies-in-waiting ran to Ralph and embraced her one-by-one making a great show of their affection for her. When they finally finished with the hugs and kisses and returned to their places, the queen stood. Ralph approached the throne. She knelt and kissed her mother's hand.

"We bid you rise," the queen said. "We are pleased you had the good sense to come home."

"I hope it is good sense, Mother. My life may be in danger. Someone killed Tam. And they may be trying to kill me."

"We were informed by Mr. Vilkas of Tam Elam's unfortunate demise. We were saddened to hear of it. But you will be safe here."

"Will I? Until we catch the killer, I certainly do not feel safe. For all I know, the killer might be here on Diere, perhaps in this very room." Her eyes swept the chamber. "None of you liked Tam."

"You suspect someone in the palace of killing him? My dear, that is nonsense. I admit we regarded him as an unsuitable match for you. But no one here would ever do him harm." She shot a glance at Commander Woad.

"That's not what I think," Ralph said. "And as long as I think it, my life may be in danger as well. That is why I have hired Oren Vilkas and his team to investigate the murder."

"Have you? Do you think that is wise?"

"Of course, I do, Mother. You hired him to bring me back."

"We did. But a murder investigation is so ... so unseemly."

"Mother, I need to find out who killed my husband."

The queen raised her eyebrows. "Oh, so you did marry. This is the first we have heard of that. Well, we understand your desire to bring the killer to justice. But really ..."

Commander Woad looked up to the queen on the throne and nodded. She leaned her head down, and he whispered something in her ear.

The queen straightened back up. "Commander Woad has volunteered to lead the investigation himself. We would find that more suitable."

"Mother! Woad is hardly a disinterested person. I insist it be investigated by the Galactic Detective Agency. They were able to chase me down twice. I don't know how they did it, but it demonstrates their ability. There is no one I trust more."

Woad stretched up to again whisper something to the queen, but this time she waved him off.

"If it is that important to you, my dear, it shall be done," the queen said. "We have no interest in antagonizing you again. And now, is Mr. Vilkas with us?"

Zastra stepped forward, bowed, and brought out the tablet. She switched it on to Oren's face.

"Mr. Vilkas," said the queen, "we want to express our deep gratitude for your assistance in returning the princess to Diere. I understand Her Royal Highness, Princess Ralph, would like to engage you to investigate the death of her ... her late husband. We would like to add our royal approval to that arrangement."

"Very good, Your Majesty," said Oren. "Then may I ask you a question or two regarding the murder?"

The queen paused for a moment as in a movie freeze frame, her face betraying not a hint of emotion. Finally, she said, "I cannot imagine how I might help, but very well."

"Your Majesty, can you think of anyone who would wish harm on the Dieren royal house?"

Queen Scythia smiled. "Mr. Vilkas, the royal family is beloved by one and all. We maintain a charitable foundation that serves the poor. We visit hospitals and factories and schools. We are the glue that holds Diere together as one people."

"And outside Diere?" Oren asked.

"We are a peaceful people. We have no enemies." She added pointedly, "Now I am sure those are all your questions, correct, Mr. Vilkas?"

Oren smiled and bowed his digital head. "They are indeed, Your Majesty."

"Good. Then would you be so kind as to meet with us in private? You and I need to attend to certain … financial arrangements."

"Of course, Your Majesty."

The queen stood and left the throne room. Zastra followed with the tablet. The crowd began to disperse.

"So what do we do?" I whispered to Yorbah.

"Just wait. They'll notice us standing here sooner or later. I'm hoping they show us to rooms. I'd love to take a shower with real water. Sonic showers just aren't the same."

She was right about them noticing us, though it was later rather than sooner. We stood there in the throne room for a good ten minutes while other people came and went. I tried to make eye contact with some of them, but as palace employees, they all seemed determined to remain as invisible as possible. Finally, a white-haired old man in knee breeches came up to us, walking bent over with the assistance of a cane.

"If you will be so kind as to follow me," he said in a thin voice, "I will show you to your rooms."

'Thank you," I said.

"Warm shower here I come," whispered Yorbah.

He led us out of the throne room to the great hall, walking at a glacial pace. He took us up a grand staircase. The steps had been designed as a sort of compromise between the dual heights of Dierens. The height of each riser was comfortable for Dieren men and humans while the width of each tread was extended wide enough to accommodate the larger feet of Dieren women. I noted some women taking the stairs three at a time, while we needed two or three steps to cross each tread.

"Will you be requiring other clothes fetched from your ship for the banquet tonight?" the old retainer asked us.

"There's a banquet?" I asked. "I don't have anything formal."

"We are celebrating the return of Princess Ralph. But every culture has a different definition of formal attire." He chuckled. "You could wear anything, and no one would know the difference." He glanced at my shirt and added, "Well, anything clean, that is"

At the top of the stairway, we turned onto a long hallway with doors on either side.

"I do have some fresh clothes in my cabin on the ship," I said. "There should be a pair of blue jeans folded up and a T-shirt that has a picture of Einstein with his tongue sticking out. That's as fancy as I have with me."

"Einstein, sir?"

"Old guy with wild hair. But I don't want to put you out and make you fetch it."

"It is my pleasure, sir. I will see to it."

At the end of the hallway, we turned onto an even longer hallway.

"And there's a book on my bunk. While you're there, would you bring that too?"

"A book, sir?"

"Yeah, a book … about yay big." I indicated the size with my hands. "It has a whole bunch of sheets of paper inside with writing on them all bound together."

"I will look for such a thing, sir."

Yorbah said, "There's a red dress hanging in a cabin on my ship, which is docked to his ship."

My head swiveled. "Red? I've only seen you in dark colors."

"Well, sometimes I'm in a mood. And you should find a pair of shoes there, too. Please bring them."

"Very good, miss. Any particular pair of shoes?"

"I only have the one other pair."

Toward the end of the hallway, he finally stopped in front of two doors. "This is your room on the left, sir, and yours on the right, miss. I will have your things sent around. When you hear two chimes this evening, come out and return to the great hall." He bowed.

"Thank you," I said with a bow back at him.

"You are welcome," he said, with another bow to me.

"Don't mention it," I said, bowing again.

We might have kept bowing to each other all day, but he finally turned his back and shuffled away.

I went into my room and stretched out on the bed. I heard the shower kick on in the next room. I decided I could use a shower myself. When I had finished in the bathroom, I found my other clothes waiting for me at the foot of the bed. I put them on and picked up the book while I waited, reading how Miss Marple solved *The Murder at the Vicarage*.

After a couple of chapters, I put down the book and began thinking about Commander Woad. He seemed to be the queen's top advisor. And whatever group it was that he commanded, they would no doubt be loyal to him. I wondered if there was a scenario in which he could ascend to the throne himself. Would that give him motive to kill Tam and Ralph? Or maybe Woad had killed Tam under orders from the queen. Surely the queen would not kill her own daughter, but would killing Tam be out of the question for her?

It all depended on motive. *Why* did someone, whoever it was, kill Tam? Was it a personal grievance against him? Did it have anything to do with royal succession? Could it be part of a complicated palace coup? Once we knew the *why*, the *who* would follow.

Much later the two chimes rang. I stepped out of my room. There was Yorbah in the hallway in a red dress as advertised. She was leaning against the wall using one hand to steady herself while slipping high-heeled sandals onto her feet with the other. An expensive-looking gold chain hung around her neck. And just like that, I felt underdressed even in my best T-shirt.

"Nice look," I said.

She smiled and took my arm. "Walk me down."

In the great hall, people seemed to be organizing themselves by gender. I asked a man in a long purple robe about it.

"Oh yes," he said. "On Diere a great many things are segregated by gender. It is because of the size difference, you know. I'm sure you would prefer using table service designed for your own proportions."

"I suppose I would," I said.

"Well, then I guess that's our cue to split up," said Yorbah.

"Sorry. I kind of feel bad for you and Zastra having to deal with huge plates and chairs and everything else."

"Yeah. We'll be like toddlers at a grown-up dinner."

She wandered off toward the group of women. I turned toward the gathering of men and spotted Jace in the crowd. He was holding the habitat with Buad and Blan. I moved to him.

"So you guys got in on this, too?" I asked.

"Yeah," Jace said. "Everybody except Oren, since he doesn't eat."

The doors before us opened, and we were ushered into a long dining room. As honored guests, Jace, Buad, Blan, and I were seated at the head table. I found myself sitting beside Commander Woad. I decided to take advantage of the situation by interrogating him a little.

"Commander Woad, I don't think we have formally met. My name is Gabriel Lake with the Galactic Detective Agency."

Woad was buttering a dinner roll. He gave me a one-second glance and returned his focus to the roll. "Lake, is it? Good to meet you. What planet are you from?"

"Earth."

"Earth? Indeed." He looked up from the roll and eyed me. "I have never met an Earthling."

"Apparently, not many of our kind venture into space. Earth is where Tam Elam was murdered."

"You don't say?" he replied. I couldn't tell whether or not his surprise was genuine. "Is that how you got involved in this matter?"

I wondered if he was trying to pump me for information the way I was trying to pump him for information. I held up an index finger since I was at the moment chewing on a bite of some kind of vegetable. It had the appearance of spinach but was surprisingly chewy. I finally got it down. "I suppose you could say so. Have you ever been to Earth?"

"No, of course not. It is quarantined, you know."

"Yes, but I understand some do break the quarantine. It is a beautiful place, Earth. Warm beaches. Majestic mountains. Quiet lakes in the middle of still forests. Lovely pink sky."

"You don't say?"

I had been hoping he would correct the pink sky bit, and then I would know he had been to Earth. But he didn't take the bait, and I could read nothing on his face. In retrospect I suppose it wasn't a very sly trick, so no surprise it didn't work. Unless saying 'you don't say' was some kind of tell for him. It might be his standard response to avoid telling a lie.

"What is this meat?" I asked. I was cautious after the chewy vegetable and that hideous drink Khan had served me back in Port Otto. Who knew what aliens might find tasty?

"It is lunkin. It is a kind of waterfowl."

"Like a duck?"

"I don't know," he said. "What is a duck?"

"A kind of waterfowl."

"Then yes. It is probably like a duck."

I tried a bite. It tasted okay. Possibly it did taste like duck, but I don't know because I've never had duck.

"I am curious about one thing you could explain to me," I said. "I take it the princess is the heir apparent to the throne?"

"Yes," said Woad cautiously.

"So what would happen if she died?"

"Nothing until the queen also died. Then that would leave us with something of a problem. The queen has no other children or siblings or even cousins. The royal line is currently extremely thin."

"Is it always a woman who reigns?"

"Almost always. At times men have ruled, but because of their size men don't often receive the respect women do."

"So if there was no one, man or woman, in the royal family to assume the throne?"

"The council would select a new royal line from among the noble families. That very thing happened some three hundred years ago. It was what instituted the current dynasty."

"Interesting. Is your family noble? Earlier today the princess said you were hardly a disinterested party in the murder investigation."

He gave me a hard stare. "My family is, in truth, one of the oldest and most respected of the noble houses. But if you are suggesting that—"

I held up my hands. "I'm not suggesting anything. I'm only trying to understand the situation. Another question, if I may. When you met our party

119

earlier out on the palace grounds, you said something to Khan. Would you mind telling me what the conversation was about?"

"Yes."

"Yes, what?"

"Yes, I would mind very much. It was a private conversation, which does not concern you."

"We're investigating a murder."

"Then by all means do so. But my brief chat with the butler has no relevance to it."

"I couldn't help but notice you seemed to be opposed to the murder investigation today. Why was that?"

"I was opposed to Princess Ralph hiring a detective agency. It is so tawdry, so common. Queens and princesses do not become involved in murders or hire private detectives. We have the honor of the crown to consider."

"And that's your only reason?"

"Why else would I be opposed to it, Mr. Lake?"

"I don't know. That's why I asked."

He pointed a fork at me. "I will tell you this, Mr. Lake. Now that this investigation is going forward, I hope it will be successful. Tam Elam was a decent enough man. It was my suggestion to the queen to allow them to marry provided Her Royal Highness also married a Dieren."

"That was your idea?"

"It was. I was thinking only of the happiness of the princess."

I grinned. "You don't say?"

Chapter 18

A Funeral on Cunedda

That night I stayed in my room in the palace. The next morning when I was walking out to the *Shaymus*, I thought it looked different somehow, but I couldn't put my finger on it. I finally dismissed the idea, assuming the ship just looked different under an alien sky. I climbed up the shaft to the office where I found Yorbah back in her dark piloting clothes sitting in one of the red leather chairs in conversation with Oren.

"All I'm saying," she said, "is I helped you return the princess. I deserve a cut."

Oren shook his head. "Our deal was based on you providing information leading to her return. Your information led us to the wrong planet. It was my deduction that led to the correct planet."

"Where I helped you find them. I tackled Khan, remember?"

"You tackled him in front of the house where they were staying … with my people right behind him. Your assistance was hardly necessary."

"I'm not saying I should get a full share. But I deserve something, right? I've been part of this."

"All right," said Oren, "a partial share, then. I can agree to that. A transfer has been made. Now, we are leaving for Cunedda this morning. If our business together is finished, you may undock your ship. What will you be doing next … if I may ask?"

"I think I'll stay here a bit. I might be able to dig up some work hauling something for someone." She stood. "It was a pleasure doing business with you."

She turned to go and smiled a crooked smile in my direction. "Maybe we'll run into each other again sometime, Gabe."

I watched her climb down the shaft, then turned back to Oren. "So we're off to Cunedda to take the body for burial?"

"Yes. We have kept that room set to morgue temperatures, but it is time we turn the body over to someone else."

"And we'll look up the girlfriend while we're there."

"Correct. And talk to Tam's family. Tell me, Gabriel, have you enjoyed working the case so far?"

"I'm not sure enjoyed is exactly the word. I've been beaten up and jailed. But I've been to three alien worlds so far, with another one coming up. I might call it exciting, mind-blowing, breathtaking, dangerous." I wagged my head back and forth. "Okay yeah, it's been fun."

"Good then. What do you think of Yorbah?"

"She's full of surprises, that one. Especially the sucker punch to the gut. But after that, we seemed to get along okay."

"Ah, Zastra," Oren said as the scaly member of our group climbed into the office, "were you able to access Tam Elam's tablet and find those messages?"

"Yeah, I don't know if I would call them threatening like the princess did. But they were easily on the creepy side of love. She wrote about how she was pining for him. She actually used that word."

We were interrupted by Kah-Rehn's voice. "The *Falcon* has undocked. Prepare for take-off. Since Cunedda is in the same solar system as Diere, we will be using the ion engine. The trip will take four hours and forty-two minutes."

I went down to my cabin and strapped in. I spent the flight practicing how to perform normal tasks under weightless conditions, such as brushing my teeth and changing clothes. Putting on pants propelled me into a midair front roll.

Cunedda was a surprise in two ways. First, it looked like what old sci-fi shows had taught me to expect alien worlds to look like. In other words, it was like a southern California studio back lot with boulders and scrub brush. The air was dry and warm, and the dirt had a red cast to it. Cunedda even had creatures that looked like they were straight out of a Hollywood props department. A pack of animals that looked like Pekingese dogs with unicorn horns were stalking a cat that sported two heads.

The other surprise was gravity. Until we landed on Cunedda I had forgotten what Oren had told me about the planet having twice the gravity of Earth, which was why Tam Elam could jump so high playing basketball. It didn't take me long to remember. As we lowered into the atmosphere, I felt pressed down into my chair like I was buried in sand. After we landed, I continued to stay in my chair nearly unable to move. Zastra went to deliver the body to the authorities, while I sat there, gasping for air. I finally pulled myself up with effort and shuffled across the room to grab my book. I lumbered over to my bunk and collapsed onto it. I could barely raise my arms enough to turn the pages.

Later, there came a *ding* from my cabin door. Still flat on my bunk and breathing with effort, I realized it was a good thing I didn't have to get up to answer it. I called, "Open," and the door slid clear. Zastra walked in.

"They will be having the funeral tomorrow morning," she said.

"Okay."

"Someone from the *Shaymus* is expected to speak since we brought the body to them."

"Okay," I said more slowly. I didn't like where this seemed to be heading.

"Oren has picked you to do it. He says you knew Tam Elam better than anyone else."

"I spoke to him for about a minute."

"Exactly. Besides, I'll be busy scanning the crowd for the ex-girlfriend."

"But ... I don't have funeral clothes. The closest I have is a clean polo shirt."

"That will be all right. Cuneddan funerals are, let's say, pretty casual."

"Fine. I'll work on something to say. It won't be much."

"You won't work on it right now. We have to go see Tam Elam's brother. On your feet."

I pulled myself to a standing position and followed her out, lugging one foot after the other. We crossed a scrub brush plain to a small settlement with a handful of geodesic dome houses. A man was outside one house working in what must have been a garden because whatever plants were growing there were doing so in straight rows. The man had horns and a flat nose like Tam. In fact, he looked exactly like Tam. He stared at us as we approached.

"We are looking for Gat Elam," Zastra said.

The man stared at us for a minute before responding, "I am he."

"We are here about your brother, Tam Elam," she continued.

Gat bowed his head. "I learned of his death."

"We are the ones who brought his body back."

"Then I thank you."

"We are investigating his death. Can you think of anyone who might have wanted him dead?"

"Well, there is his former girlfriend, Ex Awoo. That woman is a little ... shall we say ... highly strung. So there's one. And, of course, there's the entire population of Diere. So that's another 5 billion. Those are the only ones I can think of."

I spoke up. "How did his family feel about his relationship with the princess?"

"Well … Mama was upset, but only because he would be living off world, and she would never see him. The rest of us all agreed Princess Ralph was a step up from Ex. I suppose we were wrong about that."

"We're sorry for your loss," I said, parroting every cop show ever. I looked over at Zastra. It seemed Gat Elam had no more useful information.

"Thank you for your time," she said.

* * *

I spent most of the night trying to come up with a eulogy. What do you say about someone you met one time? The only thing we had talked about was being in love with a woman three times his size. That didn't give me much to work with. When Zastra and I left the ship the next morning all I had were a few notes scribbled on a scrap of paper. It would probably run about a minute and a half. I hoped that would do.

We joined a procession of mourners. At the front of the procession, four men carried a four-legged platform raised above the crowd. The body was sitting in a chair on top of the platform. Ropes tied the body to the chair, presumably to keep it from falling out onto the ground. The knife was still sticking from Tam's chest with the ropes wrapped around it on either side. As the procession moved across the ground, the body swung wildly left and right, back and forth in the chair in a weird rhythm.

The procession wound its way up a long hill. It was a challenging climb with the g-force, but at the top, we were rewarded with a beautiful setting overlooking a deep gorge. Rows of benches were arranged with an aisle down the middle. The platform was carried up the aisle and placed at the cliff's edge. The crowd moved to take seats, whispering and nodding to each other solemnly. I wondered when I would be called upon to speak.

A Cuneddan whom I assumed to be the funeral director stood and walked up beside the platform. He had the same flat nose and set of horns as Tam. I couldn't tell him from Tam other than the fact that Tam was dead, and this guy was standing in front of me.

"Friends," he said, "we are gathered here today to honor the memory of Tam Elam." He paused for dramatic effect. Then he pumped his fist in the air and cheered, "So let's get this party started!"

I gaped in shock as the crowd erupted into whistles and cheers. Peppy, cartoonish music started up from a speaker somewhere. Gat Elam stood and ran toward the platform. The music faded away. He took a minute to look at Tam strapped into the chair, then he turned to the crowd and said, "Well, it's no surprise Tam would get himself stabbed. He always was a cutup."

The crowd exploded in laughter.

"I mean, I'm Tam's brother. Tam and I grew up together. And let me tell you, if brains were antimatter, he wouldn't have enough to blow his nose."

The crowd roared again.

I leaned over the Zastra. "What gives?"

She whispered, "Didn't I tell you? Cuneddan funerals are about insulting the deceased. It's a remarkable custom, anthropologically speaking. They say it aids in the grieving process."

"You're telling me I'm supposed to tell jokes?"

"Of course. If you don't, it would be considered a huge insult."

"But I don't have any jokes prepared. I worked all night on something somber and respectful."

"Well, that was a mistake. Now shush. Pay attention."

"You know, I was thinking of Tam just the other day," Gat said. "It reminded me to take out the trash."

Gat took a bow to a howl of laughter and a round of applause and returned to his seat.

The funeral director got up again. "We are able to have this memorial this morning only because the Galactic Detective Agency recovered the body of Tam Elam from a planet called ..." He pulled a card from his pocket and squinted at it. "A planet called ... um ... Ert. And here from the agency to say a few words is an Ert person who knew Tam Elam. We welcome Gabriel Lake."

The happy music started up again. I stood and walked toward the front. My mind was racing, trying to think of every joke I had ever heard and unable to remember any of them. I stood looking at the body, trying to collect my thoughts. I stood there so long that people started to murmur behind me. Finally, I turned to them and looked out over a sea of identical-looking faces. Seriously, how did they even tell each other apart?

"I … I didn't know I was supposed to tell jokes," I said. "Um … that's not really a funeral custom on my planet."

Someone in the crowd yelled out, "Get on with it."

I forced a chuckle. "Um … Um … So a horse walks into a bar, and the bartender says, 'Why the long face?'"

Nothing. If Cunedda had crickets, they would have been chirping. "What's a horse?" a voice called. I was starting to feel flop sweat run down my face.

I said, "See a horse is … well, never mind. Sorry. Earth joke. I guess that one doesn't translate so well. Um … Um … Okay. Do you have jigsaw puzzles? Do you know what they are?" Some heads nodded. "Okay. Okay. See Tam told me he was so proud that he had finished a jigsaw puzzle in only a week. 'Cause on the box it said two to four years."

That drew some smiles and chuckles, though one person yelled out, "They told that one at the last funeral." Just what I needed, a heckler.

"So Tam married a Dieren princess. Dierens, am I right?"

A few chuckles.

"She's big. I mean, big. I was afraid she'd try to kiss Tam and end up eating him."

A few in the crowd started booing. One person called out, "Don't speak ill of the living."

"Sorry. Sorry. I'm not from this culture, remember? Um … Ah! But … um … I was talking to the princess, and I asked her, 'Do you think Tam is pretty or ugly?' She said, 'Both. He's pretty ugly.'"

That one hit the mark. The crowd roared in laughter. I decided to quit while I was ahead. Waving to the group, I took my seat. I leaned over to Zastra. "You did that on purpose, didn't you?"

"Shush," she said. "We're at a funeral."

A couple of other speakers took their turns. It was like open mic night at the comedy club. Finally, the funeral director stood again and said, "And now join me as we commit Tam's body to the soil of his home planet."

The crowd stood and solemnly surrounded the platform. They took hold of the legs of the platform and lifted it off the ground. Then, as I watched wide-eyed, they tossed it over the edge of the cliff into the gorge and cheered. My jaw dropped open.

As the funeral service broke up, everyone began heading home, chuckling and shaking their heads at all the fun they had had. Zastra and I were watching the crowd. She pointed out how Cuneddan females have smaller horns than males. We spied a young female, sitting on a boulder at the edge of the crowd and crying her eyes out. We approached her.

Zastra asked her, "Are you Ex Awoo?"

The female wiped her eyes and blew her nose before looking up. "Yes. Oh, you're the Ert person who spoke," she said to me. "Thank you for your comforting words." Sobs began to come again as she spoke. "They were hilar ... hilari ... hilarious." She buried her face in a blue lace hankie.

"Um ... thank you?" I said.

"You used to have a relationship with the deceased, is that right?" Zastra asked.

Ex looked up from the hankie and gave Zastra a hard stare. "There was no 'used to' about it. Our relationship was sometimes off and on, but we had a deep and unbreakable connection."

"You realize he married someone else, right?" I said.

"Tam would sometimes stray a bit, it's true. But he would always come back to me eventually."

Zastra looked at me and whispered the words, "She's nuts." I nodded. She certainly seemed crazy enough to be a stalker and maybe a killer.

"So have you ever met Princess Ralph?" I asked.

"I haven't met her personally. I wouldn't want to. But everyone knows her from the news feeds, the big cow. We get quite a lot of Dieren news, especially all the little tidbits about the precious royal family." She stopped and blew her nose again.

"I was wondering how you felt about Tam's relationship with her," I said. "I mean, if you couldn't have Tam to yourself, then ... well then did you think maybe nobody should?"

Her face twisted into a question. "But I *was* going to have him to myself. It was only a matter of time. We were soulmates. Honestly, I don't know what Tam ever saw in ... Ralph ..." She said the name like it left a sour taste in her mouth. "... other than possibly the wealth and power. Tell me, Mr. Lake, you're a man, right? How could a man fall in love with someone so much ... bigger?"

"I don't know. I asked Tam the same question."

"You did?" She turned her eyes up at me hopefully. "What did he say?"

I was fairly sure she wouldn't like the answer. But I needed to see her reaction.

"He said ... he said, 'more to love.' That's what he said."

Her face was still turned to me, but her eyes glazed over. She turned back to her handkerchief and sobbed loudly.

I said, "If it's any consolation, Tam was upset Princess Ralph had agreed to also marry a Dieren husband."

Ex looked back at me with slits for eyes. "She agreed to what? Oh, she would, wouldn't she? She wants the whole galaxy revolving around her."

"Miss Awoo, this is Oren Vilkas." I turned to see his face on the tablet in Zastra's hands.

She dabbed at her eyes with her hankie. "Yes, Mr. Vilkas?"

"We are thinking of returning to Earth as part of our investigation into Tam Elam's murder." This was news to me, but Oren was the boss. "Would you like to accompany us as our guest? See the place where Tam last lived?"

"Why, yes, I would," Ex said. "If it would not be a bother."

"We can easily accommodate you," Oren said. "Have you ever been to Earth?"

"Why no, I haven't."

"It is a lovely planet," Oren said. "Warm beaches. Majestic mountains. Quiet lakes in the middle of still forests. Lovely pink sky."

"You mean blue," Ex said.

"Do I?"

"Oh... Well, I ...um ... wouldn't know. I guess I just assumed it was blue ... or green. It might be green. I suppose I'll see when I get there ... for the first time."

"Doubtless," said Oren. "My associates will escort you to our ship."

"Can I see the tablet for a minute?" I asked Zastra. "You two go on ahead."

Zastra held the tablet out to me.

I took it and turned my back to them. "You sneak. So you were listening in on my conversation with Woad last night?"

"Correct," Oren answered. "You should be flattered. This time your trick worked. Woad is far too clever to fall for it, but not Miss Awoo."

"So why are we going back to Earth? I thought we covered that ground already."

"Two reasons, Gabriel. First, we have now discovered that Miss Awoo has been to Earth. We need to re-analyze the crime scene with that in mind. Do you think she could be a murderer?"

"Maybe. She could certainly be a stalker. And she might be the person who was watching from the barn. But is it wise to take a possible murderer with us?"

"There's an ancient Rhegedian proverb, Gabriel, 'Keep your friends close and your enemies closer.' We want to keep an eye on her."

"I'm pretty sure that comes from *The Godfather, Part II*."

"The proverb is no doubt true on any planet, Gabriel."

"What's the second reason?"

"Yes. That is interesting. I've been following the news from Potato. The neighbor, Henry Koster, has also been murdered."

"Duh-duh-dun!" I hummed. "The second murder!"

Chapter 19

The Second Murder

In detective stories, there is almost always a second murder. It serves to heighten the drama, turn up the intensity, raise the stakes as the detective races to catch the killer before even more people die. In some stories, it is only after the second murder that other characters begin to take things seriously. Up until then, nearly everyone has been dismissing the first murder as an accident, and only the protagonist has realized the cold hard fact that there is a killer in their midst. Only with the second murder do things become chillingly clear.

In our case, we already knew we were looking for a murderer, and the stakes were as high as a princess's life. And while the death of Henry Koster might plausibly have been a coincidence, it seemed about as unlikely as me winning the Indianapolis 500 on my bike. The big question was why. Why was Henry Koster killed? What had he done or seen or heard that was a threat to the murderer? And who did that point to?

After we got Ex settled into a spare cabin on the *Shaymus*, I went into the galley and replicated myself a cup of coffee. I was sitting there thinking about coffee with the gang back at the Buzz House on Earth when Jace strolled in.

"Looking forward to going home?" he asked.

"Well, I'd rather go home with the job done. But sure, it will be nice to see cats and dogs, pigs and cows rather than living gargoyles or Pekingese unicorns or all the other weird creatures that have skittered by us out here. It will be refreshing to see human faces ... no offense."

"I understand completely. You've been thrown into the deep end of the pool." Jace walked to the replicator. "Coffee black." He turned back to me. "I'm gonna try it, Gabe."

He brought the steaming cup to the table beside me and took a tiny sip. He made a face.

"It'll grow on you," I said.

"I don't see how." He returned to the replicator and got the coffee remade with cream and sugar.

"So, Jace, I've been sitting here trying to count on my fingers how many days we've been gone. But with each planet having its own day-night cycle, I have no idea. What day will it be when we get to Earth?"

"Just about whatever day we want it to be."

"How's that?"

"We travel through time, remember. We go back some thirteen billion years and then forward again. We can stop almost whenever we want. All these chrono journeys we've done so far, we've been going to different planets on the same day over and over again. So technically, you've only been gone one day. It's more efficient that way. It lets us solve a case in record time."

"But we've all aged like four or five days, right?"

"Sure," Jace shrugged. "But honestly you don't look a day over last week."

"So can we go back to Earth on the day Koster was killed and watch his murder? See who does it? Or maybe stop the murderer?"

"No, that we can't do. Normally, we would go back to the very next day after we left. But this time, see, we're going there to investigate a murder, which Oren says happened on the Earth date March 10. We already know about that murder. So if we went back on March 9 or even March 10 before the murder happened, it would create a causality loop."

"A causality loop? Is that a bad thing?"

Jace held up both fists and exploded them while making a blasting sound with his mouth.

"I'll take that as a yes," I said.

"Yeah, it's a bad thing. Catastrophically bad. See, we'd be going there to prevent a murder, which we know about because it's already happened. Except if we go back and stop it, then that would mean it didn't happen, so then we don't find out about it, so then we don't go back, so then the murder does happen. See? Round and round."

"Yeah. It's like an infinite loop in programming. It locks the computer up."

"Right. And we don't want to lock up the whole universe."

"No. That sounds bad. But what if we just observe and don't try to stop it?" I asked.

"Nah. Same thing. On a quantum level, even the act of observing changes things. Don't they teach quantum physics on your planet?"

"Oh, they teach it. But I didn't take it. So when are we going to? Is that how you say it? *When* are we going to? That sounds wrong. Seems like time travel makes language lock up, too."

"We're shooting for March 11."

"Okay. We left on the ninth, so I've only missed two days. If I get a chance, I'd like to check my email."

"Sure. And if you get a chance, you might pick up some of those other kinds of foods you were talking about for the replicator."

"Excellent idea. You're gonna love pizza."

Oren's voice came over the speakers. "Gabriel, please come to the office."

"Duty calls," I said.

I downed the last sips of my coffee and patted Jace on the shoulder as I left. I climbed up the shaft to Oren's face on the screen. "Have you ever thought about putting in a turbo lift?" I asked.

"What is a turbo lift?" Oren asked. "Is it powered by a turbine?"

"No. It's just an elevator in a spaceship. That's what you call it, isn't it?"

"We would call that a lift. Or an elevator."

"Okay. Anyway, that way we wouldn't have to climb."

"True. But if I had put in a lift, the princess would not have been able to get up here, would she? Besides, I don't need a lift. I can move to any screen on the ship with ease."

"Lucky you. What did you need?"

"I want you to read this news account of the death of Henry Koster. See if it means anything more to you as an Earthling than I could get out of it."

A short news item filled the screen in place of Oren's face. It read:

Henry Koster, 43, of Port Otto was found dead in his garage on March 10 under a pile of boxes. Police are treating it as a suspicious death since unexplained burn marks were found on his torso. Koster had been arrested and taken into custody by Indiana State Police the previous day, charged with reckless driving when he was observed swerving wildly across the road while hauling a load of sandbags larger than his truck could handle. He had been released after posting bond.

"Well, it doesn't give us much to go on," I said. "I'm guessing he didn't have any next of kin, at least none the newspaper knew of, or they would have been mentioned. If I know Koster, he was hauling those sandbags because he was anticipating a heavy rain and thought he could sell them at a hefty profit. There would be a police report on the arrest. If we could get it, that might tell us something more. What about those burn marks? Would a laser weapon make marks like that?"

"Yes, it would, Gabriel. That is what caught my attention."

"So how do we investigate?"

"If we can inspect the garage, we may be able to uncover clues the local police would find meaningless. Plus, we want to see if we can discover when Miss Awoo was there stalking Tam."

"Do you think she might have had anything to do with Koster's murder?"

"I don't know. If she killed Tam and thought Koster had seen her, then perhaps."

The voice of Kah-Rehn came over the speakers. "Prepare for takeoff. All crew please strap in."

"Gabriel, would you stay up here during the flight? I'd like to discuss the case on the way."

"Well ... um ... sure."

"Hey look, Buad," said Blan. "He's feeling brave enough to fly up here now."

"Yeah," said Buad, "but I'm still glad our habitat is above the floor in case he hurls."

They continued to heckle me while I strapped in. Zastra climbed into the office and strapped in at her desk. The *Shaymus* took off, shooting through the atmosphere like a bullet. I closed my eyes and whispered soothing affirmations to myself. No way was I going to appear nauseous in front of Buad and Blan.

Once the chrono engine kicked in, and we started traveling through time, Oren's face came back to the screen. "All right. Let's list our suspects. Who might have wanted Tam Elam dead and killed Henry Koster as part of a cover-up?"

"Ex Awoo," said Zastra. "She's obsessed with Tam. Plus she's loony."

"She is locked into her cabin, isn't she?" asked Oren.

"You bet she is," said Zastra. "I made sure of that myself."

"But to hear her explain it," I said, "she was convinced Tam would someday come back to her. So why murder him?"

"It could be a lie," said Oren. "She's going on the list." Ex Awoo's name appeared on-screen beside Oren's face. "Who else?"

"Commander Woad," I said. "Princess Ralph doesn't trust him, and after talking to him, I don't either. He was one of the ones against the relationship between Tam and Ralph."

"Yes," Oren said. "But according to him, he proposed the deal the princess and I worked out."

"According to him," I said.

Commander Woad's name materialized on the screen. So did the name Khan Krete.

"Khan Krete," I snickered. "Man, that never gets old. So funny."

"If Woad is a suspect, Khan is one too," said Oren. "He was against the relationship as well. And he was at the scene of the murder."

"As in the butler did it," I grinned.

Oren's face showed the slightest flicker of a smile. "You are, of course, referring to the common trope in those detective novels you love so much — murders in English country mansions where the butler turns out to be the culprit. Yes, I did my research. It is trite, but it's a possibility."

"But Khan has served the princess his whole life," said Zastra. "Would he actually destroy the man Ralph loved? She had nothing but high praise for Khan."

"Still," said Oren, "domestic workers can get some strange notions about duty."

"Yorbah," squawked Blan.

"Really?" I said as Yorbah's name appeared on-screen.

"Yes, really," said Blan. "She's the only one who knew where they were staying."

"The only one other than Khan and Princess Ralph," I pointed out. "Plus, we figured out where they were staying, so somebody else might have also. Besides what would be her motive?"

"Money," said Zastra. "She seems highly motivated by money."

Oren said, "Speaking of Princess Ralph, I'm surprised no one has yet listed her." Her name appeared with the others. "Tam was not happy about the deal in which she got to have a second husband. That could have led to an argument between them and bloodshed."

"She denied it," I said. "And Koster said he heard men's voices arguing."

"Koster might have been mistaken. A deep woman's voice is often lower than a high man's voice," said Oren. "Especially if the woman is twenty feet tall."

"Her grief seems sincere to me," I said.

Zastra smirked, "I wouldn't base too much on your judgment of women."

"What's that supposed to mean?" I protested.

Oren ignored me. "Any suspects from Earth?"

"Not if those burn marks are from a blaster," I said. "There's nothing like that on Earth. You know, I half suspected Koster for Tam's murder. He may have guessed Tam was an alien, which could make an Earthling freak out. But I suppose he's off the hook now that someone has killed him."

Oren inclined his head. "Right. There's always a possibility of two different killers, but that complicates things. I always presume a one-killer scenario until I'm forced to abandon it. Is that the lot?"

We considered the list for a minute.

"X," I said.

"We already have Ex's name up here," Oren said.

"Not Ex. X. Question mark. The person we don't suspect. The landlady, the queen, the kid at the donut shop. Or someone completely unknown to us."

"Very good, Gabriel," said Oren. "In your detective stories, the culprit is always introduced in the first act. But not so in real life. It might be someone we find out about only at the end. We would do well to keep that in mind lest we unconsciously shape the evidence to fit the persons on the list."

So there we had it.

EX AWOO

COMMANDER WOAD

KHAN KRETE

YORBAH

PRINCESS RALPH

X

Unless we were mistaken, one of them had murdered twice and might very well try to murder again if we got too close. And here we were putting ourselves right in the crosshairs, going back to the scene of the crime to look into Koster's murder.

"I have a suggestion," I said. "We won't be able to land behind the barn this time, not with an active crime scene right next door. We're going to have to park somewhere else and use a car to get around. You can drop me off at my house in the wee hours of the morning when it's dark, and I can drive my car."

"And then do what with the *Shaymus*?" Oren asked.

"There's a state forest near Port Otto. It has a lot of old gravel roads in it that don't go anywhere anymore but used to go to farmsteads back before it was a forest. If I drive to one of those old farmsteads, you can follow my signal, right?"

"We can give you a tracker."

"Good. You drop me off and fly around for an hour or so. You could go see the Great Lakes or something and then follow my tracker. I know just the spot. I went hiking through there last year. It's not fifteen minutes from Koster's house. I'll drive in any of us who need to come and be able to report back any time."

"Satisfactory," said Oren. "Kah-Rehn, do you have Gabriel Lake's address?"

"I do," responded the AI.

"Land there in the street. What time do you suggest, Gabriel?"

"Let's see. It's mid-week. Make it 4:00 a.m."

"Course changed," Kah-Rehn said. "We are approaching present day. We will be landing soon."

Chapter 20

Return to Potato

Because of tree cover the *Shaymus* couldn't land right in front of my house. Instead, they sat down in the intersection at the end of the block. In the middle of a residential area like that, they needed to take off again as quickly as possible. So I waited by the top of the ramp, and while they hovered five feet off the ground Jace opened the ramp just enough for me to slide over the edge and drop to the pavement. They swooshed back into the air, and I hustled over to the side of an overgrown cedar bush growing on one corner of the intersection. I scanned the surrounding houses. Several dogs started barking, but no one had switched on their lights. No early morning joggers or dog walkers were out. Of course, somebody might be standing at a darkened window, so you never knew. To be on the safe side, I walked all the way around the block to get back to my house.

I walked in my front door and switched on the light. The mail had been delivered through the slot and was there at my feet. I scooped it up and sorted through it quickly. Bill, junk, bill, junk, junk, a check from a client, more junk. I moved to my office, dumped the junk mail in the trash, and dropped the important stuff into my in-basket.

I decided I might as well check my email while I was here. I switched on the laptop and opened my email program. I watched fifty emails immediately get tossed into the junk folder. Another fifty stayed in my inbox and had to be dealt with manually. Most could be deleted without me opening them, ads for snoring treatments, muscle enhancers, new product sensations. That left ten emails I needed to read and probably respond to, some from clients, some from friends. I had already invested five minutes in this. I needed to get on the road. I decided to at least skim the emails from clients to make sure they didn't have pressing problems. They didn't. It could all wait until we caught a murderer.

I moved to the bedroom and grabbed my wallet and car key. I had been thinking about how I would approach the investigation, and I concluded that a classier shirt would be in order. I changed to a blue Oxford that let me pass as a professional anything. I went back to my office and dug out my DSLR camera to use as a prop. I hadn't used it much since phone cameras had gotten so good. I blew off the dust, made sure it still turned on, and swung the strap over my shoulder.

I looked around the house one more time. Was there anything else I needed? I grabbed a banana for the road and left, locking the front door behind me. I got into my car and set off for a wee-hours drive down to Port Otto. As I rolled into the little town, I glanced at the car clock. It said 5:05 a.m. Warm, welcoming lights were shining from inside the Donut Dive. I thought I could use a cup of coffee and a donut. I pulled in front of the little building, realizing I needed to be quick. I didn't want my tracking device drawing the *Shaymus* to the parking lot. Fortunately, the shop was empty. I stepped to the counter, and the girl behind it immediately made eye contact.

"Coffee and a maple bacon. Wait. Make that three maple bacons." I figured one for me, one for Jace, and one for the replicator.

"Sorry," the girl said. "We only have those on weekends."

I won't lie, I was heartbroken. "Okay. Okay. Well, make it three yeast donuts, please. To go."

She had my cup and my sack of donuts ready in seconds. I climbed back into my car, took a sip of the coffee, and headed through town toward the state forest.

The state forest isn't like a park. There are no recreational facilities. It exists solely for conservation purposes. It had been created during the Great Depression from eroded and abandoned farms. No one lived there now, though a few county roads still ran through it. Which made it a beautiful place to drive or hike, especially during autumn. The year before, Adam and I had backpacked through part of it and camped for the night on an old farmstead beside a decaying barn.

Of course, hiking to a place cross-country and driving in by road are two different things. I hoped I remembered how to find the place. But if I couldn't find that exact clearing, any clearing would do. I was driving down a steep hill, going slowly because it was still dark when I spotted a gravel lane jutting out to the right near the bottom. It looked familiar. I turned into the lane. It curved steeply uphill, and a quarter mile later the dilapidated barn appeared in my headlights. I parked and took the time to enjoy my donut and coffee.

A few minutes later I heard a *whoosh* and watched the *Shaymus* gently touch down in the clearing in front of me. The ramp lowered, and I walked inside. I called up the shaft, "Give me a minute." I climbed down to the lower level and found Jace.

"I brought you some presents." I handed him the bag. "There are two donuts in there. One is for you, and the other is for the replicator. Prepare to have your mind blown." I held out my other hand with the banana. "Run this into the replicator, too. It's called a banana, one of Earth's iconic fruits, top ten for sure."

He took the bag, opened it, and sniffed. He pulled out one of the yeast donuts and took a bite. His eyes lit up. "Oh, man! My opinion of Earth just went way up."

I nodded and climbed up the shaft to the office.

"What do you need for the investigation?" Oren asked.

"For now, I think I'll go to Koster's house by myself. I have an angle I want to try."

"Very well. I'll monitor you through the translator bots. Don't forget that Buad and Blan would blend right in if you need their surveillance skills."

"Right. I was thinking they might check out the barn. Remember Lucas thought he saw somebody in there on Saturday. I doubt if anyone has been in there since. There might still be clues."

"We're on it," said Blan. He opened the habitat with his beak, and they flew out and down the shaft.

"Do they know the way?"

"They'll find it," said Zastra. "Don't worry about them. If you get in trouble, let me know. I hate just waiting."

"I'll keep it in mind. Okay. I'll check back in later."

"One more thing, Gabriel," Oren said. "Ex Awoo is waiting for you in her cabin."

"For what?" I asked.

"Remember we promised we would show her where Tam was staying. You'll need to take her along."

I rolled my eyes. I needed her like I needed a wicker water bucket. I only hoped she wouldn't be quite so annoying today or mess up what I was planning to do. I also hoped no one noticed I was driving around with an alien woman with a flat nose and horns on her head.

The sky was growing lighter in the east as I crested the hill by the A-frame. "There it is," I pointed toward the house. "That's where Tam spent his last days."

I probably could have worded it better because Ex burst into tears again. She pulled out the blue lace handkerchief she had used at the funeral. By now it was stiff and stained with tears and snot.

"My poor Tam. My poor, poor Tam," she wailed. "His last days ... spent on this dreary planet ... with that loathsome giant ... when he could ... he could have been ... with me." She broke off into more sobbing. "How could he?" she sobbed. "How dare he?" she cried, her words taking on a different tone. "I built my whole world around him, and he ... he tossed me to the curb like trash."

"I'm picking up some anger here," I said.

She sniffed. She dabbed her eyes and blew her nose. "Anger? No, not anger. I'm just very, very hurt."

I wondered if she had been hurt enough to come to Earth and pick up a carving knife.

"Okay. You've seen the place," I said. "I need to stop next door where the neighbor was killed. Do me a favor. Slide down in your seat, so no one sees you."

She slid down, and I rolled on up the road and pulled into Henry Koster's driveway. Police tape was wrapped around the entire house like a Christmas present done up in ribbon. A county sheriff's car sat in the driveway. I parked behind it, grabbed the camera, and got out of the car.

The deputy stepped out of his patrol car. He had a moon-shaped face and a body to match. We wore a badge over the left shirt pocket of his uniform and a sewn tag over his right with the name, "Drumwell."

He said, "May I help you, sir?"

"Yeah. I hope so. My name is Chris Bacon from *The Indianapolis Star*. I was wondering if I could take a few pictures of the crime scene."

"You know we can't do that, sir. This is an active crime scene for a murder investigation."

"Oh. Well, I suppose not ... not for a murder. But I can take a shot of the front of the house, right? I mean it's publicly viewable from the county road."

"I can't stop you from taking a picture *from* the road."

"From the road. Okay. I'll do that. Are you the investigating officer, Deputy Drumwell?"

"I'm ... I'm working the case." He puffed up his round chest.

"Can I ask how the body was discovered?" I tapped open my phone's To-Do list app to take notes.

"A friend of the deceased called it in. He came by yesterday to go with the victim on a trip to buy some merchandise of some sort. When the victim didn't come to the door or answer his phone, the friend called us."

"What's the name of the friend?"

"That information is being withheld."

"What time was the call?"

"That information is being withheld."

"What's the estimated time of death? Wait. Can we say it together?"

"That information is being withheld," we both repeated.

Drumwell added, "Smart aleck."

"Hey. Don't get me wrong. I don't want to stand in the way of your investigation. But a possible murder in a little town like this is big news. Is there anything else you can tell me?"

The deputy stuck his hands in his pockets and leaned in conspiratorially. "Okay. Off the record and between you and me, you can ditch the word 'possible' because this was definitely murder."

"The burn marks, you mean?"

He nodded solemnly. "Also, those boxes he was found under. They held rolls of paper towels Hardly likely to crush a guy. But you didn't hear that from me."

I crossed my heart. "One last question, and then I'll get out of your hair. When do you think I could see the crime scene?"

"No idea. A State Police crime scene team is coming in this afternoon to go over the place. Maybe after that. But you'd need permission from the landlord."

"Sure. I know her. Thanks, Deputy."

I made a show of walking out to the road and taking a picture. Then I got into my car and drove back toward the state forest. Another breaking story from ace reporter Chris P. Bacon.

I circled back toward the *Shaymus*, deposited Ex in her cabin, and went up to the office.

"You got all that, I suppose," I said.

"Yes. What little of it there was," said Oren.

"I have a plan B, but I need Zastra for backup."

"Let's roll," she said, practically jumping from her desk. "What's the plan?"

"I'll explain on the way. You might need a blaster."

She pulled back her robe to show me one hanging from her waist.

"Good." I pulled out my wallet and dropped it on my desk. "I may not want anything identifying me."

We had turned to go when I stopped in my tracks. It had finally registered in my brain that Buad and Blan were back in their habitat. I turned to them. "Did you guys find anything at the barn?"

"Did we!" said Blan.

Zastra stepped back to her desk, opened a drawer, and pulled out a white lace handkerchief. Except for the color, it was identical to the blue one Ex had used at the funeral and this morning. They could have come from the same package. They probably did come from the same package.

"Well, what are the odds?" I said. "So she was the one in the barn."

Out in my car, I pulled out my phone and punched up the maps app. This morning at Koster's place, I had spied a woodsy area backing up to the property. I located the house on the map and noted just beyond it a green area indicating the wood behind the house. A county road twisted around on the other side of the wood. I noted the road number and set off for it. The road turned out to be gravel, which was good news since it meant few people would use it. I drove slowly down the road until my blue dot on the map sat opposite Koster's house. I parked, and we got out.

"With luck, if anyone sees the car, they'll assume we're mushroom hunting," I said.

"What kind of beast is a mushroom?" Zastra asked.

"A tasty one. Come on."

The wood was damp and muddy from spring rains, making our progress slow going. We trudged up a hill and down the other side to a stream. Zastra pulled off her boots and waded across. But the water looked cold, so I decided to look for boulders in the creek bed or some other way to make my way across without getting wet.

A hundred feet downstream I found a log that stretched nearly across. I started walking across it, found it slippery, and almost fell in. I managed to right myself and made my way slowly to the end. The log ended about three feet from the bank. I took a leap, cleared the water, and planted my heels in the sandy bank, sinking into the mud above the tops of my sneakers. I managed to pull my feet from the muck and made my way up the bank to where Zastra was putting her boots back on.

We climbed the hill away from the stream and found ourselves looking at the back of Henry Koster's house.

"You wait here and listen," I said.

"Listen for what?"

"For sounds of me getting myself into trouble."

"Then what?"

"Well, my preference would be for you to rescue me."

Old ranch houses like Henry's almost all have sliding glass doors in the back. This one was no exception. Doors like that are notoriously insecure, with a tiny latch doing its best to hold in place a huge, heavy door. They can be made more secure with such simple solutions as a piece of broomstick placed into the track. I was hoping Henry had been too lazy to do that.

I crouched and ran across the short stretch of grass between the wood and the concrete slab patio extending from the sliding door. I peered in through the door. There was no sign of movement. There was a length of 2x4 in the track, but it was a good foot or more shorter than the space. I could slip through an opening that size. I started to reach out to pull down the crime scene tape and wished I had thought of bringing gloves so I wouldn't leave fingerprints. I looked around and spotted a baseball mitt in the grass. That might work. I slipped it on and slid down the tape. I used the mitt to grasp the center edge of the door and jiggled it. The latch clicked, and I pulled the door open until it stopped against the 2x4. I dropped the mitt and squeezed sideways through the opening.

I stepped into a family room containing a TV, a worn-out easy chair, and cartons of Koster's inventory. The door to the garage was right in front of me across the room. I moved to the door and eased it open, using my shirt sleeve as a glove. I stepped down into the garage and made my way among the rows of cartons to a pile of overturned boxes. I figured that was where Koster's body had been found. I turned around in a circle, surveying the scene.

On the wall opposite the overhead door were burn marks. I'm no forensic expert, but they looked fresh to me. I pulled out my phone and took a picture, the camera flashing in the dim light. I moved to the overhead door and turned back toward the interior. If someone had stood there with the overhead garage door open and fired a weapon toward the spot of the fallen cartons, those burn marks would be right in the line of fire. The killer had found Henry working in his garage with the door open as I had the previous Sunday, walked up to the door as I had, and shot him dead as I unquestionably had not done. I glanced down at a muddy boot print on the floor. Henry had been wearing Crocs when I saw him. I suspected it was his go-to footwear. So this boot print might belong to the killer. I knelt and took a picture of it.

It was time for me to go. I made my way back along the rows of cartons and stepped into the family room. That's when I noticed my muddy footprints trailing across the family room carpet. Oh well, the cops would know someone wearing ten-and-a-half-sized shoes had been here, but not necessarily me.

I slipped back through the partially open sliding glass door. Then I turned around and found myself looking into the barrel of Deputy Drumwell's service revolver.

"Mr. Bacon," said Drumwell, "you are under arrest."

Chapter 21

My Run-in with the Deputy

I raised my hands and looked around, expecting Zastra to come charging out of the woods right then. She didn't. Maybe she didn't want to do anything while Drumwell had his pistol drawn. More likely, she wanted to make me sweat a little. If so, she was succeeding. I mean, I've been pulled over for speeding before. But this was different. This was serious.

"Turn around and put your hands on the back of your head," Drumwell said.

Wow, it was just like in the cop shows. I suppose cop shows get their lines from real police procedures. Though it's possible it sometimes goes the other way, that Drumwell had picked up the line from watching TV. In any case, now wasn't the time to ask. I put my hands on my head and turned. He grabbed my right wrist, pulled it down, and slapped on a handcuff. Then he pulled down the left wrist and slapped it into the matching half of my new steel bracelets.

Keeping one hand on my arm, he moved back to look through the sliding glass window. "You've tracked mud all over my crime scene," he groaned, "and you went through to the garage where the murder happened. This is gonna cost you, Bacon."

He shut the sliding glass door and marched me around to the front of the house. With his hand on my head, he pushed me into the back of the patrol car. I looked through the steel mesh grate separating the front from the back. Despite being anxious about being under arrest, I have to say I was impressed and awed. I mean, cop cars are undeniably cool, and they have all this neat gear in them — two-way radio, radar speed gun, dash camera, buttons for lights and siren. Taped to the dash was a picture of a smiling golden retriever. I thought I could use that to try establishing some rapport.

"Is that your dog? Man, goldens are awesome dogs, aren't they?"

Drumwell said nothing.

"I had one when I was a kid. That dog followed me everywhere."

No response.

"His name was Bailey. He was a great dog. What's your dog's name?"

Nothing. It was like I wasn't even there.

He let me sit and stew while he took a long sip from a travel mug. Then he pulled out the microphone for the two-way and said, "This is Deputy Drumwell. I have a 10-15, prisoner in custody. Over."

A voice came back over the radio. "Do you need assistance? Over."

"Negative. I'll write it up and run him to the jail."

I was sure the bit about jail was for my benefit. He re-clipped the mic and flipped open a laptop computer mounted in front of the dashboard on a swivel. He double-clicked a shortcut, and a browser opened to a website. I read the URL in the address bar: *arrest.in.gov*.

"What's the website?" I asked.

This time he decided to answer if only to taunt me. "It's how you're getting booked for breaking and entering and criminal trespass and obstruction of justice and anything else I can think of. This here is the Indiana Comprehensive Arrest Database Tracker. You get arrested by any police agency inside the borders of Indiana, and you will be written up in INCADAT."

"Interesting," I said. That meant Koster's arrest by the State Police would be in there somewhere.

I gazed through the steel mesh. I couldn't believe it. Drumwell had the laptop facing the backseat, so I could see everything he was typing. He logged in with the username ldrumwell@WhitcombCo.gov. Of course, the password he typed didn't appear on the screen as clear text, but I noted it was only six characters.

"All right," said Drumwell. "Name?"

"Gab … No … Whew! Man, I am all shook up by this. I mean Christopher Bacon."

"Middle name?"

"P … um … Paul."

"Home address?"

"Um … One four seven Shaymus Street. That's with a Y. Indianapolis."

"Eyes?"

"Two."

"Don't be a wise guy."

"I mean … brown."

Drumwell took another sip from the travel mug. He sighed and shook his head. "You know, Bacon, I tried to do you a solid earlier by giving you a little information, and you see where it gets me. That's why I don't like reporters. In my experience, they just get in the way of law enforcement and operate way too much in the legal gray areas. Let me assure you, Bacon, we take these kinds of things very seriously."

It was all eerily familiar. It was Xox all over again. Was there some interstellar handbook they all read?

Drumwell wiggled his fingers and set to work typing up the description of the arrest, speaking the words out loud as he slowly typed with two fingers.

"On March 11 at approximately ..." He glanced at his watch. "9:30 a.m. officer was on duty guarding the former home of Henry Koster, deceased, of Port Otto. The house was sealed as a crime scene awaiting the arrival of state crime scene investigators. Officer observed what appeared to be a camera flash coming from inside the garage. Officer proceeded to investigate. Upon reaching the back of the house, officer encountered suspect leaving through a sliding glass door. The glass door was known to have been previously locked and—"

He was interrupted by something exploding somewhere outside the patrol car. Bits of dirt rained down on the windshield. Drumwell flinched. He slid down in his seat and unholstered his service revolver. He peered out the windshield and checked the rearview and side mirrors. Another explosion hit. This one struck the driveway a few feet in front of the car, creating a mist of concrete dust that filled the air. The fog cleared to reveal a three-foot-wide crater in the driveway and Zastra standing behind it with her blaster pistol pointed toward the car. Her hood was thrown back, her full lizard face on display.

She jerked her head to the side as a signal for Drumwell to get out of the car. He did. I couldn't see his face, but I could imagine the look of shock it must have registered at the sight of a lizard woman with a blaster aimed at his head. Zastra nodded toward the service revolver in his hand. He dropped it. She stepped closer and kicked the gun away. She nodded toward the backseat. Drumwell got me out.

"What is that thing?" he whispered to me with terror in his eyes.

"You got a dog. I got her."

Zastra said, "Are you calling me your pet? You know, I could leave you here with him."

"All he hears coming from you is hissing," I replied. "Just let me handle this." I turned to the deputy. "I can keep her from hurting you, okay? First, take off these cuffs and put them on yourself."

"You know I can't do that," Drumwell said.

"Oh yeah? I think what you can't do is let her put a hole in you matching the one up there in the driveway. She'll do it. She isn't bound by Earth laws."

Drumwell took a long look at Zastra. "She's ... she's an alien?"

"No, she's from France." I shook my head. "Of course, she's an alien."

He removed the cuffs from me and put them on himself. He started to put the handcuff key back in his pocket.

"No, no," I said. "Drop it on the driveway."

He grimaced and complied.

"Now climb in the backseat."

He climbed in. I shut the door with a hip.

Now I had to think. I turned to Zastra. "Could we use that memory-erasing thing on him?"

"What memory-erasing thing?"

"The thing Oren told you to use on me if I didn't take the job."

"Oh, that. Yeah, that isn't real."

"It isn't real?"

"Nah, Oren made it up to convince you to take the job."

"Oh for crying out loud. You know, this is why I have trust issues. Well, anyway, Drumwell is cuffed and unarmed, and I'm fairly sure he can't open the door from the inside. That should keep him from pursuing us or calling for help. But someone might be checking on him at any time. Especially since he radioed in."

"Then we need to move."

"Wait. I need to think. Have I touched anything and left fingerprints? He opened the door for me. My fists were clenched the whole time I was in the back seat. I was careful inside the house. Okay. I think I'm good. I hope I didn't drop any DNA. Wait. The dash camera. I'm not sure it's turned on, but if it is it has my face. No, I remember I was looking at the ground as we came around the house. I thought I needed to watch my step because with my hands cuffed, I wouldn't be able to catch myself if I tripped. I bet it got a pretty picture of you, though. I almost hope the camera was turned on just for that. Otherwise, no one is gonna believe this poor guy's story. He's never going to live this one down."

"Are you ready now? We can't stay here." She was impatient but with good reason.

"Yeah. Yeah. Let's roll."

We dashed around the house and across the grass to the wood. We ran up and down the hills and splashed through the stream as quickly as possible. I would have liked to clean our footwear before tracking mud in my car, but I didn't want to take the time. We accelerated away. My adrenaline was surging, and I had to keep one eye on the speedometer to keep from speeding. I didn't want to get pulled over by some other cop.

"So did you find anything interesting inside?" Zastra asked.

"Inside what?"

"Inside the house you broke into. What do you think I meant?"

"Oh, sorry. At the moment, I'm kinda focused on my new career as a fugitive from the law. I'm trying to figure out how to avoid getting arrested, now with new and improved charges. But yeah, I found a couple of interesting clues inside."

"Good. So there's that at least. Otherwise, this would be a fiasco."

"You're telling me."

When we reached the *Shaymus* we left our shoes — well my shoes and Zastra's boots — on the ramp and climbed up to the office.

Oren was already on the screen. "That was quite an adventure you had there."

"Yeah, and it's not over yet. I have to get myself and my car back to Indianapolis somehow. They'll have a description of me, and they think I'm an Indy reporter. So they'll be watching the highways between here and there. They might even set up a roadblock since this involves a murder and now a possible alien invasion. Of course, you could just fly me back to Indy, but that would be more of a risk. They would eventually find my car here, track it to me, and match me with the description of the guy they're hunting. So I don't know what to do. It's too bad we can't load the car onto the ship."

"We can," Oren said.

"How? It wouldn't even fit up the ramp."

"Not in its present state."

"You mean disassemble it? I'm no mechanic, and I don't want Zastra blowing it to pieces."

"There's an easier solution."

Jace stuck his head up the edge of the shaft. "You called for me, boss?"

"Yes. I need you to help Gabriel with a little project."

* * *

Ten minutes later Jace and I were standing on the ramp. He was holding a long wand connected to a hose snaking back up into the *Shaymus*. You might think he was going to give my car a power wash, which it did desperately need after a long Indiana winter. But that's not what this wand was for.

My phone buzzed. It was a text from Sarah. I told Jace, "Let me check this before we proceed. It might be relevant." I tapped the screen open. The text said:

How RU?

I texted back.

OK. Why? What have U heard?

I pressed Send and waited. A few seconds later the phone buzzed again.

Nothing. Should I?

I texted back.

No. Just kidding. Ha Ha.

I started to put the phone back in my pocket and say something to Jace when it buzzed again. It was Sarah again.

When will you be home?

I texted back.

IDK. Hope to make Friday coffee.

She texted back a thumbs up and a smiley face.

I realized with a sinking feeling that my phone had been pinging off some nearby cell tower this whole time. If police started looking at me as a suspect, those pings would tie me to the scene of the crime. I should have turned it off before ever coming here. But there was nothing I could do about it now other than live and learn for my next crime spree. I put my phone away and turned to Jace.

"Now, you're sure this will work, and you can put it back together again?" I asked.

"Sure. We've done this before. Well, never with an automobile. But other stuff."

"'Cause it isn't paid off yet."

"Relax. I know what I'm doing."

"Fine. But only because the other alternative risks jail time."

Jace pushed a switch on the wand. It made a buzz. There was a ripple in the air between the wand and the car. Then the car simply disappeared.

I grabbed his arm. "Where'd it go?"

"It was turned into a compressed solution of quarks and electrons and sucked inside the replicator."

"And you've kept the pattern so you can replicate it later, right?"

"Just like the coffee. Don't worry, Gabe."

"Wow!" I shook my head. "So could that work like a transporter to beam me to a different location?"

"Technically, yes. Somebody could send your pattern as data and replicate you at the remote location using quarks and electrons already located there. But, and this is kind of important, it would have to kill you at the first location and recreate you from scratch in the new location. Otherwise, there would be two of you."

"I don't like the sound of that."

"Yeah. And it requires a huge amount of energy. For your car, it would have been much, much cheaper to simply drive it back. But in this case, we needed something stealthier. Well, we're done here. Hey c'mon, I programmed in those donuts you brought back. I'll make you one."

"Will the donut be made from the quarks and electrons you sucked in from my car?"

"Very likely. But it'll still taste like a donut."

The *Shaymus* flew off. It was still before noon, but they didn't want to fly directly to Indy and have to replicate my car during the day when someone might see them. So I had them fly out west on a tour of the Grand Canyon. Afterward, we put down outside a little town in New Mexico, and I walked into town to pick up some tacos and pizza, partly for lunch and partly for the replicator.

We were eating in the galley, Zastra, Jace and I enjoying the excellent tacos and pizza when Oren's face appeared on the galley screen.

"So about the clues you found," he said.

I hurried to swallow a bite. "Right. More signs of a laser blast, so clearly the murderer was an off-worlder. Plus, I found a boot print where the killer probably stood. Our only suspect who wears boots is Woad."

"And Yorbah," said Oren. "But any of them might have worn boots for the occasion."

"Right," Zastra said. "One should always have proper footwear when committing murder."

Chapter 22

Back in my Element

I didn't make it back to my house until after midnight. We landed in the familiar industrial park where Jace replicated my car back into existence.

"Well," I said, walking slowly around it. "I think it looks like it did before. To be honest, I could have done without the dirt getting replicated back on it."

"Sorry. That's how it works," Jace shrugged. "Try turning it on."

I got in and was pleased to find that it started right up. In fact, after being reconstituted at the subatomic level, it might have even run better.

I cruised slowly down my street, scanning for signs of a police presence. I thought I recognized all the cars parked along the street and in driveways. Of course, the cops might be crouched in the bushes waiting for me. But I decided I couldn't keep hiding forever. I needed to just go for it and see what happened. I pulled into a spot and walked boldly to my door.

If someone stopped me, I had a receipt for a candy bar in my pocket from a mini-mart outside La Crosse, Wisconsin to give me an alibi for the day. The story was I had gone there to meet with a potential client, but he never showed up. It was weak as alibis go. I didn't have an email or phone record or text from the imagined client to back it up. I guess I would say the guy wrote me a now-destroyed letter, which, of course, wouldn't seem likely to anyone.

I let myself into my house, checking the street behind me one more time as I closed the door. I walked through the living room and down the short hallway to my office. We had essentially wasted the afternoon and evening hiding out. Now I was in a mood to find some answers. That meant turning to my old friend, the Internet. I flipped up the screen of my laptop but immediately realized I didn't want to do this from my own IP address. That would tie Gabriel Lake to the events in Port Otto. There was only one thing for it.

I muttered to myself, "No rest for the weary."

With a sigh, I shut the laptop, unplugged it, and headed back out to my car. On the way out the door, I grabbed a baseball cap for a disguise of sorts.

I drove to a strip mall where there was a restaurant I remembered had free Wi-Fi. The restaurant was closed at this time of night, but the router would still be on. I parked a couple of rows back from the entrance, close enough to get a signal but far enough away to be out of sight from a security camera.

I slouched down in the seat below the headrest so I couldn't be seen from the street. I opened the laptop and logged onto the Wi-Fi. I launched a browser in incognito mode so there wouldn't be a history stored on the laptop. I typed in the web address, arrest.in.gov, the web application Drumwell had used. I typed in the deputy's username, ldrumwell@WhitcombCo.gov.

Now, I asked myself, what would he use for a password? I knew it was only six characters, which was weak. So that would make guessing easier. What I didn't know was if this system would lock me out after a few wrong attempts. If I only had three or four tries, I would need to be both smart and lucky. The most commonly used passwords, believe it or not, are things like 12345, abc123, password, iloveyou, and qwerty (the top letters across the keyboard). Let's face it, people are mentally lazy.

I knew from watching Drumwell's hands move around the keyboard while he typed that it wasn't 123456 or 654321 or qwerty. I didn't know his middle name or his mom's maiden name or his favorite team or other things people use for passwords. But I knew one thing from the picture on his dash. He had a dog, a golden retriever. I tried typing the word golden. The system came back with the message, "Invalid username or password."

Then I remembered he had typed the arrest report in all capital letters. Drumwell was a Caps Lock guy. I tried GOLDEN and this time was rewarded with a welcome message on the screen. Seriously. That was one crummy password, no mixed upper- and lower-case letters, no numbers or special characters. If I had been hired to write the system, I would have made sure the users set up stronger passwords.

But I was in. I grinned. I couldn't help but feel like I was back in my own element again with a keyboard at my fingertips. This was how I worked, how I made my living. A wizard on the keyboard. Moses with a mouse. I'm no hacker, but this was much more familiar ground for me, at least compared to flying across the galaxy or running from the cops.

One of the menu choices was "Search by Name." I selected it. It gave me boxes for First Name and Last Name. I typed in Henry and Koster. The laptop sent the search request off to the Internet, and a few seconds later three records popped up. One was his arrest by the State Police. One was his murder. The third was for the arrest of one Christopher Paul Bacon for breaking into his house. Again, I was surprised by the lack of security. You wouldn't think a county deputy should be able to access data on a State Police arrest without some kind of authorization. But it was all to my advantage in this instance.

I brought up the State Police report. The arrest had been for reckless driving. He had been carrying so many sandbags that the front wheels of his truck were barely touching the pavement, causing him to swerve all over the road. Most of the report was standard police information. But there was one interesting bit. During his interview, he tried to make a deal for his release by saying he had information about an invasion by space aliens. One part read:

> *Suspect told officers he had a neighbor with horns on his head. That he had first thought they were transdermal implants until the previous Saturday evening when he saw the neighbor from across the pasture remove his human-looking nose to reveal a very alien-looking nose underneath. At the same time, he had seen a gigantic green face appear in the neighbor's window and say something to the neighbor. Suspect also claimed to have seen another man with green skin outside on a previous day, and then the man had disappeared. Suspect was referred for a drug screening.*

That was it. Nothing about Tam's murder. And apparently the cops, not surprisingly, had been skeptical of his alien invasion story. There was nothing in the report that should have gotten him killed by Tam's murderer. The motive for Koster's murder must have been something else.

A set of headlight beams swept across the line of storefronts. I quickly closed the laptop and slid even lower in the seat. I closed my eyes so that if this turned out to be the cops, I could tell them I was sleeping. Of course, I would need a story for why I was sleeping at a strip mall, and no reasonable excuse was coming to mind. The car pulled up to a shop a few stores down. I opened one eye a slit and glanced out the window. The driver had gotten out and was staring into the shop window using his car's headlights to light it up. Was he getting ready to break in, or was he just checking the store hours? He stood there a minute, then turned and walked back to his car and drove off.

I opened the laptop again and brought up the report for Koster's murder. They didn't have any suspects and no clues other than the ones I already knew.

There wasn't much more in it than there had been in the newspaper and in the few tidbits Drumwell had given me, which maybe wasn't surprising since I had badly contaminated the crime scene. But this murder wasn't going to be solved by the local cops anyway, not if it had an alien perpetrator. The report did mention that police had found the garage door up, which lent credence to my suspicion that Koster had been working in the garage that day as he had been when I talked to him.

For fun, I brought up my arrest record, or rather the arrest record for Chris P. Bacon. I've read a lot of fiction but never anything as creative as that report. No mention of Zastra, and no explanation for the potholes she blew in the driveway and yard. Instead, it said Bacon had managed to overpower Deputy Drumwell and had fled on foot. I checked the description of the suspect — average height, brown eyes, brown hair, stocky build. Stocky? Stocky? I definitely wouldn't call myself stocky. For the record, I had slid through a twelve-inch opening in the sliding glass door. Could a stocky person do that?

The good news was that such a generic description would match thousands of people in central Indiana. Drumwell had even worked with a police sketch artist, but the resulting drawing looked more like my old high school social studies teacher than it resembled me. I figured I was safe.

I still had my DSLR camera in the car and used it to take pictures of all the relevant parts of the reports. That kept any evidence off my hard drive. I drove home yawning. The excitement of the day was starting to catch up to me. Except for a nap while flying back from the Grand Canyon, I had been up for more than twenty-four hours, keeping myself going on replicator coffee. I was ready to hit the hay. It felt wonderful to sleep in my own bed that night.

The next morning, I woke up feeling remarkably normal for the first time in days. For a moment I thought the whole thing might even have been some strange, vivid dream. But there was my DSLR sitting beside the laptop. I turned it on and thumbed through the screenshots from the police database. Yup, it had been real. And I needed to make a report to Oren.

I printed off the photos and deleted the files from the camera. It probably wouldn't fool a digital forensic expert, but I was feeling more confident now. I got myself cleaned up for the day and made my way by bus to the warehouse. I said, "Open sesame" to the ramp on the *Shaymus,* and it responded. I climbed up to the office, showed Oren the photos, and gave him my report.

"I agree with you," he said. "It appears Mr. Koster was grasping at straws to get himself released by the police. If he had known anything about a murder, he would doubtless have used that instead of some unbelievable story about space aliens."

"Then he wasn't killed because of something he knew about Tam's murder," Zastra said.

"Not because of what he knew," said Oren. "But perhaps because of something the killer thought he knew."

"Or," I suggested, "maybe Koster killed Tam because he found out Tam was an alien, and then somebody like Ex or Princess Ralph killed Koster in revenge."

Oren frowned. "It is possible, but I don't like it. First, it requires two murderers, which rankles me. But the more important point is that it requires the revenge killer to have deduced Tam's killer, which is highly unlikely. To date even we haven't discovered the killer. The only way Koster's killer could have learned such a thing would be from Koster himself or from someone else on Earth to whom Koster had confided. And none of our suspects, none of us even, know anyone from Earth other than you, Gabriel."

"And I can't tell what I don't know," I said. "So how do we figure it out?"

"This is going to require a good deal of consideration on my part. Excuse me while I think." The slightly blue Dwayne Johnson face went still on the screen.

I stood up. "Well, if he's going to be thinking for a while, I might as well return to my cabin and do some reading."

"Wait a second," said Zastra.

"What for?"

Just then Oren said, "I have it."

"Already?"

"In this digital form, I can think rather quickly."

"I guess so. So who did it?"

"I need one piece of information first. But I can obtain that while we travel back to Diere. Let's go reveal a killer."

Chapter 23

Who Done It

When we landed on Diere, I was dispatched to arrange an audience with Queen Scythia and request that she command Ralph, Khan, and Woad to be present. If I could also find Yorbah, I was to use my supposed influence with her to convince her to attend as well. With Zastra bringing Ex, we were rounding up all the suspects like in an Agatha Christie novel. After getting the shindig set up with the queen, I found myself walking out of the palace as Yorbah was walking in.

"Hey, stranger," I said. "I see you're still here hanging around on Diere."

"Still here? You left yesterday. I've hardly had time to go anywhere."

"Oh yeah. I still get confused with the chrono drive. Well, it's been longer than that for me. It feels like a month, but I know I've spent a couple of days at least, including one super long day where I got arrested and ran from the law."

"That sounds more like my life."

"It seems to be turning into a regular occurrence for me too. If you recall, I was arrested on Girsu ... because of you as a matter of fact."

"Because you didn't identify yourself before you started tossing out accusing questions," she countered.

"As I remember it, all I said was we had some questions."

"Yeah. I didn't like the sound of that. So have you solved the murder?"

"Oren has. He's going to announce it in the throne room in a few minutes. Do you want to see us unmask a murderer?"

She bit her lower lip for a minute. "Sure. Sounds like fun. I wouldn't miss it."

I went back to the *Shaymus* and told Oren everything was set up. "Are you going to clue us in before everyone else?" I asked.

"I don't think so," Oren said. "I suppose I am a showman at heart. I want you to be part of the audience."

"What if you need the culprit grabbed?"

"We have the entire palace guard for that."

* * *

"Your Majesty, Your Royal Highness," Oren said with a bow of his head to the queen and princess, "and everyone else in attendance, thank you all for being here today."

The throne room was filled with Dieren dignitaries apparently here for the show. The queen sat on her throne with Woad standing beside her with military correctness. Ralph sat near the queen with Khan standing beside her. Oren was being projected on a screen on the side wall with Zastra, Ex, and I standing opposite it. I had the habitat with Buad and Blan beside me so they could be a part of this as well.

Yorbah made her way through the crowd and sidled up beside me. "Have I missed anything?"

"Just starting," I whispered.

"This has been a puzzling case with very few clues," said Oren. "At first I wondered if we would ever get a lead on the killer. But as sometimes happens in situations like this, the killer finally contributed the breakthrough by killing again. That is what provided us with a line of inquiry and allowed us to amass sufficient clues to unmask the murderer today."

It was an impressive opening. This was like Poirot and Nero Wolfe and Sherlock Holmes all rolled into one. It was like I was inside one of my books. But unlike reading in bed, a real murderer was going to be named here, and things could become dangerous.

"As we all know," Oren said, "the first murder was that of Tam Elam, late husband of Princess Ralph. The second murder, of which many of you are not aware, was of their onetime Earth neighbor, a Mr. Henry Koster, which occurred only two Earth days later.

"Two murders within a few days of each other in two houses on Earth only a few steps away. Could that be a coincidence? When I first learned of Mr. Koster's murder, it seemed unlikely. After investigating it, it seemed a near impossibility because Mr. Koster was killed with an energy weapon, the kind of which cannot be found on Earth. He had burn marks on his chest. There were burn marks on the wall behind him. No Earth weapon can do that.

"Therefore, it was certain Mr. Koster was killed by someone not from Earth," said Oren. "And that would tie his murder to the death of Tam Elam and suggest they were killed by the same person."

"So who was it?" asked Woad. "Get on with it already. Name the person."

Oren raised a palm. "Please, Commander Woad, I need to do this my way. I do not have a police force with power granted by the state. I cannot act as judge and jury. I need to explain this to all of you here so Diere can prosecute the culprit. Now, where was I?"

"They were killed by the same person," said the queen.

Oren bowed his head. "Thank you, Your Majesty. Yes. We were not yet near a motive for the murder of Tam Elam, but perhaps we could detect a motive for the murder of Henry Koster. We knew three things about Mr. Koster that seemed relevant to the case. One, he had seen Tam Elam's horns and real nose and the princess's Dieren-sized face and Khan's green skin, and he was suspicious he might be living next door to aliens. Two, the night of Tam's murder he overheard the sounds of an argument, the voices sounding to him like that of two men. Three, he had recently been arrested by the Earth authorities on an unrelated issue and had tried to get his charges reduced by spinning a story of a possible alien invasion."

"I deduced from those facts that Mr. Koster actually knew little about the death of Tam Elam, or else he would have given information of the murder to the Earth authorities. All he had heard that night was the sound of an argument, not any actual words. But the killer could not be sure of that."

Princess Ralph interrupted. "Do I still need to be here, Mummy? This is getting boring."

"You need to be here, dear," said the queen. "You hired Mr. Vilkas, and this is what you get. Besides, I expect we are getting to the interesting part."

"Indeed, we are, Your Majesty," Oren said. "If the killer thought Mr. Koster had overheard the words of the argument, that *would* be a motive for murder. But who knew that Koster had heard an argument? Outside of the members of our agency, the fact was known only by Princess Ralph and Khan Krete."

I suppressed a giggle. That name.

"We had asked them about it in our interview with them," Oren continued. "Assuming they told no one else, those were the only ones who knew."

I thought to myself that Yorbah also knew about it. Plus, she knew someone had been watching from the barn. She knew because I had told her myself. I had given her confidential agency information because ... well because I kind of thought of her as part of the investigation and, if I had to admit it, because I found her attractive. I realized I had a lot to learn about being a detective.

"Mr. Vilkas," said the queen, "I'm certain you are not accusing Her Royal Highness of killing her own husband."

"Your Majesty, I was simply trying to eliminate her as a suspect, though I might point out that the spouse is always considered a possible suspect. But in this case, it all depended on the actual words of the argument, the words Mr. Koster did not hear, but the killer might have thought he had heard. However, there was another person there that evening. There was someone who was watching the house from the barn. That person was Miss Ex Awoo. In her infatuation with Tam Elam, she had placed a tracker in a gift she had given him. So she knew he was on Earth, and she hired a pilot to take her there. A handkerchief, identical to the one we saw her use, was found in the barn on Earth, and she has confessed it all to me."

Ralph jumped up and pointed at Ex. "You followed us to Earth? You put a tracker on him? How obsessed can you be? No wonder he left you. That's why he loved me instead of you. You were too obsessive, too clingy, too ... too psycho. You killed him, didn't you? And you would have killed me, too!"

"I didn't kill him," Ex yelled back. "You killed him. You killed my Tam."

I put my arm around Ex, to both comfort and restrain her.

Oren said, "Your Royal Highness, Miss Awoo could not have murdered Mr. Koster. She probably did not even know Mr. Koster existed. Even if she did, she had no reason to suspect that Mr. Koster or anyone had seen her in the barn. We would not have known of it except for an exceptional little boy. However, Miss Awoo did have valuable information. I interviewed her and asked her what, if anything, she had heard of the alleged argument. Miss Awoo, please repeat for everyone what you told me."

"I ... I didn't hear much," she said, seemingly shy after her outburst. "Only snatches of conversation. But I could tell it was Tam, and he was talking to that butler fellow."

"Khan Krete," said Oren.

"If you say so. The butler fellow was telling him, 'Stand up for yourself. Don't let her go back.' I made out that part distinctly. And Tam said, 'I'm surprised you don't take her side.' They went back and forth like that."

"Did you know what they were talking about? Why exactly Tam Elam was to stand up for himself?" Oren asked.

"Not really. But it had something to do with going back to Diere."

"Yes. Thank you, Miss Awoo," Oren said. "As she said, 'It had something to do with going back to Diere.' Earlier that day I had negotiated an agreement with Princess Ralph allowing her to return to Diere and keep Tam Elam as her husband provided she also took a Dieren husband. I could tell at the time—"

"Oh, you would, wouldn't you?" screamed Ex at Princess Ralph. "Tam wasn't enough for your big fat ego. You never loved him like I loved him."

"Oh, I loved him," Ralph spit back. "You don't know what love even is. What you called love was just some kind of mania, some kind of psychosis."

"You wanted a second husband!"

"That was merely politics. You know nothing!"

"Ladies, please, please," said Oren. "It is crucial I proceed." His eyes darted from one to the other. When they both appeared under control, he continued. "I could tell at the time when we discussed the plan that Tam Elam was not overly pleased with the arrangement, but he gave into Her Royal Highness. That is why Princess Ralph would never have killed him. Tam Elam always gave in to her wishes. He agreed to her idea to marry on Earth. He agreed to the plan to come back to Diere, even though he would have to share her with another man. Why would she kill someone so accommodating to her?

"What Tam Elam realized that evening in the argument was that the princess's own butler was not nearly so accommodating as he was. Khan had served Princess Ralph her whole life. He professed a deep loyalty to her. Why then was he telling Tam Elam to stand up to her and refuse to go back to Diere? Why was he, of all people, trying to keep her from going back?"

Khan cleared his throat and said calmly, "The girl misheard. I never said Tam should not agree to Her Royal Highness returning to Diere. I only advised him that he should not return."

Ralph turned her huge head toward Khan. "What? You advised Tam to break up our marriage?"

"M'lady."

"Don't m'lady me—"

Oren broke in. "In either case, you advised Tam Elam to contradict Princess Ralph, the person to whom you swore loyalty. That was when it clicked for him, wasn't it? That phrase 'I'm surprised you don't take her side,' that was when Tam Elam realized you were not acting as a faithful butler would. He figured out you were disloyal. What happened, Khan? Did he threaten to expose you to her? Is that why you stabbed him?"

A general commotion began. People began talking over each other. Woad signaled to the guards, who were now approaching Khan from all sides.

Oren's commanding voice overpowered them all. "And then when you learned that Henry Koster might have overheard you, you went back to Earth and killed him too! But why, Khan? What induced you to turn against the princess you had served for years and then kill to cover it up?"

The guards were steps from Khan. Some were reaching out toward him. Some had raised weapons. All of a sudden, some kind of huge rodent the size of a Great Dane appeared from somewhere and scuttled across the dais. It knocked a guard down. It ran between the legs of a Dieren woman who screamed and jumped into the queen's lap. Everyone started shifting and shouting. In the midst of the commotion, Khan had disappeared.

"Where did he go?" yelled one of the guards.

The rat thing shot through the crowd. People were screaming, jostling each other, jumping on chairs. Zastra and Yorbah un-holstered their weapons, trying to maneuver for a clean shot, but none could be found. The guards turned and pursued it, but it disappeared through the crowd and out the door.

I didn't know what had happened. But one thing was clear. In the confusion, Khan had escaped. I had to say it. I clenched my fists and yelled out in my best Shatner impression, "KAAAHN!"

Chapter 24

The Shape of Things

So the butler *had* done it.

The crowd in the throne room was still in an uproar. Everyone was pushing and yelling. People were standing on chairs in fear. Princess Ralph was crying and being comforted by her ladies-in-waiting. Seemingly the strain of losing her husband and then finding out her butler had killed him was too much for her. Ex Awoo was wailing something about if only Tam had stayed with her. Zastra was excitedly scanning the crowd, looking for any sign of Khan. Woad was shouting orders, and the guards were scurrying to follow them. The only person who looked at all calm was Queen Scythia. No doubt she'd had a lifetime of practice in keeping a stiff upper lip.

"I should have seen it," Oren said from the screen of Zastra's tablet. "I should have seen it. Quickly now, Gabriel, have Woad show you to Khan's quarters. Zastra, release Buad and Blan to search for him, then follow Gabe to the quarters and bring me along."

I ran up to Woad. He was busy barking commands. "Secure the palace. Send word to the space port and the train station. Shut down all transport off the planet. Put out an alert for Khan. And somebody, calm this crowd. Get those people out of here."

"Hey! I need you to show me Khan's quarters," I said to him.

Woad glared at me. "Surely you don't think he would simply return to his quarters. You saw him disappear in front of our eyes. You saw that creature appear. This was some kind of magic, and he's used the distraction to make his retreat. He'll be heading for a space port to escape."

"Look, I don't know what I saw or what I think. I just know Oren told me to go to Khan's quarters."

Woad grimaced. "Very well. But it's pointless. He's long gone." He motioned for one of his guards to come over. "Take this man to Khan Krete's quarters."

As I turned to go, I spotted Yorbah standing where I had left her. Her gaze seemed a thousand miles away. I managed to make eye contact as I left the throne room, and she nodded at me. The guard led me through the great hall, along a hallway, and down a back stair. The lower level of the palace, which must have been where the help was quartered, was more cramped and not anywhere near as ornate. We took a right, then a left, another left, another right. I hoped I didn't have to find my way out by myself. Finally, the guard stopped at a door and knocked on it politely.

"Seriously?" I asked. "He's been exposed as a murderer. You think he'll answer our knock." I moved past the guard and pushed through the door.

It was immediately clear he wasn't ever going to answer our knock. On the floor was the body of Khan Krete. It was badly bloated, and the flesh had desiccated from sage green to a charcoal gray. The stench inside the room was overwhelming. I found myself backing out of the door at the same time Zastra came through.

The guard muttered, "The guilt of betraying the princess must have been too much for him. He came back here and died by suicide."

I stared at the guard and shook my head in disbelief. "Are you crazy? This body has been dead here for days, maybe weeks. That wasn't Khan upstairs. It couldn't have been."

"Then who was it?" asked the guard.

"It was a shapeshifter," Oren said from the tablet.

"There really are shapeshifters?" asked the guard. "My granddad used to tell me scary stories about them, but I've never seen one. I didn't think they existed."

"Neither did I," Oren said. "But they must exist. We just encountered one in the throne room."

"Then that rodent thing?" asked Zastra.

"That must have been him," Oren said. "That thing appeared when Khan disappeared. He changed into it."

"Okay. Just so I understand," I said, "'cause you all seem surprised by this. I'm getting that shapeshifters aren't a common thing, right? There isn't like a whole planet of them the next star system over or something?"

"Correct," said Oren. "As the guard says, there have been legends of them for centuries, but no one believed they existed. We need to meet with the queen and

Princess Ralph immediately. Go back to Woad and arrange it. Have him join the meeting too if he isn't too busy quelling a riot."

As I left the room Oren was contacting Buad and Blan. "Gentlemen, you are no longer looking for Khan. We are dealing with a shapeshifter. The only thing you can look for is someone who changes their appearance. It's a long shot, I know, but good luck."

I dutifully made my way back to the throne room, getting lost only three times in the maze of hallways. I found Woad going over a map of the city with his subordinates. He was setting up a house-to-house search.

"You won't find him," I said.

"And why are you so sure?" he sneered at me.

"Because you won't know what to look for. Turns out he's a shapeshifter. The real Khan is dead down in his quarters, as Oren suspected."

Woad collapsed in a chair. "Now what do we do?"

"Oren wants to meet with the queen and the princess right away. Can you be there, too?"

He nodded.

I turned to go and found Yorbah beside me. "What's going on?" she asked me.

"I'm not sure. Want to tag along and find out?"

* * *

A few minutes later we were in what they called the queen's drawing room, a smaller but just as ornate sitting room behind the throne room. Woad was there along with the queen and princess, Zastra, Yorbah, Oren on the tablet, and me.

"I bear responsibility for this," Oren was saying. "There were clues. That Earth neighbor said he saw a green-skinned man who seemed to instantly disappear. I did not take those words literally. I should have. But then I have never known of a shapeshifter before."

"I have," said Queen Scythia. All eyes turned to her in surprise. "That is why you should not take responsibility, Mr. Vilkas. There once was ... or perhaps still is ... a shapeshifter named Rells Partian who bore a deep grudge against the royal house."

"Begging Your Majesty's pardon. I did ask you about enemies at the outset of this investigation."

"I know. I know. But I thought he was dead. It all happened when I was a little girl in the days when my grandmama was still on the throne. A strange spaceship crash landed on Diere, carrying two very odd-looking passengers. As soon as they saw Dierens, they transformed to take our shape, well, the shape and size of our men. They told us they were from a distant galaxy. Their ship had been thrown into a wormhole. They emerged from the wormhole inside Diere's gravity field and tumbled into the atmosphere. They could not regain control of their ship but managed to eject themselves and parachute to the ground. Grandmama welcomed them and told them they could make Diere their home. I believe she viewed them as potentially powerful allies should we ever find ourselves at war. But we were at peace, and the shapeshifters, Rells Partian and his mate Rells Demetian, spent their days in more pleasant pursuits. They were an endless source of entertainment to me as a small child. They would transform themselves into animals or people that I knew. I found it delightful."

The queen sighed, smiling at the memories.

"I remember they could not transform into something very large or very small. It had something to do with the conservation of mass. So they could not, for instance, take the form of my mother or a tiny animal."

"So that's why when he became a rodent, he became a huge one," I said.

"How did they become enemies, Your Majesty?" Oren prompted.

"It was an accident, as is all too common on Diere with women being so much larger than men. A woman will roll over in bed and smother her husband to death. Or a woman might accidentally sit on a man and crush him."

"Yikes!" That came from me.

The queen shrugged. "Well, these things happen. In this particular case, my mother who was princess at the time was arguing with my father. I don't know what it was about. Mommy said things. Daddy said things. The result was she stormed out of their rooms in the palace in a huff and rushed through the great hall, blinded by rage and tears, and threw herself on a couch. She never even noticed Rells Demetian sitting there. Poor Demetian. All that was left was a sheet of ooze. She tried to reform, but apparently the core organism in her had been crushed, so she could not come together in any form. Rells Partian went crazy with grief. He called all of us Dierens freaks because of our size. He blamed the royal family especially. He said we were vain, self-absorbed, and unconcerned for others. I suppose he had a point. My mother could be like that. Rells swore revenge against us and then transformed into a huge bird and flew off. No one knew if he ever left the planet on a transport ship or stayed here, hiding in some form."

"And now after all these years," said Oren, "it appears that Rells has undertaken to seek his revenge."

"Not exactly after *all* these years, Mr. Vilkas," said the queen. "There was an assassination attempt once while my mother was queen, a bombing. There was a spaceship, a passenger liner, being ceremonially launched, and she was to do the honors. As it happened, she was running late. As she was pulling into the shipyard, the entire launch pad exploded. It killed fourteen workers, but she was uninjured. They suspected Rells was behind it, but they couldn't prove anything or find him anywhere. Then nothing at all during all the years of my reign. I supposed he must have died or at least was too aged to attempt anything."

Oren closed his eyes. "That is the missing piece. I could not discern a motive for Khan being disloyal to the princess. Now it makes sense. It was not Khan."

"Poor Khan," said Ralph. "All this time he was lying there … dead. You know, now that I think about it, it was Khan, or Rells masquerading as Khan, who suggested to me I run away from Diere. I was surprised when he said it because he had always lectured me about my duty to Diere. But he had never given me bad advice, so that's why I did it. But now …" Her voice trailed off.

Oren said, "But now it appears that was Rells trying to separate you from Diere. Princess Ralph, I believe you were the real target all along. Perhaps Rells waited all these years for his revenge because he still had fond feelings for your mother, whom he remembered as a little girl, and did not blame her for what happened. But he was determined to bring down the royal house. So when word of your romance with Tam Elam became known around the galaxy, Rells saw it as an opportunity to separate you from the palace guard and kill you."

"But then why did he kill Tam?" Ralph asked.

"Because Tam realized his disloyalty. And in any case, he had to get Tam out of the way before he could deal with you. After killing Tam, he was probably planning to kill you too before you could leave Earth. But something stopped him. Perhaps Yorbah arrived too soon."

All eyes turned toward Yorbah.

"Like I told you," she said, "when I arrived there Khan had another knife in his hand."

"Yes," said Oren. "You weren't suspicious about that?"

"He was a butler. They work with kitchen utensils, don't they?"

Zastra said, "Then Yorbah took you to Donovio, where weapons aren't allowed."

"And not even good kitchen cutlery," said Ralph. "Very strange place, Donovio. So that must be why he convinced me we needed to leave for Astrid."

"Where he bought a blaster rifle," I said. "If we hadn't come upon him when we did, you would have been a goner."

Ralph's eyes grew large. "I owe you all my life."

"Your Majesty," Oren said. "You said something about a core organism in the shapeshifters. Can you explain that? Do you know how they manage their shape-shifting abilities? That might help us find and stop Rells."

"I only know the way Rells explained it to me as a child. Consequently, I can give you only a child's understanding. He said they were composed of millions of tiny organisms. I got the impression it was like an insect colony where a hive mind controls all the individuals. When they shift to a new shape these microscopic organisms crawl to certain locations. Then they extend connective tissue to each other. They grasp the connections from each other, and that is what allows them to maintain that shape. The microorganisms take on the functions of the new shape. They become a beating heart, a stomach that can digest food, eyes that see, and so on."

"And there is a core organism that controls it all?"

"Yes. I suppose if you could control that core organism, you could control the shape."

"If we had any idea where it was located."

"I hope that helps you apprehend him," said the queen. "But please do not kill him unless it is the only way."

"Your Majesty!" said Woad. "This thing is trying to kill your daughter."

"I know. I know," said the queen. "And he must be stopped. Ralph must be protected above all else. But he was once my dear friend so many years ago."

Oren said, "We will use all the restraint we can, Your Majesty."

Chapter 25

The Stakeout

So the butler didn't do it after all.

And now we had a shape-shifting killer to apprehend. How do you fight someone who can take any form and, as we witnessed in the throne room, can do so in nearly the blink of an eye? How do you even go about looking for him?

We were back on the *Shaymus* planning our next move. Zastra and I were at our desks, talking to Oren. Yorbah, who had stayed close to me since the big reveal was perched in one of the red leather chairs. Buad and Blan were out flying around looking for anyone of any shape who was acting suspiciously.

"We will assume for now," said Oren, "that Woad got all the off-world transport shut down before Rells could escape. If he is still on Diere and he is still bent on revenge, he will perhaps come to us."

"Are you suggesting using the princess for bait?" I asked. "I doubt the palace will be thrilled about that."

"We are not using her as bait," Oren said. "She already is bait. If Rells is trapped here, he will probably make an attempt on her life. He'll try to finish the job."

"Do you think he would walk right into the palace?" Zastra asked.

Oren shrugged. "He could walk right in looking like anyone he chose to impersonate, and who would know? He could do it at any time, but my best guess is he'll do it at night when the chances of him running into the person he is masquerading as would be lower. Perhaps tonight."

"What do you propose?" asked Zastra.

"I propose we guard Princess Ralph. We'll station Buad and Blan in the great hall to watch for anyone looking suspicious. I want Zastra in the upstairs hallway. Gabriel, you will be the last line of defense in her chambers."

"I'm not sure I'm comfortable being in her bedroom," I said.

"You won't be. Her Royal Highness has an entire suite of rooms. You'll stay in the outer room."

"Do I get a blaster? It seems like I should have a blaster."

"What experience and proficiency do you have with firearms?" Oren asked.

"My uncle used to take me out in the woods, and we'd shoot pistols at tin cans."

"Did you ever hit them?" Zastra asked.

"As a matter of fact, I did … sometimes. Uncle Aaron said I wasn't too bad."

"So you were 'not too bad.' That's clearly high praise," said Zastra in a sarcastic tone. "We don't want you accidentally shooting the princess."

"I won't."

Yorbah said, "I'll stay with him. I can handle a blaster."

Zastra shot a concerned look at Oren.

Oren said, "I would rather not have outsiders included in this, but you could come in handy in a fight. I'll permit it as long as you agree that you are under Gabriel's orders."

"Of course," Yorbah said. She turned and shot me a wink.

I said, "I still get a blaster, right?"

"Fine," said Zastra. "I'll take you to the arms locker to pick something out and take you out for some practice. But keep it set on stun."

"We should all keep weapons set on stun," said Oren. "We want to apprehend him, not kill him, as per the queen's orders."

"So do we just stun anyone acting suspiciously?" I asked.

"I have been researching the problem. I have read all the old Dieren news reports on when Rells was here. I even read old legends about shapeshifters from around the galaxy."

"And?" I asked.

"And I have found nothing useful. Magic spells. Gold amulets. Noting a birthmark or tattoo that appears on the creature in all forms. It's all nonsense and old wives' tales. But for you at least, Gabriel, you should stun anyone who gets inside the private chambers. Out in the hallway, Zastra will have to use a bit more discretion."

"Well, discretion is her strong suit." I grinned.

Her eyes narrowed. "In fact, I'm exercising considerable discretion at this very moment."

Zastra picked out a blaster for me that could only be fired on stun, which was annoying since she and Yorbah had much more powerful weapons. Still, it was my first ray gun, and I was excited. I even found a shoulder holster that fit it.

There was a firing range on the palace grounds where I practiced for more than an hour. Firing a blaster was different from firing a handgun. There was no recoil and much less noise. But it still required precise aiming. With practice I was able to hit the target ... most of the time, at least.

That evening Yorbah and I walked through the palace to the princess's chambers. In the hallway outside her door, I looked around for Zastra. I couldn't see her. "Zastra, are you here?" I asked.

She stepped out right in front of me and nearly made me jump.

"Where were you?" I asked.

"There's an alcove behind that statue. We're supposed to keep out of sight, you know."

"I know, and you're doing excellent at that."

Yorbah and I moved to Ralph's door and knocked. The door opened. It was Ralph herself.

"You don't have a new butler yet?" I asked.

"It isn't safe yet," she grumbled. "Khan could simply kill the new butler and take his form. I can't even be sure about you two. How do I know you are who I think you are?"

"Well, I'm me for sure," I said. "Yorbah, are you you?"

"Yes, I am," Yorbah said.

"Well, there you have it," I said. "Look, at most only one of us is Khan. And we'll be keeping an eye on each other. So that should be reassuring."

"Sort of," Ralph said. "Well, I'm retiring now. Make yourselves at home out here."

We looked around. The room was built to the princess's scale. In other words, it was about the size of a basketball court. You probably could have pushed back the furniture and put up some hoops because there was even a wood floor, which I caught glimpses of here and there between the fine thick rugs.

The room was filled with huge couches and chairs, whose seats were at the height of my head. But there were also some that were human sized. We picked out a couch that was screened from the outside door by larger pieces of furniture but had a direct line of sight to the inner door through which Ralph had gone. Plus it was close enough to the fireplace to be cozy.

I sat down at one end of the couch. Yorbah sat down close and leaned against me.

"What's this?" I asked. "We're supposed to be working here."

"We are. I figured you'd be more likely to stay awake if I'm close like this."

I felt her warmth and caught the scent of perfume. "You might be right about that."

"Besides, it's a good thing I'm here. I didn't like the way Her Royal Highness smiled at you when we came in. You may need a chaperone."

"No worries there. I mean, I like tall women, but not that tall."

"So tell me about yourself. We have time. Do you live in Potato?"

"It's Port Otto. Why does everyone think it's Potato? No. I don't live there. I live in Indianapolis. It's not far away, but it's a much bigger town."

"And you're a detective there?"

"No. This is kind of a side hustle for me. I mainly work with computers."

"Well, you're good at this."

"I just do what Oren tells me to do." Why was I getting the distinct impression she was flirting with me? When we first met, she had sucker punched me in the gut. Now she had her head on my shoulder. In my experience, I wasn't all that irresistible.

* * *

The evening wore on into night. We talked about our childhoods. Turns out mine had been a lot easier than hers. She asked me tons of questions about Earth. Hours passed. Sometimes I would stand and walk around the room to keep myself awake. Sometimes the conversation lagged, and we each dozed off for minutes at a time.

The palace was quiet. A clock somewhere in the room had just chimed fourteen. Yeah, that's right. I counted the chimes, and it was fourteen. I don't understand Dieren time, so who knows? I felt chilly and got up to poke the fire back into life again. When I got back, Yorbah had flopped down at the other end of the couch asleep.

I settled back onto my end. That's when I heard the *creak* of a door. I shook Yorbah by the boot. She started to murmur something, but I lunged toward her and put my hand over her mouth. Her eyes flipped open.

I whispered, "I heard something."

I rolled off the couch into a kneeling position and pulled out my blaster. In the corner of my eye, I saw Yorbah sit up and un-holster her weapon. I could make out no sound of footsteps, but that wasn't surprising given the thick rugs. I would have to rely on seeing something in the dim firelight.

I crept closer to the line of travel someone would take if moving from the outer door to the princess's bedroom. There had been only the one squeak. Had it been my imagination? Maybe it was just the sounds that a centuries-old palace inevitably made at night. If it were Rells, how could he have gotten past Zastra? I started to worry about her. But there was no time for that now.

A shadow moved in front of the fireplace. It didn't look like Khan. It was shorter and bulkier than Khan. But Rells could look like anything. Whoever this was, they shouldn't be here in the royal chambers in the dead of night.

I took aim and fired. I missed. The energy beam from my blaster hit a log in the fireplace sending sparks into the air and lighting the room more brightly. The figure turned and looked in my direction, holding a blaster in his hand. He took a shot in my direction. A flaming hole burst through an upholstered chair beside me as the figure raced toward the inner door to the bedroom.

I dashed after him. I made it to the fireplace, turned, and spotted him. I aimed and fired again. I missed again, but this time the energy beam swept past him mere inches from his chest. He jumped back and darted under a giant couch.

The bottom of the enormous couch came up to his waist. In the faint light, I could see his legs underneath. I threw myself on the floor on the other side of the couch, raised my blaster, and fired. I scored a hit right on his butt. I expected him to fall over stunned and unconscious, but he didn't. What he did do nearly stunned me. The stocky two-legged figure began to deform and then re-form into another shape, the shape of a giant insect.

The insect jumped up and disappeared from sight. I looked up to see it perched on the back of the couch. It began skittering down the front toward me. I took aim and fired again. Another hit. It began to transform again, this time taking the shape of a giant sloth-like creature. What was going on here? Was my blaster doing that to it?

I rolled under the couch away from the creature. The sloth dropped to the floor and began to reach in toward me with long sharp claws. The paw was inches from me when I shot it, and the creature began to morph again. This time it took the form of a snake. It slithered under the couch after me. I rolled away fast to the other side of the couch, got to my feet, and ran. A human-sized table was not far away. I jumped onto the top of it. I turned and fired at the snake. It writhed and transformed into a Rhegedian with blue skin and dark hair who looked like Jace. By now I was fairly sure my blaster was triggering these transformations. Was there something about the stun setting that somehow reset the connections between his micro-organisms and caused him to reform?

The Rhegedian stepped toward me and again transformed, this time not in reaction to my shot but by its own will. It became the spitting image of Yorbah. The fake Yorbah winked at me and flashed me a smile. It picked up the blaster it had dropped as an insect and aimed at me. I dropped to the tabletop as the blast passed over my head and sent a chandelier behind me crashing to the floor in shards. I rolled off the table and fired back.

Just then the real Yorbah came into view. She fired at the fake Yorbah. The shot sailed past it and struck an ornate chair, kind of a Dieren version of a Louis XIV chair. It exploded into smithereens.

"Hey," I yelled. "Stun setting."

"Is there any doubt who this is?" she yelled back. "He's been shooting at you."

"Stun," I said. "It forces him to transform."

The fake Yorbah ran off around the end of the couch. I signaled to the real Yorbah to guard the princess's door. I would follow Rells. I dashed after him, peering around and under and over the pieces of furniture that filled the cavernous room.

I came around the corner of a giant table and found myself face-to-face with Yorbah. Was this the real one or the fake one? I had told the real one to guard the bedroom, but then she wasn't always big on following orders. Oh well, it was only a stun. I fired and struck her. She transformed into an alien with gray skin and large black eyes like out of so many sci-fi shows. The gray darted through the furniture, turning back to fire a shot at me. The blast caught the edge of my jacket and disintegrated a hole in it.

I followed. I ran through the room, ducking around furniture. This time I couldn't find him anywhere. After a minute of futile searching, I decided I should check in with Yorbah and make sure the bedroom door was being guarded. I started to move toward it when I heard my own voice coming from up ahead.

"Have you seen him?" I heard myself say.

"No," Yorbah said.

"We have to be ready," my voice said. "He can pop out at any time, looking like anything. He could even look like me."

I rounded the corner of a chair and saw the back of my body, which is a weird thing to see by the way. It was facing Yorbah, less than four feet from her. My doppelganger had the blaster in his hand pointed toward the floor. He began raising it toward her.

I had but a split second. I fired. As my beam hit his back, his blaster tilted upward, fired, and blew a hole through the door above her head. Yorbah hit the ground. Rells writhed and twisted and took the purple blobby shape of a Donovian, like Xox.

Now I began hitting him with shot after shot faster than he could respond. I have to admit, turning him into one thing after another was fun. It was kind of like a video game.

"I can keep this up all day, Rells." I stepped closer and fired again, watching him transform into a human-sized turkey. "And I can tell Woad's guards how it works" I fired again. This time he became a five-eyed, green-feathered creature with bird legs. "You'll never get to her now." I fired again. He transformed into a six-foot-tall rabbit standing on its hind legs.

The rabbit made a mighty hop toward a nearby window before I could shoot again. The glass burst and the rabbit fell through. Yorbah and I ran to the window and leaned out. There was no sign of splattered rabbit on the pavement below. But a huge bird rose up to the window on giant wings.

The bird glared at me and said, "Does it feel good to have stopped me, Lake? Perhaps you should feel the grief I have felt all these years. Perhaps you should learn what it's like to lose someone you care about. The pain never goes away, you know. But you'll see. You will see."

I fired at it, hoping he would transform into a pallet of bricks and crash to the ground, but the bird whirled in the air and the shot went wide. I watched it fly off across the palace grounds and out across the city.

Yorbah threw her arms around me.

"Ahem." It was Zastra's voice behind me.

"Thank God you're safe," I said. "How did Rells get past you?"

She shook her head, her mouth in a grimace of disgust. "I don't know. He got the jump on me and stunned me. I just now woke up and came running in here."

"He only stunned you? I'm pretty sure he didn't have it set on stun when he was shooting at me. Things were exploding left and right."

Zastra smiled. "I guess that's what you get for smarting off to him so much."

She was probably right.

Chapter 26

The Truth Comes Out

So I had fought a space alien. Which was awesome, especially since I didn't get killed along the way. But — and as buts go this was a huge and ominous one — his last words were a threat against someone I cared about. Was it only an idle threat, or was he actually planning to do something? If so, who could he mean?

Who did Rells know that I cared about? He knew everybody in the Galactic Detective Agency, of course, and also Yorbah. But I figured they could all take care of themselves. Who else did he know?

Then it hit me. No! No, no, no, no! Lucas. Lucas had been at the A-frame with me. Rells had seen him. Rells had heard Oren call him an "exceptional little boy." Of course, Lucas was on Earth, and Diere was still on lockdown, so his leaving the planet seemed unlikely.

At least it did until the next morning. I was in the *Shaymus*, and Oren was responding to my report about the night before.

"The stun setting is designed to render humanoids unconscious," he said. "But for Rells it must somehow have stunned the bonds between his microorganisms and forced them to break and reform. Or perhaps it simulated a command from his core organism to take a new shape."

"Can we use that?" asked Zastra.

"I don't know," said Oren. "It would be better if we could force him *not* to shapeshift so we wouldn't have to keep changing our tactics for each form he takes, and so he couldn't simply fly away in the form of a bird."

"So what's the plan when we catch up with him again?" I asked. "Just keep stunning him?"

"We need more than that. Forcing him to shapeshift doesn't get him captured."

"No, but it sure is fun. Also, his reaction to it lets us know it's him. We could pick him out of a crowd with that."

"Are you proposing, Gabriel, that we stun large groups of Dierens just so we can pick out the one who doesn't fall down unconscious but rather turns into a chicken or a frog?" asked Oren.

"Well, when you put it that way, it doesn't sound like a perfect plan," I said.

"What we need," said Zastra, "is a way to contain him. We know he always takes the shape of something that is about the same mass. So if we can contain him in one form, that should still contain him in any form he takes."

"Yeah, well mass is not the same thing as shape," I said. "One of his forms last night was a giant snake, which could wiggle between the bars of most cages that would hold a human. Maybe a steel box or something like it would hold him."

"Let's bring in an engineering perspective," Oren said. "Jace."

Jace replied over the speaker, "Yes, sir?"

"Jace, a question for you. If a blaster set on stun forces a shapeshifter to take a new shape, can you think of a way that might keep him from shape-shifting at all?"

"Let me think about that," Jace replied. "I'll get back to you."

Oren turned his eyes back to us. "At least Princess Ralph is protected now. I briefed Commander Woad on your technique."

Zastra said, "But if Rells is intent on taking revenge against the boy—"

"Lucas," I corrected.

"If he's intent on revenge against Lucas," she said, "all he has to do is wait on Diere until the lockdown ends, hire a pilot, and go to Earth."

"But we can reach Earth ahead of him and take precautions, lay a trap," said Oren.

"I'd rather capture him here, and not let him anywhere near Lucas," I said. "But even if he could reach Earth, how could he even find Lucas? There are seven and a half billion people on the planet, six or seven million in Indiana. He saw Lucas only in Port Otto. He doesn't know where he lives."

Oren shared a glance with Zastra and frowned at me. "Gabriel, do you remember the clothes you were wearing the day we visited Princess Ralph in Potato?"

"Yeah, I think so."

"Are they on the ship?"

"Yeah."

"Go check them."

"What for?"

"Anything you didn't put there."

I didn't like the sound of that. I climbed down to my cabin and went through all my clothes. In one pair of jeans, I found a little piece of black plastic about one inch square. It was tucked into the little pocket on the side, what they call the watch pocket, though nobody carries a pocket watch anymore. I carried it back up to the office and held it up.

"That is a tracker," Oren said. "It has no doubt been relaying all your movements back to whoever put it on you, probably Rells."

"So then he knows my house and Lucas's apartment and the warehouse where you hid the *Shaymus* and every other place I went."

"Correct. He doesn't know which location is which, but once on Earth it wouldn't take him too long to figure it out."

"Did he plant a tracker on anyone else, or only me?"

"I found one this morning in my robe," Zastra said. "That must be how he got the drop on me last night. Hand that to me. I'll disable it."

I passed it over. She disabled it using the heel of her boot.

"It's a good thing you didn't wear those pants last night," Oren said "He would have known you were in Princess Ralph's chambers, and things might have turned out very differently. Both you and the princess would probably be dead now."

We were interrupted by the sound of banging reverberating through the hull of the *Shaymus*.

"What the devil is that noise?" asked Oren.

His face disappeared from the screen and was replaced by a view of the outside of the ship. Yorbah was standing beside the ramp, grim-faced, pounding on the ship with both fists.

"Open ramp," Oren commanded the ship.

The ramp began its slow descent. Yorbah jumped onto it long before it reached the ground. A few moments later her head appeared over the top of the central shaft.

"What did you do with my ship?" she barked.

Oren's face came back up on the screen. "We've done nothing with your ship."

"Well, it's gone."

"Doesn't your ship employ security?" Oren asked.

"Of course, it does. I'm not an idiot. I'm the only one who can enter it."

"So why do you suspect us?"

"You might have hacked my security while we were docked."

"That is ludicrous. We would have no possible interest in doing that. But you say you are the only one who can enter your ship. How is that validated? Fingerprints? Retina scans?"

"I can't afford tech like that. It uses my image."

"Which a shapeshifter could copy."

The color drained from Yorbah's face.

My stomach sank. "Then he's on his way to Earth," I said.

"Highly likely," said Oren.

"We have to go after him!"

"We will. Gabriel. But there is no need to rush off in haste. Remember, we travel through time. We can arrive on Earth at the same moment whether we leave now or in an hour or even a day. We need a plan first. Let's see if Jace comes up with an idea."

"I'm coming with you," said Yorbah.

I turned to her. I took a breath and let it out. "No, you're not."

"Yes, I am. It's my ship. And, besides, we're a great team." She flashed me a smile.

"Oren, you say we have time before we have to leave?" I asked.

"I do."

"Then I have time to say this right. We're not a great team, Yorbah. We're not a team at all. We aren't playing for the same side. We aren't working toward the same goals. It just now hit me. How did Rells get back to Earth when he went to murder Koster? He didn't have his own ship. He couldn't use a commercial flight because of the Earth quarantine. He had to hire a pilot."

"What are you saying?" asked Yorbah. "He didn't hire me."

"I think he did, or you offered your services. After we brought the princess back to Diere, after Oren told Ralph and Khan what Koster had said about the argument, and after I told you that someone was watching from the barn, the next morning after that, I was walking to the *Shaymus*, and I thought the ship looked somehow different. At the time I couldn't figure out what it was. It finally dawned on me when we were talking about the *Falcon* being gone. That morning the *Falcon* was not positioned quite the same way on top of the *Shaymus* as it had been the day before. It must have been undocked in the night and flown somewhere."

"That doesn't mean it was flown to Earth, or that I took Rells there," Yorbah said. "He probably stole it then, too."

"We can check that," said Oren. "Jace."

Jace's voice came over the speaker, "Yeah, boss?"

"The night when we brought Princess Ralph back, the night Gabriel and Yorbah stayed in the palace, did Yorbah come take her ship that night?"

"Let me check the security video." There was a pause as we all watched each other uneasily. "Yeah, she and Khan took her ship out for a while."

"It's not what you think," Yorbah said.

"You knew Khan wasn't Khan all along," I said. "You knew he was a shapeshifter."

"How could I have possibly known that?"

"Because you transported him and Ralph and Tam to Earth. Ralph was in the cargo hold, and it was so cramped Tam couldn't stay with her. That meant Tam would have been put in your guest cabin. So then where was Khan during the journey?"

"I put him in my cabin."

"I don't think so. The kind of messiness you had going on in your cabin, that's a form of marking territory. You weren't going to put someone in there. And you didn't have any other place for him, or at least not a place where he would fit and be comfortable in the form of Khan. He must have shapeshifted into something that could curl up in the corner of the bridge."

"I didn't know he was a shapeshifter!"

"Was it a little secret between the two of you? Or did he try to hide it from you, but you found out all the same? I'm guessing it's the second. He wouldn't tell you, not with him planning murder. But you know every inch of that ship, don't you? And if something didn't add up, you would check it out. Especially if there might be a way to make money from it."

"You're wrong, Gabriel." Her face looked stricken.

"I was wrong to treat you as part of the team. I was wrong to confide in you. You knew he was not who he pretended to be. You knew about the argument Koster overheard. You put two and two together. It meant that Khan, or Rells, was the likely killer. But did you tell us that? No, you didn't. Maybe you approached Rells about making a deal, or maybe he approached you. Did Rells hire you to take him back to Earth so he could kill Koster? Did you blackmail him with what you knew and then help him return to Earth just to keep the blackmail going?"

She had been staring at the floor. Now she looked up and shrugged. "It's like I told you before, a girl's gotta eat. I suppose it all looks black and white from where you stand. But you've got two sources of income, being a detective here with Oren and the computer stuff you do back on Earth. I've had to scratch for everything I've ever had, and it hasn't been easy. I can't be so choosey with my morals."

"That's why you weren't using the stun setting last night. You were trying to kill Rells before he had a chance to implicate you. I've been thinking about this since you started flirting with me, cuddling up to me after Oren revealed Khan as the killer. Why was I so desirable all of a sudden? It was all an act to distract me and try to keep me from seeing the truth."

"No, Gabe," she said, "that part was real. I really do like you."

"Yeah. I like you too. But that doesn't change the fact that you helped him murder a guy. And now a kid I care a lot about is in danger." I turned to Oren, "What do we do with her?"

He replied, "Zastra, take her to the palace and turn her over to Woad. She is an accessory after the fact in the murder of Tam Elam, which either Diere or Cunedda will want to prosecute."

Yorbah went for her blaster, but Zastra already had hers pressed against Yorbah's back. Yorbah let the weapon clatter to the floor.

"What about the *Falcon*?" Yorbah asked.

"We will bring it back," Oren said. "You should probably sell it and hire a good attorney."

Zastra escorted Yorbah off the ship. As her head disappeared down the central shaft, she gave me one last stony look.

I turned to Oren. "Classic *femme fatale*. If that had been in a book, I would have spotted it a mile off. How long have you known?"

"I knew something about her story was a lie after you inspected the *Falcon*. I came to the same conclusion as you did on the quarters."

"But much sooner. And you were waiting for me to figure it out for myself."

He shrugged. "I remember what it was like to have romantic feelings. But now, as soon as Zastra gets back, we do need to set off for Earth. I hope Jace has thought of something we can do to capture Rells."

Chapter 27

Showdown on the Canal

We were in orbit back around good old Earth, and it felt great to see the old familiar continents below me. We would be landing in the late afternoon of March 12, which was the earliest time we could come back. It had been earlier that same day when we left Earth, after our investigation of Henry Koster's death. Rells could, of course, have come back sooner. He hadn't been to Earth since he killed Koster on March 10. I was hoping it had taken him a while to track down Lucas. I was anxious to get on the ground and make sure Lucas was okay.

But first, we needed to go over our plan or as much of a plan as we had devised. We were floating weightless in the office. On the view screen, the curve of the Earth stretched away below us. The sun peaked over the horizon, beginning a new day somewhere on Earth. I hoped it would be a good day for us.

"I don't really know if this will work," said Jace. "It isn't based on science because, well, we know so little about shapeshifters. It's based on a story my mom used to tell me. It was a story about an evil shapeshifter that was chasing a family. He chased them through a forest at night, changing into horrible monsters as they ran in terror. He chased them through a meadow all the next morning, changing into the form of a wolf and leaping after them through the tall grass. But in the afternoon, they reached an arid plain. The sun burned down hot upon the desert land, and in the heat, the shapeshifter could not transform. And between the heat and the thick fur of his wolf shape, he could no longer pursue them. I think it was supposed to teach me the value of perseverance or something. But if that story has a kernel of truth to it, perhaps a blaster put on the heat setting would prevent him from transforming. Possibly if one person hit him with a stun ray to force a shapeshifting and another person hit him with a heat ray to prevent a shapeshifting, he might get stuck in an in-between state."

"It is worth a try," said Oren. "I like it. Zastra and Gabriel, each of you take two blasters. Set one on heat and the other on stun. Preferably, you would work together."

"If he gets stuck in an in-between state and can't reform, that would be like how his mate died," Zastra said. "Does that violate the queen's command to not kill him?"

Oren shook his head. "I believe we are well beyond that. He has killed twice. He has attempted to kill Princess Ralph and Gabriel and Yorbah. And now he may have kidnapped a child. Do what you have to do. Now, Gabriel, what do you have for us?"

I pulled out a piece of paper. "I drew this for Buad and Blan. It's a rough map of the section of Indy where Rells is most likely to be, between my house and Sarah's apartment. I've drawn in some landmarks to help you get your bearings — the motor speedway, the Colts stadium, the monument downtown, stuff like that. We don't know for sure what Rells will look like, though he'll probably impersonate me to get to Lucas. You guys remember what Lucas looks like, right?"

"Of course, we do. We spent a whole morning in the backseat of a car with him," said Blan. "You know this is a decent map, knucklehead. Don't worry, we'll spot him."

"Where should we land, Gabriel?" Kah-Rehn asked.

"I was thinking a central location would be Victory Field. It's a baseball park downtown. The season hasn't started yet, and there are high walls around most of it, so I don't think anyone will see us once we land. The downside is there will be plenty of downtown traffic. So there's a chance someone could look up and spot us landing. But under the circumstances, what choice do we have?"

"Agreed," said Oren.

"I think our best bet would be to come in from the south through the factories and warehouses along the river."

"I can come in low and fast to minimize detection," said Kah-Rehn. "You'll want to hang on."

"Oh, goody." I wasn't looking forward to another wild ride.

We strapped in and began our re-entry into the atmosphere. Kah-Rehn came in high over the hills of southern Indiana and then dropped like a rock once we passed inside the I-465 beltway. Skimming along the river we dropped into

Victory Field. As I heard the ramp lower, Buad and Blan shot out of their habitat. I pulled out my phone and checked for cell service. I dashed off a text to Sarah.

Hi. How RU? How's Lucas?

I hoped her response would say he was sitting beside her with a book. I didn't have long to wait for a reply.

Isn't he with you?

"Beans!" I said. "Rells already has him."

"Don't tell her anything about Rells," cautioned Oren. "She won't have any useful information for us in any case. Anything Rells told her will be a lie."

"But it's her kid who's in danger."

"I know. But the odds are she would call in the police who are not equipped to deal with Rells. There would only be more loss of life and more danger to Lucas."

"Okay," I agreed reluctantly. I texted back to her.

Yeah. Yeah. I meant how is he doing? He seems quiet.

She texted back a shrug emoji with:

IDK. He's been OK I guess. Why RU being weird?

I answered.

Sorry. Tough week

I put the phone back into my pocket but immediately pulled it out again and texted Adam.

Hey I'm gonna need a big favor no questions asked. Can you drop everything and come? I'll text the when and where in a bit.

I tapped the send button and prayed he wasn't tied up in a meeting. A minute later I got a reply.

Sounds ominous. But sure.

I texted back.

THX Stand by

Now I just had to wait.

Zastra said, "Let's go get those blasters."

We had finished arming ourselves when I heard Buad in my head, "I think we have them. They're down in a park area below the street level. They're sitting on a bench beside some water and a bunch of little boats. Rells has taken your form, which I just have to say is a poor choice for anybody."

"Those little boats," I said. "Are people peddling them around with their feet?"

"Yeah, there's a few of them out on the water."

"I know the place. It's the Canal Walk. That's only a couple of blocks from here. We're on our way."

Zastra pulled up her hood to disguise herself. We dashed down the ramp, across the baseball field, and out on the street heading north. I texted Adam as I ran.

Historical Society by the canal. Now! Wait there for Lucas.

We raced down the steps to the canal and spotted them. The bench was facing away from us, but Rells must have seen our movement in the corner of his eye. He turned as we approached, grabbed Lucas by the arm, and set off running. He darted around some planting beds and up steps toward a bridge over the canal.

Lucas saw me. A question swept across his face, but only for a second. He shouted out, "Gabe!"

I yelled back, "Don't worry, buddy. I'm the real Gabe, and I'll save you."

Rells pulled at him. "Don't listen to him. I'm the real Gabriel. That is an evil phantom."

But Lucas yelped, "You're hurting me. Gabe wouldn't hurt me."

Rells ran with Lucas across the bridge and began running north along the other side of the canal. I remembered another bridge a block or two north.

I said to Zastra, "Follow them. I'll cut them off."

She shot over the bridge after them. I turned and ran back north along my side of the canal. I ran as hard as I could, dodging around pedestrians and cyclists. I saw Rells over my shoulder running with his hand clamped on Lucas, Zastra in pursuit.

It was further to the next bridge than I recalled. But I needed all that distance. I had to get enough in front of them so I could run up the steps to the street, cross the canal, and run back down before they got past me. Only then would we have them surrounded.

I was starting to run out of steam when I finally reached the steps. I glanced over my shoulder and figured I had enough time to make it. I darted up the steps, taking them two at a time. I dashed across the bridge and ran down the steps on the other side, stopping at the last step to lean against the railing and try to catch my breath.

Rells stopped in his tracks not twenty feet from me. Zastra halted another twenty feet behind him. He was hemmed in by the canal on one side and a five-story apartment building on the other. He pulled a blaster out of a jacket pocket and placed the business end of it against Lucas's head.

"If you shoot a stun blast at me, it will make me flinch," he said. "You don't want me to flinch, do you?"

"Just let the boy go," I said. "You and I can settle this man to man, or man to whatever you are."

"Gabe," Lucas said, tears welling up in his eyes, "what's going on?"

"It's okay, buddy. Just pretend you're in a cartoon where crazy things happen. Like that Bugs Bunny cartoon we watched the other day. Remember when the gangster pointed a gun at Bugs?" I hoped Lucas got the message.

"Yeah, I remember," said Lucas.

"Well, there you go, buddy. Make it just like that. Just remember what Daffy is."

"Daffy?" asked Lucas. "Daffy wasn't in that cartoon. Oh, wait. I get it. Daffy is … a duck!"

On the word duck, Lucas stomped on Rells' foot like Bugs had stomped on the gangster. He ducked out of the way before Rells could fire or grab at him and ran to my arms.

"Good job, Lucas," I said, hugging him with one arm while I kept my blaster trained on Rells with the other. "Now I need you to do one more really brave thing. Run up this bridge and over to the other side. Go back up the stairs by the boat rental. You'll see Adam up on the street. Call to him when you see him and let him help you cross the street. Stay with him until I come get you."

"How will I know it's really you?" he asked, looking up at me.

"Excellent question. Smart question. Tell you what, ask me to do my Elmer Fudd voice. This guy doesn't know Elmer Fudd."

Lucas grinned. My Elmer Fudd voice was a favorite of his. "Okay."

"Off you go now."

Lucas ran. This would be the tricky part. I knew Rells could transform into a fish and swim across the canal, then transform again and grab him. Or transform into a giant bird and fly across the canal and soar off with him in his claws. But I had to get Lucas out of here to safety before the shooting started. If Rells tried something, my only recourse would be to fire the moment he started to transform and hope I didn't miss. I kept my eyes trained on him until Lucas was out of sight. Then I pulled out my phone and texted Adam.

Lucas on way to U. Don't give him to me unless I answer a programming question.

I turned back to Rells. "We're taking you back with us."

"I don't think so," he said. He transformed, picking the form of a snake, which would be the hardest for us to shoot. He slithered quickly toward the canal. Zastra and I both shot and missed as he disappeared into the water.

"Buad and Blan," Zastra called. "Look for a large snake in the water."

One of them darted overhead, wheeled in the air, and took off north. "This way," he said.

Zastra and I sprinted north. I was running with one eye on the Avanians in the air and one eye on the canal. A giant fish leaped from the canal. He must have shapeshifted in the water so he could make the leap. Rells began to shapeshift again in mid-air, taking the form of a tiger. The tiger touched down on the pavement, pivoted, and lunged toward me. I hit it with the stun blaster, causing it to transform again, this time into a giant turtle, which smacked down on the pavement. Zastra and I caught up to it as it was starting to transform yet again.

I called out, "Stunning it," and hit it with a stun blast.

Zastra said, "I've got heat," and shot her blaster.

The turtle had been in the process of transforming into a giant bird. The shell was flattening and turning into feathers, the front legs spreading into wings, the turtle's beak extending into that of a bird. In the blast of both beams, wings and legs and feathers and all of it began to turn lustrous and shiny. A second later it seemed to liquefy. It melted into a puddle of goo that spread across the pavement.

A guy riding a bike along the other side of the canal stopped and said, "What did you do to that turtle, man?"

I said, "Turtle? That was no turtle. You should have seen it up close. That was an alligator, dude. It was coming after me."

The guy said, "You're kidding me. No way."

"For real. Probably somebody bought it as a pet and flushed it down the toilet when it got too big. What's wrong with people, anyway?"

"Whoa." The guy shook his head. He got back on his bike and rode off.

I peered at the pavement. The goo was still goo.

"What do we do with it?" I asked Zastra.

She glanced around to make sure no one else was around and then blasted it a few more times for good measure. "Jace," she said through her translator bots, "Could you bring out some towels and a big bucket? We got him, and now he's … he's nothing but slime. Let's sop it up and take it back to the ship."

Zastra turned to me. "Go take care of the kid, Gabe. Jace and I will clean this up."

"Okay. But don't let anyone see you."

"Not a problem. It's getting toward evening now."

I took a breath. It was over. Just then a shadow flew over me. I looked up to see a hawk bearing down on the Avanians. "Buad and Blan, watch out!" I yelled. "A hawk!"

Buad and Blan swung around to face the predator. The hawk was four times bigger than they were and at least that much heavier. It was no contest. Buad and Blan tore into that hawk like it was a Sunday chicken dinner. The hawk screeched and shot off in retreat. The boys cackled overhead.

I walked back up to the street and texted Adam.

Ready to pick up Lucas. Where RU?

He texted back.

In the Python language, what's a complex data type?

I texted back.

Beats me. I don't know Python.

He replied.

That's what Gabe would say. We're on the circle.

It was an eight-block walk to Monument Circle, giving me just about enough time to take some deep breaths and force my heart rate back to normal. I spotted them sitting on the steps of the Soldiers and Sailors Monument eating ice cream cones.

As I crossed the brick street I yelled out, "Ice cream? Seriously, Adam? It's a school night."

They both eyed me suspiciously. Adam yelled back, "What kind of values can a string variable hold?"

I stopped in my tracks, causing a car to have to swerve around me. The driver honked. I answered in my best Elmer Fudd voice, "Wetters and numbas, you wascally wabbit."

Lucas giggled.

Chapter 28

The Last Chapter

"So are you going to tell me what was going on?" Adam asked as he licked his ice cream.

"I'll text you later. I need to get Lucas back to his mom."

"What are you going to tell her?"

"I don't know, Adam. But I can't pretend nothing happened. Would you drive us to my house so I can get my car and take him home?"

"Sure." Adam crunched down the last bite of his ice cream cone and stood.

We walked back toward the canal where Adam's car was still parked. Lucas walked slowly, still working on his cone.

"I just realized I don't have a kid car seat," Adam said.

"Oh, right. Well, put him in the backseat in a seat belt and drive super carefully." It was one more law I was breaking. This was starting to become a habit.

We got back to my house without incident. Lucas climbed into the car seat in my car, and we headed toward Sarah's apartment.

Lucas asked me, "Was that your evil twin?"

I considered the question. It would explain the situation. But telling him I had a twin, evil or otherwise, might lead to inconvenient questions later if I ever talked about family get-togethers. Besides, I didn't want to give twins a bad name.

"No. But he did kind of look like me, didn't he?"

"Kind of? He looked exactly like you. Who was he?"

"A bad guy. But you probably already figured that out. The important thing is he's gone now and won't come back, and I'm gonna make sure nothing like that ever happens again."

"He fooled Mom, too. Boy, is she gonna be mad when she finds out."

"Yes, she will. You better let me tell her. This is all on me."

We rang the bell on Sarah's door. She opened it and gave me a mom look. "Where have you two been all this time?"

"I have a confession to make," I said.

"What?"

"Lucas was with Adam for a while, and he gave him ice cream."

"Oh brother. Lucas, run on up to your room. I'll be up as soon as I read Gabe the riot act."

"Goodnight, Gabe," Lucas said. "Thanks for saving me." He ran up the stairs.

Sarah raised her eyebrows. "Saving him? What was that about?"

"I have another confession to make."

She looked me dead in the eyes.

"That wasn't me who picked him up from you. It was someone else in disguise. Someone who was a threat to Lucas because of me."

She didn't say anything. She just stared at me for a minute. Then she began beating on my chest with the bottoms of her fists. And let me tell you, she was hitting me hard. I stood there and took it. I deserved it. Finally, the punches trailed off.

"You said you'd be careful. Instead, you brought the danger to Lucas."

"I know. I am so, so sorry."

"How much danger was he in? Wait, don't tell me. It would probably ruin our friendship."

"It won't ever happen again."

"How can you be sure?"

"The job is over now."

"Are you going to take any more jobs like that?"

"I doubt it. This was a special situation. But if by some chance I ever do, I won't let you or Lucas within a trillion miles of it. I've learned my lesson."

"A million miles," she said. "The phrase is a million miles. It has the alliteration of the m's."

"Yeah, well a million miles doesn't cover as much territory as I used to think."

I looked at her, and a smile swept across my face.

"What's with the goofy grin?" she asked.

"I don't know." I really didn't. Perhaps it was all the adventure, all the danger, all the adrenaline of the last few days. But standing there with her in her doorway I finally felt like I was home again.

I took a breath and let it out with a sigh. "Um … I was wondering if maybe we could go out to a nice restaurant this weekend. Just you and me."

She stared into my eyes. "Are you asking me out on a date?"

"Yes? I think so."

She was quiet for a moment. "Yeah. Yeah … Gabe, please ask me again some other time. Sometime when you haven't just put my son in harm's way."

I nodded. 'Right. I get it."

She was quiet again. Then she said, "So you really saved him?"

"Well, I don't want to throw around the word *hero* or anything."

* * *

I was back in my bungalow by 7:30 and already changing into pajamas. This had been some day … or some week … or whatever it was. It was hard to keep track of time when you kept time traveling thirteen billion years. I picked up my phone and started browsing for an e-book to read in bed with the lights off. All my normal mystery authors came up as suggestions. Somehow, though, I wasn't in the mood for mayhem and danger. Maybe some light comedy. I was interrupted by a text from Adam.

So?

I remembered I had promised to text him with an explanation of what was going on. I texted back.

Lucas and I were playing a spy game.

Adam texted.

No you don't. You didn't make me leave work early because of a game.

He had me there. If I could share the truth with anyone, it would be him. But it was all more than I could get into right then when I was exhausted. Maybe later.

If I told you the truth, you would still accuse me of lying.

He came back with:

Seriously?

I responded.

Hey I know it's real and I still don't believe it. Give me time to wrap my head around it. I'll tell you eventually. Maybe.

It took a few minutes for him to reply.

But it all had to do with that investigation job, right?

I texted back:

192

Yup

One more text from him came in.

Coffee 9 AM Buzz House. B there.

It sounded like a command, which was okay by me. I owed him after tonight. I just hoped I was awake by nine. I switched on the TV and promptly fell asleep in front of it like somebody's grandpa. I woke up after midnight and shuffled off to bed.

* * *

I didn't wake up the next morning until the sun was shining in on me. I opened one eye and gazed out the window at Earth — beautiful, normal Earth. I couldn't remember what day it was. I grabbed my phone, and it said it was Friday. I remembered I had coffee at the Buzz House. I wondered what that would be like with Adam and Sarah and all the questions I would not be prepared to answer. The phone also told me I barely had enough time to shower and make it to the coffee shop.

I found them waiting for me when I got there. Adam had a fedora on the table in front of him.

"What's with the hat?" I asked.

"It's a present for you," he said. "A private detective needs a fedora. This was my grandfather's. Take care of it. It has to be a good sixty years old."

"Don't encourage him in his fantasies, Adam," Sarah said.

"I can't take that," I said. "It's a family heirloom."

"I have more heirlooms than I have room for in my house. Try it on."

I tried it on, pulling it down at a rakish angle. "What do you think? Am I a hat guy? I've never been a hat guy."

"I'd say you're a hat guy," Sarah said, nodding her head approvingly.

Adam said, "Very Sam Spade. Gabriel Danger-Is-My-Middle-Name Lake. If you want, I'm still up for being your Watson and writing about the case. I always wanted to be an author."

"Sorry. The story is a little too unbelievable."

"That's why it needs to be told. If not by me, then write it yourself."

"Maybe. But I'd have to change the names and stuff and make it sound like fiction." I took off the hat. "Anyway, I think my detecting days are behind me now. And I'm looking forward to my normal boring life of writing programming code."

"Boring!" exclaimed Adam. "You think information technology is boring! Why just the other day, one of the company systems started crashing for no reason. I had the company brass all over me. 'When will it be fixed?' 'What's going on?' The company's reputation was on the line. Let me tell you, I had to think under pressure and think fast. I don't mean to brag, but I got it going again."

* * *

I was leaving the coffee shop when I heard Oren's voice in my head. "If you come by the warehouse, I have payment for your services."

I diverted to the warehouse, opened the ramp to the *Shaymus*, and walked in. I first climbed down the ladder instead of up to say hi to Jace. A large metal barrel was in the middle of the control room.

"That's Rells," said Jace following my eyes. "Or what's left of him. No sign of him being able to take a shape. But I'm keeping my eye on him. I also have some heat running through it, just in case. We'll take it back to Diere and let them decide what to do with it."

"Well, I just came by to pick up my paycheck and say goodbye."

"So it's goodbye then?"

"I suppose. They hired me as an Earth expert. I doubt you get a lot of cases having to do with Earth."

"No. This is the first one." He stuck out a hand toward me. "Well, nice working with you. And thanks for programming the Earth food into the replicator. Every time I have a taco, I'll think of you."

"You do that." I shook his hand.

Buad and Blan were the only ones in the office when I got up there.

"Hey, guys," I said. "Impressive work with the hawk by the way. Remind me not to mess with you guys."

"No worries," said Blan. "We'll be happy to remind you of that any day."

"Where's Zastra?"

"On her way back to Diere with the *Falcon*. We flew around looking for it early this morning. It was on the top floor of a parking garage. I'm surprised it hadn't been discovered and hauled off by the military."

194

Oren's face came on the screen. "Gabriel, good to see you. There is a case under your desk with your payment and also the clothes from your cabin."

I looked down at it. This briefcase was even larger than the first. It could even be called a suitcase. I picked it up. It was much heavier than just my clothes.

"Thanks," I said.

"Not every job pays this well," said Oren. "But we were working for a royal family this time. Would you be interested in doing other jobs with us, should the need arise? You have excellent instincts. And you fit well with the team."

"Says you," cackled Blan. Oren smiled but ignored him.

"I just got back home," I said. "I have about ten emails from anxious computer clients. I have to keep my Earth life going, too."

"Think about it," Oren said.

I said my goodbyes and lugged the gold down the shaft to my car. That afternoon I worked on software, adding some features, fixing data issues, checking out problems. It felt good to be doing something where I wasn't getting shot at.

* * *

It took me most of the next day to catch up. But by late afternoon my to-do list was clear. I thought about taking a bike ride. But if the last few days had taught me anything, it was the importance of running. I changed my clothes and went out for a jog. I won't lie; it was difficult getting motivated to run when it wasn't part of a life-and-death chase.

The day was turning to twilight when I got back. As I approached my house, I noticed a dark figure standing on my porch.

Truth be told I had kept the blasters. I figured now that I was a known figure in the galaxy, I could use some high-tech protection. One blaster was in my car's glovebox. As I passed my car, I clicked the clicker on my keys and reached in for it. That was when the figure stepped down from the porch into the light, and I recognized it as Zastra.

"You're not here to shoot me with something again, are you?" I asked.

"It crossed my mind," she said. "But no. Someone contacted us about a stolen gemstone. Oren wants to know if you are interested in helping?"

"I don't know. What are the odds of this case ending up in murder and mayhem?"

"I'd say the odds are fairly high. That sort of thing seems to happen on most of our cases."

I grinned. "Alrighty then. I just need to duck inside and grab my fedora."

Please review this book on Amazon and/or Goodreads.
It really helps spread the word and would make my day.
You can follow me on Instagram at garyrandolphstoryteller
and Facebook at GaryRandolphStoryteller.

Final Word and How to Get a Free Book

I hope you enjoyed reading *A Town Called Potato* as much as I enjoyed writing it. It was fun to do a mash-up of sci-fi and detective fiction while throwing in a dash of comedy. It sometimes hurt my head to keep all those plates spinning, but it was a blast.

I want to thank Ariana Moffitt for the awesome cover design. And I want to thank my grandson Gabriel who not only is the namesake for Gabriel Lake but also said to me one day while we were playing with absolutely no context, "a town called Potato."

I would love to hear what you think about the book. Leave a quick review of it on Amazon and/or Goodreads. Please! It genuinely helps to spread the word, and it would mean the world to me.

Let's be honest. The real reason you're reading this page is the free book offer. It's an ebook of short stories, *The Brief Detective Career of Reg Wilson and Other Stories*. Among its one dozen tales, it has two Galactic Detective Agency stories and one story each from my Pelham and Blandings series and my Molly Nolan Mystery series. Plus stories of ghosts and Christmas and Celtic warriors. There are even some short pieces about my life that I use in my storytelling performances.

All you have to do is go to my website at grstoryteller.com and subscribe to my mailing list. Now before you say no, I email subscribers only a few times a year. And I solemnly swear I will never sell your name to somebody else. I hate that sort of thing as much as you do.

Also by Gary Blaine Randolph

The Galactic Detective Agency

Gabriel Lake is just a regular computer guy from Indianapolis ... until he is recruited into this series of lighthearted murder mysteries in space. Under the guidance of the brilliant Oren Vilkas, the Galactic Detective Agency hops from one weird world to another to take on quirky aliens and solve interstellar crime.

Book 1 – A Town Called Potato

Book 2 – The Maltese Salmon

Book 3 – Return of the Judy

Book 4 – The Big Sneep

Book 5 – Murder on the Girsu Express

Book 6 – The Cormabite Maneuver

Book 7 – Trouble in Paradox

Book 8 – The Wrath of Kah-Rehn

Book 9 – Double Indumbnity

Book 10 – Bumps in the Night (coming Summer 2026)

Alien World

If you were stranded, all alone on an alien world, if you were forced to hide your identity and try to blend in, how would you do it? What would it cost you? What would you long for most? *Alien World* is an exploration of what it would be like to be a stranger stranded on another planet and forced to live out decades there, trying to blend in while staying one step ahead of the authorities.

Pelham and Blandings

Pelham G. Totleigh is an unlikely hero. His species, Haplors, are smaller than most others in the galaxy. And as his Aunt Agutha constantly reminds him, he is hardly the smartest or most industrious of Haplors. He also has an unfortunate habit of stumbling his way into the most outrageous and hilarious predicaments. Fortunately, his faithful valet Blandings has enough brainpower for both of them and is always there with a brilliant idea and an excellent cup of tea. This series is a loving tribute to and re-imagining of the Jeeves and Wooster stories of PG Wodehouse. Join Pelham and Blandings on their comic misadventures through space.

Book 1 – Viva Lost Vogus

Book 2 – The Importance of Being Pelham

Book 3 – The Code of the Totleighs

The Molly Nolan Mysteries

Molly Nolan had a plan all charted out for her twenties, and it had been going so well. College, check. Dream job teaching high school math, check. An apartment of her own, check. But then things began unwinding. The job went away, and a personal tragedy forced her to move back to the Indiana town of her childhood to live with her dad. And now, she keeps getting involved in murder mysteries. At least her logical mind and her enthusiasm for true crime podcasts give her an edge there. Follow Molly as she navigates getting her life back in gear, solving mysteries, and the problems of dating in a small town.

Book 1 – The Death Before Christmas

Book 2 – Molly Undercover